THE PEARL KING

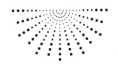

SARAH PAINTER

Siskin
Press

Published by Siskin Press Limited

Cover Design by Stuart Bache

ALSO BY SARAH PAINTER

The Language of Spells
The Secrets of Ghosts
The Garden of Magic

In The Light of What We See
Beneath The Water
The Lost Girls

The Crow Investigations Series:
The Night Raven
The Silver Mark
The Fox's Curse

For my family

CHAPTER ONE

Lydia looked around the packed room of The Fork cafe. She did not know how to finish the story she had begun, or how the audience was taking the tale so far. Uncle Charlie had his arms crossed and his expression was unreadable. Lydia almost wished he would interrupt or start an argument, anything except the terrifying stillness of his face and body. She was glad he had his sleeves pulled down and that she couldn't see the tattoos which covered his forearms. They moved when he was angry or worried and Lydia wasn't sure whether that was something that everybody could see or whether it was another facet of her own abilities. She was so used to keeping those under wraps and secret from Uncle Charlie and the world, that it was just a habit now.

She hadn't slept in twenty-four hours and her eyes were gritty. She kept making eye contact as she spoke, though, and made sure her voice stayed strong and clear. She was a Crow. More than that, she was the daughter of Henry Crow, who was the rightful head of the

Family. If she couldn't put on a good show, who knew what would happen next? She had been arrested, set up by the Fox Family, and if that didn't constitute a violation of the truce which had been in existence for eighty years, then Lydia didn't know what did.

It was all horrendously complicated, of course. She had been working for Paul Fox in good faith, developing a trust and a rapport that nobody in the room would believe or be pleased about. When she had been set-up for murder, one of Paul's brothers had given the police a false witness statement to bolster the case. Lydia still wasn't sure whether he was working alone, or whether she had been duped by Paul. All she knew was that she had to calm things down and make sure that nobody in the room went off on a revenge mission against another Family. Or the police.

She had to tell a good story and fast. 'In the story of the crow and the fox, the fox outsmarts the crow. He plays on her vanity and gets her to drop the food from her beak. I got close to a Fox,' Lydia looked around, daring them to judge her. 'You all know this. And I'm not ashamed. They are just people, good and bad to varying degrees like anybody else. The point is, though, that I have spent time with the Fox Family and I have learned something very important.' She paused for effect. 'Crows are smarter.' There were a few nods. Lydia ploughed on, putting every ounce of conviction she could muster into her voice. 'That means we've got to make the smart move now.'

'What's that, then?' Uncle John had his arms folded. He probably still saw Lydia as a tiny child and was anxious for the grown-ups to speak. Lydia fixed him with a stare and held it until he was forced to look away first. She wasn't afraid of silence. She wasn't afraid of her Family. She was afraid of being locked up in a tiny box, again, of hearing the cage door slam shut, but in this room, with these people, she felt strong.

AN HOUR LATER, Lydia was beyond exhausted. She dragged herself up the stairs, feeling like every step was a mountain. Her mum and dad had said their goodbyes privately, waiting at the door leading to Lydia's flat while the crowd dispersed. Her mum had kissed her cheek and hugged her tightly, while her dad peered at her in confusion before giving her a formal handshake. 'Good to meet you,' he said, and the last of Lydia's emotional reserves drained away.

There was one last thing to do before she could pass out, though, and that was check on her flatmate. Jason was a deceased entity and her presence seemed to power him up, making him less ethereal and wispy and more able to make mugs of tea and, on occasion, save her life. He was sitting on the sofa in the room that Lydia used as both an office and a living room. Lydia could see the fabric of the sofa through Jason and she went and sat next to him. She was too tired to speak and was very grateful when Jason seemed to sense this and didn't ask her any questions. Perhaps he had been floating at the back of the crowd downstairs and had heard it all. Either way, he gave her a sympathetic grimace and put his hand on the chair next to Lydia, palm facing up. Lydia put her hand on top of his, feeling it become more solid by the second. It was exceedingly cold but Lydia squeezed it gently and let her head flop onto the back cushions of the sofa. She would just close her eyes for a moment. There was the smell of coffee and fried bacon, something which seemed to permeate the whole building from the cafe kitchen on the ground floor, and Jason's chilly hand was in hers. She was home.

THE NEXT DAY, Lydia got up early. She hoped that all had magically been sorted during the night but, of course, it had not. Lydia didn't live in a Disney movie and friendly woodland creatures hadn't appeared while she slept to sort out her problems.

Lydia made coffee and toast, slathering on a thick layer of butter and carrying it out to eat at her desk. Everything ostensibly was the same. The piles of paperwork she never got around to filing, her laptop and portable hard drive and the tangle of cables which seemed to breed in the night, and her Sherlock Holmes mug. But nothing felt the same. She didn't blame Fleet for doing his job, especially since he had tried to warn her, tried to give her time to do a runner, but those panicked few minutes before the arresting officers had arrived had thinned into something unreal. She couldn't hold onto the memory of Fleet's voice concerned and urging her to run, only the uniforms that followed. And the fact of his freedom while she had sat alone in a locked cell. Charlie had always warned her that they were from different worlds and now she couldn't stop replaying the moment when he had led her out of her flat, surrounded by his police crew. It made something shift inside. Something vital and delicate and very hard to replace.

As if sensing her thoughts, her phone buzzed with a text. It was Fleet.

Lydia finished her toast before reading it, and then went to make another two slices. She still felt empty inside, as if she would never be full again. One night in the slammer and she was utterly wrecked. She kept breaking out in shakes, remembering the feeling of being trapped. Caged.

Licking buttery crumbs from her fingers, she allowed herself to focus on Fleet's text.

Bridge? Midday? Please.

Lydia waited for the anger she expected. It didn't come. She pictured Fleet, his beautiful smile and warm eyes and waited for the usual mix of affection, longing, excitement and desire. That didn't come, either. Instead of being flooded by feel-good hormones or righteous fury, she felt blank. Nothing.

Hell Hawk. It would pass, she was almost sure, just a momentary lapse due to exhaustion and the after-effects of being arrested, but what was worrying was the feeling that she didn't want it to pass... She could feel her resentment solidifying. She knew that she was excellent at compartmentalising, keeping everything in her life separate. Some would argue she was a little too good at it. She could feel that mechanism kicking into gear, moving Fleet from the box marked 'significant other' to 'useful acquaintance'. That felt nice. Less painful.

IN BURGESS PARK Lydia approached the Bridge To Nowhere. She was early but Fleet was already there, waiting in the middle of the footbridge which spanned the grass. There had once been a canal here, back in the day, but it had been filled in years ago and the bridge was a souvenir. A reminder of how things used to be. Fleet wasn't in his work suit. He was wearing a smart long grey coat to protect against the cold but Lydia could see he had jeans and a jumper on underneath. She wondered if that had been a deliberate choice on his part, wanting to avoid reminding Lydia of his work persona. If so, it hadn't worked.

'All right?' she said, as he turned to greet her. He went to hug her and she took a step back.

He went still. 'You're angry.'

'Not with you,' Lydia said. But she felt the lie, bitter on her tongue.

'I'm so sorry,' Fleet said, his gazed fixed on her face, 'there wasn't anything I could do.'

'I know that,' Lydia said. 'And you warned me.'

He closed his eyes briefly. 'I can't believe-'

'Don't,' Lydia said, interrupting him. 'It's in the past.'

There was a pause and Lydia looked out across the park, unable to focus on Fleet for any length of time. She felt numb but knew it was a fragile protection, liable to crack at any moment. 'And I'm out now. It's done.' Lydia had accepted Charlie's offer to get her out of trouble which put her squarely in his debt. The price of his help had been entering the Crow Family business, something she had been at pains to avoid. To make matters worse, she had then been offered immediate release by a man she barely knew but suspected worked for the secret service. Desperate for freedom, she had shaken the man's hand. Now she owed him 'friendship', whatever that meant. A small part of her blamed Fleet for the mess, however unfair that was.

'I'm sorry I didn't come to see you,' Fleet's voice was quiet, earnest. 'I had to keep working the case.'

'My case.'

'Yes. Sorry. I had to keep working and I was worried it would make everything worse.'

'I understand,' Lydia said, although she didn't. Not entirely. There had been a sense of rejection, she realised, now. Fleet had always worked with her, always turned up and backed her up. In this case, she had felt abandoned. She hated how needy and vulnerable that realisation made her feel and consciously stuffed those feelings down as deeply as she could.

'What can I do to make it up to you?'

'There's nothing to make up,' Lydia said, forcing herself to look at Fleet. 'You had to do your job. I understand. I knew what I was getting myself into when I dated a copper.'

'That sounds horribly like past tense,' Fleet said, his eyes damp.

Lydia shrugged. 'We had a good run. Longer than I expected.'

'No.'

The pain was there, circling, but Lydia felt a calm, blankness at her centre. 'I think so. No hard feelings?'

'Stop it,' Fleet said, angry now. 'Stop talking like we've only just met. You can't just throw us away over this. We have a solid relationship, we can get through this. We just need to talk about it properly. I know you will need some time-'

'Honestly, I'm fine,' Lydia said.

'I'm not,' Fleet said. 'I'm not fine and I don't want us to be over.'

'I'm sorry,' Lydia said. 'But we are.'

CHAPTER TWO

Lydia walked back to The Fork. Rain began to spit and she allowed herself a bleak smile. Of course it was raining. She had broken up with her boyfriend and now her hair was getting wet; she was a walking cliché. The feeble attempt at humour didn't help. She still felt wretched. That was the word. She knew she must be upset and in pain, but the dreadful numbness was still there. A blankness where feeling ought to be. Perhaps she was a sociopath?

A small girl was walking with an adult just in front of Lydia. The child stumbled on a piece of uneven pavement and fell. Her tear-streaked face was filled with pain and surprise, her mouth opening in a pitiful wail, and Lydia felt her own eyes fill in sympathy. Not a sociopath, then. Just a wreck.

Lydia knew she ought to reach out. To phone her best friend, Emma, or her mother, but she had never been good at opening up when she was in a bad way. She tended to forge on alone, and sort things out for herself. Independent, her mother said. Bloody stubborn, her Uncle Charlie called it.

Back at The Fork, she trailed up the stairs to her flat and went straight to her bed to lie down. Just for a moment. She stretched out and counted the cracks on the ceiling, her mind carefully empty.

After a while she must have fallen asleep, because the next thing she knew, her left shoulder was freezing cold. She opened her eyes to see Jason next to her, his hand on her shoulder, shaking her gently.

'You were having a nightmare,' he said.

'Was I?' Lydia was still disorientated. A fragment of her dream was at the edge of her consciousness but when she examined it, it disappeared.

'You were shouting.' Jason looked worried. The familiar crease appeared between his eyebrows and Lydia wanted to reach out and smooth her finger over it, erasing it.

'I'm fine,' Lydia said, sitting up.

Jason moved away and while it was nice not to be flirting with frostbite in her shoulder, she missed the contact. He was looking at her warily. 'You look weird.'

'Charming.' Lydia scrubbed at her face with her hand, trying to wake herself up. Her eyes were gritty and filled with flakes of sleep and her cheeks were damp. She must have been crying in her sleep. Or drooling.

'Coffee? Toast?'

'I'm not hungry,' Lydia said. 'I ate half a loaf earlier. But thanks.'

Now Jason looked really concerned. 'What's happened? Are you having flashbacks?'

'Flashbacks? From what?'

'Being in jail?'

'No,' Lydia shook her head. 'Honestly, I'm fine.'

'You don't look fine,' Jason said. 'I'll make you a tea.'

'Coffee,' Lydia said.

'You need tea. With sugar. You don't look right.' He hesitated by the bedroom door. 'Is it from our trip?'

Lydia took a moment to realise what he was referring to. So much had happened since Jason had hitched a ride in her body and they had gone to visit a ghost in the disused tunnels of the London Underground. It had been unsettling, and a physical challenge, but it paled in comparison to everything else. 'No,' she shook her head to add weight to her response. She took a breath, preparing to tell Jason about Fleet, but then realised that she couldn't say the words. Not yet.

LATER, after two mugs of disgustingly sweet tea, which she drank only to reassure Jason, Lydia sat at her desk, fully-dressed and ready for distraction. She couldn't bear to think about Fleet and, as if conjured into being by Jason's sweet concern, she kept having flashbacks to being trapped in the cell at the police station. Lydia's tried-and-tested approach for dealing with any sort of emotional upset was to throw herself wholeheartedly into something else. In the past this had resulted in a love affair with Paul Fox and a short-lived career as a pet-groomer. Now, it meant one thing - work. She pulled up her client list and scanned the case notes. She would dispense justice, she would ferret out truths, she would solve enigmas. And, if she buried herself with enough of them, perhaps she would begin to feel normal again.

Her files weren't very encouraging. There wasn't much in the way of enigmas, more a depressing list of infidelity cases, spousal uncertainty and background checks for companies doing due diligence on prospective employees. Those were the worst of all, in Lydia's opinion, entailing, as they did, a dull hour or two online and in databases and nothing else.

At that moment, Jason trailed in from the kitchen with a mug. 'No more tea,' Lydia said, as kindly as she could manage. 'Honestly, I'm fine.'

'It's coffee,' Jason said, putting it down on the desk. 'Are you sure you don't want anything else?'

'Actually,' Lydia looked up at him, a thought forming. 'How are you getting on with your laptop?'

Jason brightened. 'Great. I love it.'

'How do you feel about taking on a few clients? Just the background check ones. It's all computer work so it doesn't matter that you can't go out and about.'

'You'd trust me with that?' Jason's expression was radiant. It made Lydia feel bad that she was asking him for selfish reasons. He looked like she was giving him a gift.

'It's super-dull,' she warned him. 'Really routine. I'm passing them onto you because I hate doing them. You can say no.'

Jason made a grabby-hands gesture. 'Give them to me. And the log-ins so I can access the databases. Are they standard checks? Criminal, financial, and driving histories, right? Confirmation of identity?'

Lydia blinked. 'You've really been paying attention.'

Jason grinned. 'Yes, boss.'

LYDIA HAD SET up a proximity alarm for her flat. It was hidden underneath the carpet on the stairs so she would have warning when someone was approaching. Now she was wondering about getting her money back as someone was knocking on the glazed door to Crow Investigations without the alarm having been tripped.

She knew before she opened the door that it was the man who had sprung her from the police station. The one with the strange, unidentifiable power which made Lydia feel unwell.

'No parcel today?' This was in reference to the fact that he had been masquerading as a courier. In his line of work it was probably called 'deep cover'.

'Can we talk?'

Lydia stepped aside and gestured for him to enter. The hit off his power was as destabilising as always, but she was braced for it now, which helped. Plus, it was becoming familiar. She could separate its notes - the flash of canvas, whipping in the wind, the feel of rolling waves, and the glint of gold. It was a ship, she realised. That was probably why she had felt so sick the first few times she had encountered him. He made her seasick.

'You shouldn't be here,' Lydia said. 'If my Family see you...'

'I'll say I'm delivering something,' he said. 'But I take your point. I've got a safe house.'

'Of course you have,' Lydia said, trying not to be impressed.

'It's not *mine* mine,' he said, looking slightly abashed. 'It comes with the job.'

'And what is that exactly?'

He smiled, looking utterly assured again. 'I was thinking a regular check in would be best. Same time, same place. Then, if you don't make it, I know something has happened.'

'What if I'm just busy?'

'You won't be,' he said in a tone which spoke volumes.

'And what should I call you?' He had refused to give her his name in the police station, saying that whatever he said would have to be a lie and that he didn't want to lie to her. All very mysterious and quasi-noble, but not entirely practical.

'You choose,' he said.

'Living dangerously, there,' Lydia said. 'How do you feel about Cuddles? Or Mr PrettyBoy?'

He didn't rise to the bait, just smiled. 'You think I'm pretty? That's nice.'

'Mr Smith,' Lydia said. 'That's a good spook name. And I don't know you well enough for first names, anyway.'

'I hope that's going to change,' Mr Smith said.

He gave her an address in Vauxhall, not far from Kennington Park. Not a million miles away from the MI6 headquarters by Vauxhall Bridge, either. 'Close to your office, then,' she said. 'Handy for you. Or are you MI5?'

He looked blank, but that was likely the first thing you learned in spy school.

'Thursdays at eleven. Here's a key.'

'Seriously, though, what happens if I can't make it? Do I call you or-'

'No phones. No missing your appointments.'

'But my job,' Lydia began, appealing for him to be reasonable. 'I get caught up in stuff all the time. If I have to do surveillance for a client-'

'You'll manage,' he said. 'You are a resourceful woman.'

'Once a week is excessive,' Lydia tried another tack. 'Things just aren't that exciting around here. We'll have nothing to talk about.' She knew he wanted information on the Families and that she had agreed to give him some, that didn't mean she was going to make it easy.

'I'm sure we'll think of something,' he batted back and Lydia had the distinct impression that resistance was futile. Mr Smith wanted her to meet him every Thursday and that was exactly what was going to happen. At least until Lydia could figure out a way to get out of her obligation to him. On the plus side, she was as curious about him and his motives, as he was about her and her Family's. Part of her, the part which was always getting her into trouble, saw it as an opportunity.

'You had better be providing coffee and pastries.'

After Mr Smith had gone, Lydia poured herself a large whisky, figuring that she deserved it after that encounter. Every nerve was jangling and she didn't feel able to clear the mess off her desk, let alone face her client files or accounts. Passing on the outstanding background check work was a relief, but she still had a business to run.

As if eager to prove its worth, Lydia's proximity alarm beeped and, a moment later, there were footsteps on the landing. Lydia had a clear view from behind her desk to the front door, with its 'Crow Investigations' lettering and a tall shape appeared through the obscured glass.

She opened the door to a young Crow. Aiden was one of Lydia's many cousins. Or maybe nephews. She had never tried to keep track of her wide circle of relatives but supposed that would be something else she had to change, now. He looked older than she remembered, with a scruff of beard and wary eyes, which made her feel positively ancient. Lydia offered him a whisky, which he declined, and he took the client's seat by the desk, not the sofa, indicating that this wasn't a social visit.

Lydia sat down opposite and folded her hands. 'What can I do for you?'

Aiden was sitting forward on the chair, his spine straight. 'I want to know what you told the police.'

'I'm sorry?'

'You were arrested. And then you were let out.' Aiden paused, letting it grow as if he had asked a question.

'Yes?' Lydia said eventually. 'Your point?'

'What happened? Police don't just give up like that.'

'They do when they don't have a case,' Lydia said. 'And I didn't give them anything.'

Aiden shifted in his seat. 'That's not what people are saying. Everyone is nervous.'

'Well they shouldn't be. Everything is fine.' Lydia was trying to keep a lid on her sense of offence. The worst thing she could do would be to ramp up the tension in the room. She had to smooth the waters. Play nice. 'I already went over this,' she added, trying to sound calm.

'Yeah, but everyone knows you've been seeing a copper. You were with him, right? We've got a right to know what you've told him about the Family.'

Lydia was on her feet and around the desk before her mind caught up. She got her face up close to Aiden's and said, very quietly. 'Are you questioning my loyalty to my family? Think very carefully before you answer.'

Aiden swallowed. His eyes were flicking around, not meeting her stare. 'Course not.'

Lydia moved back a fraction. 'Good.'

'It's just... You've got to see... I mean, you can see why people are wondering. Crows don't get arrested. It just doesn't happen.'

'That's right,' Lydia said. 'They made a mistake. That's why I was out so quickly.'

'But-'

'Aiden,' Lydia said, leaning on the edge of her desk and crossing her arms. 'You've got two choices here. Either you decide that Lydia Crow, daughter of Henry Crow and endorsed by his brother, Charlie, head of the Family, is a trustworthy member of the Crows and you fly away now to tell everybody exactly that. Or-' Lydia waited a beat, watching Aiden squirm. 'Or you make an enemy.'

Aiden swallowed again, his Adam's apple bobbing.

'I'm waiting,' Lydia produced her coin and flipped it lazily in the air. She could make it spin slowly and with non-Family-members this was enough to put a little bit of 'push' behind whatever she was saying. She could make somebody answer a question truthfully or accede to her request. She didn't know if this was Crow magic or just their old reputation as fixers brought sharply into focus or a mix of the two, but she had never tried it on a fellow Crow before and was curious to see Aiden's reaction.

'I meant no offence,' Aiden said, his voice thin. 'I'm just passing on concerns. I said I would. And I have.' He was babbling, nerves overcoming the veneer of youthful cool that he had worn walking into Lydia's office.

'Pass on the good news,' Lydia said, smiling her own version of Charlie's shark smile. She had practised it in front of the mirror and was pretty proud of it. 'All is well in the Family. I am working closely with Charlie to ensure our continuing success and I am fully recovered after my wrongful arrest. We're all squared away with the other families and there is no call for retribution of any kind.'

'That's a separate issue,' Aiden said, rallying. He straightened in his seat. 'We can't let it stand-'

'I'm not letting anything stand,' Lydia cut across him. 'But the last thing we need right now is some idiot going off at the wrong person at the wrong time. Delicacy, strategy, negotiation.' She counted the words off on her fingers. 'Nobody is to make any kind of move against another Family. I thought I had already made that clear.'

Aiden's lips compressed into a thin line but he nodded.

'Good.' Lydia leaned back in her chair and tilted her head to indicate that the meeting was over. Another Charlie move.

She waited until Aiden was crossing from her office to the hall before adding. 'Spread the word.'

CHAPTER THREE

It was a cool morning and Lydia had Fleet's hoodie on over her unicorn-print pyjamas. The pyjamas had been a gift from her mum and they were fleecy and warm which, at this moment in time, trumped the fact that they were messing with her image. Jason was sitting at her desk in the main room, hunched over his laptop and tapping away on the keyboard. He had taken to the background checks like a duck to water and had powered through the backlog overnight. It was incredible. 'Fair warning,' he said without looking away from the screen. 'Your uncle is outside.'

'Outside?' Lydia had only just woken up and her synapses still weren't firing. 'Outside here?'

Jason nodded his head toward the roof terrace.

'How long?'

Jason shrugged, engrossed, again.

'Wait. How did he get in?' Lydia hadn't heard her alarm. More importantly, how had Charlie got into the flat and then out to the terrace? The connecting door was in Lydia's bedroom. She ran over her morning so far and realised that he must have strolled in while she was in the shower. Well that was creepy.

'Jason,' Lydia said, more sharply than she intended. She could taste the tang of Crow magic in the air, now, and was annoyed with herself for not picking up on it sooner.

He looked up. 'Sorry. Can't stop. I'm speaking to the head of mathematics at Harvard about code theory, he's only got twenty minutes before his next lecture,' he looked proud and incredulous. Like he had won the lottery. 'I bloody love the internet.'

Jason's face was glowing with pleasure and Lydia felt a rush of happiness for him, obliterating her irritation and fear and misery, just for a moment. It was nice to know that she was still capable. She held up her hands. 'I'll leave you two alone.'

Online contact, of course, was the ultimate equaliser. Nobody knew the colour of your skin or whether you were in a wheelchair. She looked at the ghost tapping away, his face lit by the blue light of the screen. Or whether you were even alive.

'You're a literal ghost in the machine,' she said out loud and, understandably, Jason ignored her.

After making a mug of coffee, more to warm her hands and to give her a little more time to gather her wits than any desire to drink it, she went out to the tiny roof terrace which looked out onto the narrow back street and found her uncle sitting and smoking. There was a folded newspaper on the small bistro table and an espresso cup which he must have brought up from the cafe downstairs.

'I see you've made yourself at home,' Lydia said. 'How did you get in?'

'I do own the place,' Charlie replied. He was wearing a mid-length black coat which looked like it was made of fine wool, maybe even cashmere, and had a grey scarf tucked around his neck. He looked perfectly comfortable while Lydia felt as if the cold had rushed straight through her clothes.

'I pay rent,' Lydia said, taking the seat opposite Charlie. The metal was icy against her legs and she twisted them together in an attempt to maintain body heat, hunching her shoulders inside her layers. 'I get that you'll have keys for emergencies, but you can't just let yourself in whenever you feel like it.'

'Not anymore.' Charlie clasped his hands.

'What?'

'I'm not taking rent payments from you. That's over.'

Lydia had started paying rent so that she wouldn't have to do jobs for Charlie. Now, of course, she had told him she would be 'all in'. That had been the deal in order for him to get her out of the police station where she had been held overnight. In the end, Mr Smith had offered her a deal, too, and she had taken it. The fear of being locked up for another second longer had been overwhelming. Lydia was ashamed of her terror and the way she had been unable to control it, but there was nothing she could do about that now. Except make damn sure she was never put in a cage.

'About that,' Lydia began, but Charlie held up a

hand to stop her. He stood up and reached for the external light bolted onto the wall, fiddled for a moment, and then sat down again.

A second passed before Lydia realised what had just happened. 'You've got a camera out here?'

He shrugged. 'I told you I would keep you safe.'

'And you could keep an eye on me.'

Uncle Charlie nodded, utterly unembarrassed. 'Naturally.'

Lydia began to run through every conversation she had ever had on the terrace. She had spoken to Jason out here. What had Charlie seen? Her carrying out conversations with nobody? 'Listening, too?' She tried to make her voice casual, even while her whole body was vibrating with fury.

He shook his head slightly. 'That would be an invasion of privacy.'

Lydia widened her eyes, telegraphing disbelief.

'I don't lie to you.' He spread his hands. 'Lyds. You ask, I answer. It's not my fault if you never asked the question before.'

'I'm taking it down,' she said. 'While we're being honest.'

He shrugged and Lydia wondered how many other hidden surveillance devices he had hidden around the flat. 'I'm asking now. Do you have any other cameras or bugs in this flat?'

'No,' Charlie said. His eyes stayed fixed on hers and didn't flick away.

She was going to tear the place apart. Lydia took a moment to calm herself, to make sure that her voice wouldn't betray the tension in her body. She unclenched her jaw with an effort of will, helped by sheer stubbornness. Charlie wanted her rattled, on the back foot, and she didn't want to play his game. 'What did you want, anyway? I have to warn you, I'm not in the best of moods.'

'I heard,' Charlie said. 'Sorry to hear about your copper.'

'No, you're not,' Lydia said. She wasn't going to ask how he knew about her and Fleet. Wasn't going to give him the satisfaction.

'No,' he agreed. 'It's for the best.'

'So, what can I do for you this fine day?' She rubbed her hands together and blew on her fingers. Partly because she was freezing and partly to try to hurry Charlie along.

'I thought we should get started,' Charlie said. He leaned back in the chair, looking completely relaxed. 'Now you've joined the business, I thought I should bring you up to speed. I'm not saying you have to get involved practically,' he stressed the word. 'At least not immediately, but there's general background information you should know to start giving you a feel for the organisation.'

'Not a good idea,' Lydia said.

'How do you figure that?'

'You have to keep the business details away from me.'

Charlie tilted his head. 'What aren't you telling me?'

'Just that. Keeping me in the dark is for the good of the Family. I'm known to the police, now. Doesn't make sense to bring me into anything compromising. At least not right away.'

'I don't know if you remember our conversation. It was a few days ago. You were in Camberwell nick and I agreed to get you out. You told me you were 'in'. This doesn't feel a lot like 'in'. This feels a lot like evasion. Like going back on your word.'

Lydia flinched. She had been brought up outside the Family Business and protected from most of it but everybody knew that you didn't go back on your word with Charlie Crow. 'I know how it sounds,' she managed, skin prickling with a warning. 'I wasn't lying and I'm not going back on my word.'

Charlie was very still. His wool coat was hiding the tattoos on his forearms, but Lydia could imagine them writhing in displeasure. 'Explain,' he said, quietly.

'I'm in,' she said. 'But that means you have to listen to me and trust me when I tell you this is in the Family's best interests.'

'I'm going to need a little bit more than that,' Charlie said.

Lydia shook her head. 'Not now. But I would never do anything to hurt you or anybody in the Family. I'm trying to protect you.'

'Is this to do with your copper?' He said, after a long moment of silence.

'No,' Lydia said, honestly. Being in Mr Smith's pocket was nothing to do with Fleet.

He nodded. 'Right, then.'

'Are we okay?'

'For now,' Charlie said. Then he smiled.

It wasn't entirely reassuring.

AFTER CHARLIE HAD REFUSED to give her his spare
key for the flat, refused to tell her how he had obtained
the key after she had had the lock replaced when her
new door was installed or how he had managed to get
through her flat and onto her roof terrace without
alerting her, just smiling in an enigmatic way and saying
'You have your secrets, Lyds, so I'm keeping mine', Lydia
checked her bedroom for cameras and got dressed. She
put on her standard work uniform. Jeans and a strappy
black vest with a loose t-shirt layered over the top. She
added a grey jumper and checked that the radiators were
on before sitting at her desk and trying to get her head in
the game.

Jason had moved over to the sofa and was instant
messaging with his new maths friends like he had been
born to it. The sound of his rapid tapping further under-
lined her lack of activity. Lydia got up and went through
the flat, checking for cameras and bugs. She was as thorough as possible and she checked her own surveillance
that she had installed on the outside doors downstairs.

Back at her desk, with the activity having removed
most of the furious energy Charlie's visit had raised,
Lydia finally felt ready to concentrate. She clicked on
her client file folder and was instantly derailed by the
buzzing of a phone call on her mobile.

'I need to see you tomorrow.'

Lydia hadn't intended to answer the phone to Paul
Fox, but curiosity had got the better of her. In the story

27

of the fox and the crow, it was pride, not curiosity, that was the crow's downfall. But either vice would do the trick, no doubt. She had to remain vigilant. She had thought he was on her side, that they were working together and that when he said he meant her no harm, he truly meant it. That was before. The fury and hurt came flying back, along with the taste of fur in the back of her throat.

'I don't think so,' Lydia said.

'I have something important to tell you,' Paul said. 'Face-to-face.'

'Whatever it is, you can tell me now. I'm hanging up in one minute, so you had better be quick.'

An exhalation. 'Little Bird, please.'

Paul Fox saying 'please'. Wonders would never cease. She opened her mouth to tell him to slink back to his den and die there quietly, when another thought occurred. She had her meeting with Mr Smith on Thursday. While she had no intention of telling spy-guy anything important about any of the Families, her first priority was protecting the Crows. If he really pushed her, having some little pieces of gold about the Fox Family might be handy in a tight spot. She didn't want to be a rat, but she would do whatever was necessary to protect her family. 'Fine,' she said. 'I'm not crossing the river for you, though. You have to come here.'

'Not Camberwell,' Paul said. 'Neutral ground. How about Potters Fields?'

The park was right next to the Thames, with a view of London Bridge. It was, technically, probably a bit closer to Whitechapel, but Paul would be the one crossing the river, so Lydia felt like it balanced out. She wondered if Uncle Charlie had to think like this all the time and whether he ever got tired of it. 'Okay,' she said. 'But it can't take long. I'm busy.'

'Tomorrow afternoon, then. I'll text you a time, I'm not sure when I'll-'

'I will text you a time,' Lydia corrected. 'Don't be late.'

CHAPTER FOUR

L ydia had gone to bed early, nursing a fresh bottle of whisky and the sweet quiet it afforded. She knew she wasn't coping brilliantly with her break up with Fleet, but she had no idea what coping well would even look like. She dragged herself out of bed in time for a shower and two strong coffees before it was time to leave for her appointment with Paul Fox.

The sky was clear blue, but there was an icy nip in the air. Autumn was over and winter had arrived so Lydia added a woolly scarf to her leather jacket and jeans and Dr Martens ensemble and stuffed a beanie hat into her pocket. She didn't pick up her bag, wanting to stay light on her feet if she had to run.

'I don't like it,' Jason said. He was in front of his computer, and hadn't moved from that position all night, as far as Lydia was aware. Could ghosts suffer from RSI? Lydia added it to the big list of things she didn't know.

'It'll be fine,' Lydia said, aware they had had this

conversation before and that Jason had been proved right too many times for Lydia's liking.

Jason's attention was already being dragged back to his screen. 'Am I interrupting something important?' She said, a tiny edge to her voice.

'Sorry,' Jason said, pulling his gaze back to her. 'I've done those checks you asked for. All the information is in the shared drive.'

'We have a shared drive?'

'Yes,' Jason said. 'And a password manager. Yours weren't secure enough.'

'How do you know my passwords?' Lydia said.

Jason raised an eyebrow. 'Please. Anyway, I've been practising a few things. Ways of getting into places we're not usually allowed. Databases. Staff records. Accounts.'

'That sounds useful,' Lydia said. 'And illegal.'

'Little bit,' Jason said cheerfully. 'But if we want to find out more about JRB, we're gonna need some moves. SkullFace310 has been telling me about rootkits, it's sick.'

'It's what? And who is SkullFace? That doesn't sound like the sort of person you should be chatting with,' Lydia stopped speaking, aware that she sounded like somebody's mother. Jason was a fully grown adult. Ghost. Whatever. And he appeared to have taught himself computer hacking in the time it took most people to work out how to do a mail merge. Besides, she had been investigating the shadowy organisation, JRB, all year without much success. 'Brilliant,' she finished. 'Carry on.'

Jason beamed at her and then turned back to the screen.

IT WAS mid-afternoon when Lydia arrived at Potters Fields. Too late for the lunchtime crowd and too early for the post-work rush. The cool morning had warmed, giving way to a bright winter's day. A couple of intrepid mothers with their assorted offspring were walking and chatting with takeaway coffees, while their small children ran in and out of the herbaceous borders shrieking. It wasn't a pleasant sound and Lydia could only imagine how much worse it would be in a confined space like a flat or coffee shop. How people did parenthood without losing their minds was beyond her. Perhaps it was a switch that was flipped when you got broody. A switch which turned down the dial on your hearing and up on your tolerance. Although, having said that, she had witnessed enough terrible parenting to believe the switch had to be faulty in many cases.

Tower Bridge looked especially fine against the blue sky and Lydia took a couple of deep breaths. London air, daylight, and a pleasant park to look at while she waited. She could still taste the panic she had felt when locked up in the cell at the police station, the sense of being trapped and having had her free will stripped away. The big sky was inviting and she felt as if she could rise up into it, the blue stretching all around, full of possibility.

The only thing that could spoil her afternoon was, at this moment, slinking into the park by the entrance nearest the Thames. Paul Fox looked gratifyingly tired, at least. There were lines of tension around his mouth and shadows under his eyes. Lydia had been sitting on a bench and she stood before he spotted her, wanting to be ready to move. Ready to run. Her hand slipped into her pocket and closed around her coin. She gripped it tightly and felt her spine straighten.

'Little Bird,' Paul said. He looked happy to see her and was radiating a relief which looked genuine. She didn't trust him, though. Not anymore. She had been so stupid to do so in the first place and that burned all the way down her throat and into her stomach.

She lifted her chin. 'Say your piece.'

'Can we walk?' Paul said, 'I've been travelling for the past twenty-four hours and need to stretch out.'

Lydia didn't answer, but they fell into step, walking along the path which led past a group of silver birches, their slender white trunks contrasting with some purple ground cover that Lydia couldn't name, and along to the more formal planting with low box hedges and a riot of autumnal reds and oranges, that was still clinging on even this late in the season. Global warming or possibly just the weird climate of the city.

'There has been a change,' Paul said. 'I know you don't trust me and won't believe anything I say, but I wanted you to hear it from me.'

'We're done,' Lydia said, 'you don't owe me anything and all I want is to keep far away from you and your siblings.'

'I understand,' Paul said, squinting at the sky. 'But we don't always get what we want and the word is that you are the new head of the Crow Family.'

'Not the head,' Lydia said. 'That's an exaggeration.'

'You have a significant role,' Paul said. 'You are Henry Crow's daughter.'

Lydia ignored that. She didn't know what she could say which wouldn't sound like she was protesting too much.

'You know we don't have a leader?' Paul continued.

'So you say,' Lydia said. 'But your dad-'

'I'm the new one.'

Lydia stopped walking. Paul took a couple of steps before he realised and then he stopped, too, and turned to face her.

'What do you mean?' There were bands around Lydia's chest stopping her from taking a proper breath.

'I told you I would find who was responsible for what happened to you. I told you I would make them pay.'

'I don't understand.'

'My father,' Paul said simply. 'He told the family that you needed to be protected from Maria Silver, as per my wishes, but that a little bit of rough-housing would be a good idea. To demonstrate, conclusively, that we were not allied.'

The little bit of rough-housing had been a moderate kicking, administered in broad daylight after Maria Silver had attempted to abduct Lydia. It had been the lesser of two evils, but still frightening and painful. Worse, though, had been the thought that Paul had actually been working to set her up on a murder charge.

As if reading her mind, Paul continued. 'And then there's the other matter. I had a frank conversation and he explained that setting you up for Marty's death had simply been an opportunity too good to miss.'

Lydia shook her head. 'You set me up.'

Paul closed his eyes briefly. When he opened them again and looked directly into her own, Lydia felt a bolt of electricity from her scalp to her toes. 'I did not.'

Lydia began walking again, needing the motion.

'This park has a bad reputation,' Paul said after a moment, his tone conversational.

Lydia gave him side-eye. She was still trying to process Paul as the head of the Fox Family, her mind spinning with what must have happened between him and Tristan for that to happen. Where was Tristan? He wouldn't take it lying down. She felt a spurt of fear for Paul's safety which was infuriating.

'People think it's called 'potter's field' because it was a pauper's graveyard, but it actually refers to potteries which used to work in the area. It's a funny phrase 'potter's field'. Do you know why it means common burial ground?'

'I have a feeling you're about to tell me.'

'It comes from the Aramaic meaning 'field of blood'.' Paul raised an eyebrow. 'I think that's why people don't like the name. But it's actually got a perfectly innocent history. Just people making bowls and mugs and all that. A case of mistaken identity.'

'I think people don't think about the name and if they do, they haven't the faintest idea of the Aramaic.'

Paul tutted. 'Don't underestimate human instinct. Right now, for example, the hairs on the back of your neck are raised. That's because I'm a Fox. I'm no threat to you, but your instincts keep warning you nonetheless.'

'Are you trying to tell me I can trust you or remind me that I shouldn't?' Lydia said. 'You need to work on your argument.'

Paul set off from the main path to the edge of the park and a line of lime trees which sheltered it from the buildings and road beyond. Lydia followed, wanting to hear what he had to say, despite everything, despite the warning she could feel in her skin.

'I'm not trying to do anything except be your friend,' Paul said, leaning his back against one of the tree trunks and looking down at Lydia. The light, filtered through the tree leaves made dappled patterns on the planes of his face. 'I'm being as honest as I know how and trusting that you will see the right path to take. You're clever, Little Bird, I know you'll work it out. I'm just saying that just because something has a bad name, doesn't mean it deserves it.'

Lydia tilted her head. 'Where is Tristan?'

'Japan.'

'Seriously,' Lydia said. 'Where is your father? You say he wanted to set me up or was happy to do so when the opportunity presented itself. Was it just his idea or did somebody suggest it?' Lydia didn't think it had been Paul, not in her heart, but it could have been one of the other Families or the Fox clan as a whole. She needed to know what she was up against and where the next attack was likely to spring from.

'My father is in Tokyo. At least, that is where I last

saw him. He could be out in the countryside by now, or one of the other cities, Nagoya, perhaps, or Kyoto.'

'Does he even speak Japanese?' Lydia realised as soon as she spoke that this wasn't the most important question, but she was scrambling to keep her place in the conversation.

'You know, I forgot to ask. He'll manage. Foxes always do.'

'I don't understand what you are telling me.'

'My father put you in danger. His part in the violence against your person and the involvement of the Met in falsely accusing you was directly against my wishes. He knew this. I told him that I would not tolerate any act of aggression against you and I am a man of my word.' He flashed a lop-sided smile. 'Even if you don't believe that.'

'I still don't get Japan. You forced him to go on holiday?'

The trace of the smile vanished and Paul looked suddenly very dangerous. Lydia wanted to take a step back, but she forced herself not to move. It was getting easier with practice, this overriding of her fear with bravado. Maybe eventually she would bypass the fear altogether, become like Uncle Charlie. Or her dad.

'I banished him. Tristan Fox will not set foot in London for the rest of his natural life.'

'Banished?'

Paul smiled thinly. 'I gave him the choice. He could leave the country or he could die. He chose well.'

That made Lydia pause. 'You threatened to kill your own father?'

'I was pretty sure he would take the travel option, but yes.'

'He believed you, then?'

'I don't make threats unless I mean them. He knows me well enough.'

Lydia was still struggling to process this. 'You threatened Tristan Fox. And he was frightened enough to leave London.'

'Yes.'

She had always known that Paul was a powerful member of the Fox Family. The next in line after Tristan to take over, despite all his protestations about them not being a hierarchy or as organised as the other Families. But still. This was overwhelming. 'Why did you do that?'

'You know why, Little Bird.'

'I don't know what to say.'

'Just that you trust me.'

'I can't say that,' Lydia said. 'I'm sorry. I know this is a big gesture.'

Paul laughed and it was a harsh sound. 'I wouldn't call it a gesture. I would call it a stake in the ground. A marker. A line. Tristan's way is over. I'm head of the Family, now, and no harm will come to you.'

'I thought you didn't have a leader.'

'Things change,' Paul said.

'You're not wrong there,' Lydia replied. She blew out a breath of air. Paul was very close and Lydia could taste the tang of Fox and feel the physical pull he exerted. Despite everything, he still had a disturbing effect on her animal side. 'So, you sent him to Japan?'

'I took him to Tokyo,' Paul corrected. 'Twelve-hour flight each way. I just got back.'

Lydia frowned, but before she could ask the question, Paul answered it.

'You're wondering why I went on the plane? You don't just wave somebody off when you banish them. You have to root them somewhere new. Give them a new territory, sort of thing. Otherwise it's a death sentence.'

Lydia couldn't tell if Paul meant this metaphorically or literally. This was one of the many problems with the Families. Myth and hyperbole were part of the language, it was so difficult to know what was reality and what was a story from the old days.

'He's free to move wherever he likes within Japan, although Tokyo is his new den. He can travel, too, anywhere. Just not this island.'

'Britain?'

Paul nodded. 'Exactly. You never have to fear my father again.'

Lydia's automatic reaction was to say 'I never feared him in the first place', but Paul's revelations deserved respect and that meant not lying to his face. She nodded instead. 'That's... I don't know what to say.'

'Just say that you will consider an alliance between our Families.'

'I told you, I'm not the head of the Crows-'

'Still,' he shrugged. 'You are the person I want to hear it from.'

'Yes, then,' Lydia said. 'I will consider it.'

CHAPTER FIVE

Lydia's landline rang while she was in the shower. It was eight forty-five which was a little early for a client. They often called at nine, the moment the day switched from personal to professional time. She could imagine them, waiting and watching the seconds tick by until they imagined her walking into her office or a receptionist donning a headset, ready to take their call. A lot of people rang first thing and Lydia understood it. The decision to contact a PI wasn't an easy one and was usually born from desperation. Once a person had made that leap, they were anxious to get on with it.

Whoever it was didn't leave a message which was, again, not unusual. When the same number called again, half an hour later, it was definitely not a run of the mill conversation.

'I need to speak to Lydia Crow.'

'Speaking,' Lydia said, opening a fresh notebook and picking up a pen.

'Are you a detective?'

'I am a licensed private investigator,' Lydia said. 'I offer a confidential service and the initial consultation is free.'

'You're a Crow, though? Or is that just a business name? Crow Investigations. I looked you up, but I wasn't sure-'

The voice on the line was deep and scratchy. He was speaking very quietly, too, which made it even harder to hear. Lydia pressed the phone tighter against her ear and covered her other. 'What? Sorry, can you say that again?'

'My name is not my name. But I can't remember my real one. I want to tell my mum and dad that I'm here, but I can't. Nothing is right. Everything seems different, it doesn't smell right. No, not smell. Not that exactly. But not right.' The voice got even lower. 'They might be imposters. I'm not sure if they're real.'

'Who are imposters?'

'Everyone. It just doesn't seem... Like things are right. I can't explain it. I need help to figure things out. I want to go home.'

A voice interrupted in the background and there was a muffled sound and then Lydia heard the man say, 'I asked if I could. They said I could.'

A moment later, the voice was back. 'My name's Ash. Not my real name, but the one they gave me. It'll do for now. You can find it out, you can help me remember it.'

'I'm sorry,' Lydia said. 'I don't understand what it is you need help with, can you-'

'You can reach me on this number or ask for ward fifteen at the Maudsley.'

'You're in hospital?'

'Just at the minute. That's why I need your help. I can't do this myself. We're allowed to use the computers in the room and I got your number from the world wide web. I found you on yell.com, it used to be a yellow book, I think, but they said you don't use those anymore. Just type it into the search bar and it comes back. I liked the thin pages, they felt nice when you leafed through them, like you were really getting something done. Do you remember the yellow book or is it something I made up?' Animation broke through his measured tone. 'They're being nice but I can't tell if they're real. They might not be real nurses and doctors. They might be them in disguise.'

Lydia didn't know what to say. She settled on a question. 'Who are you talking about? Are you afraid of someone?'

'Against the rules, but that's not the point. I think I'm back but nothing seems right. I might not be back at all.'

'I'm sorry, I'm not sure I can help you. If you're in hospital, the staff there will look after you. They are good people. You are safe.'

'I can pay. I'll be out of here soon enough, it's a seventy-two hour hold they said, and then I can go to the bank. I can pay you. I had a job at the newsagents. I was saving up all summer. It will still be there, the money, won't it?'

Lydia had her fair share of crank calls and time-wasters. This didn't feel like either, but it also didn't feel right. It sounded like a mental health issue. Plus, she was up to her neck in her own Family business and her investigation into JRB. 'I'm really sorry,' she said. 'I'm fully booked at the moment. And I don't think this is something an investigator should handle. If you decide you really want one, I can give you a number for another investigator. Really good guy, excellent work and very reliable.'

'No, no, no,' Ash said. Not distressed, just in a monotone. 'You're not listening. I need your help. This isn't normal. This isn't for just any one. This is for you. You're a Crow, you'll know what to do.'

'I'm sorry,' Lydia said, thoroughly rattled by that. 'I'm fully booked. I'm sorry I can't help.'

LYDIA THOUGHT that she had successfully put Charlie off for a few days at least, but he was the next phone call of the day, telling her to 'get herself downstairs pronto'.

'I'm working,' she tried, but Charlie was having none of it.

'Just a little outing with your uncle. I'll buy you lunch. You need feeding.'

It was smart to know when to choose your battles, so Lydia laced up her DMs and headed down to The Fork.

Seeing Uncle Charlie happy was a new experience for Lydia. Walking down Denmark Hill he seemed even taller than usual and when they got to their destination, an unpretentious pizzeria, he had barely stopped talking. 'African, Lebanese, Persian, fish and chips,' he was listing the restaurants as they passed. 'You can get anything here. And there's another pharmacy. And a

Co-Op. It's a proper neighbourhood. A real place for people to live and thrive. You can get your clothes dry-cleaned, your haircut, visit the doc, place a bet, walk in the park, get a decent coffee.'

Lydia wanted to say 'you love Camberwell, I get it,' but there was no point poking the bear. She would let him enjoy his ebullience and bide her time. Eventually, he would tell her the real reason for their impromptu lunch.

Outside La Pietra Charlie paused. 'Quick stop,' he said, and led the way next door, into Aristotle's Mini-Mart. It was one of those shops which is packed from floor to ceiling and seems to sell everything from cigarettes and groceries to screwdrivers and haberdashery, plus an ever-changing stock of oddments which had clearly spent most of their lives on a slow cargo ship from China or Hong Kong. Small ceramic pigs painted with splotchy blue flowers, Japanese-style lucky cats, bumper packs of cocktail umbrellas and paper fans, and whatever was the latest craze amongst the tween crowd. Fidget spinners or loom bands or Pokémon cards.

'Mr Crow!' The man behind the counter was already half-way out to greet them. He was half Charlie's height and twice as wide, but he squeezed through the narrow aisles of the shop with practised grace. He was smiling and Lydia couldn't help but smile back.

'Tea? Lemonade?'

Charlie leaned down and hugged the man, clapping him on the back. 'We're not staying. Just wanted to introduce you to my niece, Lydia. Lydia, this is Ari.'

'Nice to meet you,' Lydia said. She knew that

Charlie was teaching her something, but she hadn't worked out what, yet.

'Place looks great,' Charlie said, looking around. 'You can't even tell.'

'I know,' Ari was beaming. 'I can't thank you enough, Mr Crow-'

'Charlie, please,' Charlie said. 'And you don't have to thank me. That's what I'm here for.'

Ari ducked his head. 'Still,' he said.

Charlie nodded. He took Ari's hand in both of his for a moment and there was a moment of silent communication between them. Or benediction. Lydia spent the moment wondering how many £2.50 china pigs Ari had to sell in order to make the rent.

It was the same story at the restaurant. Wide smiles, manly hugs, and clasped hands. The chef came out to pay his respects to Charlie and the manager, a woman with enormous hoop earrings and perfect eyebrows, poured their table water herself. 'I will leave you in the capable hands of Mark,' the woman indicated a waiter who was hovering nervously to her left. It sounded like a question, not a statement, and Charlie nodded very slightly. 'I'm sure you are very busy.'

'The books,' the woman said, nervous energy pouring from her. 'You know how it is.'

'I do,' Charlie said. 'I have a guy, though. I could get him to swing by, help you out a bit.'

'No, no, no,' the woman said, taking a step back. 'I mean, that's so kind. So kind. But I can manage them.' She gave a laugh which wasn't a laugh. 'I just need a few hours in my office and a strong coffee.'

Charlie nodded and the weird tension dissipated.

After Mark had given the menus and taken their drinks order, Lydia lowered her voice to ask: 'What was that about?'

Charlie hadn't opened his menu. 'You should have the sea bass. It's very good here. Or the Linguini.'

Lydia pointedly opened her menu and took her time perusing it. Annoyingly she did fancy the fish, but she chose a risotto instead, just to be contrary. She had already lost the battle to choose her own drink, as Charlie had ordered wine for them both.

He took a sip and nodded to Mark who was hovering. 'Run along, son.'

'The books,' Lydia prompted.

'You know we run a fund for the good of the community?'

Lydia nodded. She knew that if people needed money in Camberwell and they couldn't get it from the bank, they came to the Crow Family. Specifically Uncle Charlie. She also knew that every business, even those who hadn't been loaned their start-up money, owed an extra business tax. Some people might call it a protection racket and in the bad old days that might have been accurate, but now it was more like a non-optional Rotary Club. At least, that was Lydia's understanding. Her Dad had been light on the details of the business, having abdicated his position when she was born, choosing a life of safe normality in suburbia.

'Well, it's my responsibility is to make sure it's fair. It only works because everybody pays in their percentage. Everybody benefits, so everyone has to play their part.'

Lydia nodded to show she understood.

Charlie smiled as if she was endorsing the whole system. 'But sometimes I hear little whispers. Maybe this person is doing better than they are reporting. Maybe they are trying to keep their percentage amount as low as possible, so they are padding out their expenses, making it look like they're making less than they really are.'

'So you look at their books?'

'I don't,' Charlie said. 'I send someone.'

At that moment, Mark appeared with their meals. Lydia wasn't at all surprised when he put down two plates of sea bass. This entire day was a performance exercise. Charlie was setting out the new world order, one in which he said 'jump' and Lydia said 'how high?'.

'Really?' she said, indicating her plate.

'It's good for you,' Charlie said. 'Brain food.'

Lydia picked up her cutlery and began to separate fish from bone. 'What happens if you find out the whispers are true?'

Charlie stopped, a fork of sea bass halfway to his mouth. 'They don't do it again,' he said flatly.

CHAPTER SIX

It was a cold morning with the promise of rain as Lydia skirted Kennington Park. She had a coffee in a reusable takeaway cup, courtesy of Angel, and was wearing fingerless gloves and a gigantic scarf along with her usual leather jacket and jeans. It was late November and the shop windows were filled with decorations and every retailer was playing the Christmas Greatest Hits album. Lydia had retained a childlike love of Christmas but she didn't like to shout about it. It was unseemly for a hard-bitten private eye. She also knew that not everybody had the Crow Christmas memories. The burning log, candles filling the house for the special Christmas Eve dinner. If you went back far enough, Crows were Nordic and they still held onto the old Yul traditions. Light in the long darkness of winter was very important. That and strong alcohol.

The address was off Kennington Road, in a large red-brick Georgian terraced building with uniform rows of sash windows. It didn't have the feel of a residential building, more one which had long ago been subdivided into offices. There were plain blinds visible at some of the windows, no curtains, and Lydia glimpsed strip lighting. Letting herself in using the key, Lydia was not surprised to find herself in an anonymous entranceway with beige carpeted stairs leading up and a printed notice on the first door to her right which said 'Kennington Council Reception. Appointments Only.' To the best of Lydia's knowledge, there was no 'Kennington Council' as the area fell under the jurisdiction of Lambeth.

She took the stairs up and up again, arriving on the third floor and in front of an unmarked door with a Yale lock. Using the second key, she opened the door. Inside was a plainly furnished flat. Living room with a black leather sofa and matching armchair, kitchen-diner with a square beech-effect table and chairs which looked like they had been bought in IKEA ten years ago, and two bedrooms, both with twin beds. If it was a safe house, it would make sense that it would be set up to sleep the maximum number of people, Lydia supposed.

Having deliberately arrived an hour before her appointed time, Lydia spent the next forty minutes going over every inch of the flat. She looked in the drawers and cupboards, not really expecting to find clues to Mr Smith's employers, but knowing she had to try. Then she did a sweep of every light fitting, smoke alarm, plug-socket, and switch, looking for surveillance equipment. She didn't find anything. Of course, if Mr Smith was MI5 or MI6, the chances of them using the same level kit as Lydia has access to and would recognise, was slim, but Lydia felt more in control, anyway. She heard the key in the front door and straightened up from her position in the kitchen. She had just prised the baseboard off from under the built-in oven to check the space beneath the kitchen units, and she kicked it back into place before crossing the room to sit in one of the chairs and picking up her coffee. It was cold now, but she took a small sip as Mr Smith walked into the kitchen.

'You're early,' he said, his gaze roaming the room before settling back on Lydia.

'So are you,' Lydia put her coffee down but didn't move to stand up.

Mr Smith nodded and took the seat opposite her.

Lydia had braced herself for the effect of his strange signature and was pleased to find it definitely wasn't having as strong an effect as before. She was getting used to him. Or developing an immunity. A pleasant thought.

'I was hoping you could do me a favour?' Lydia said, having decided offence was the best defence. He might have dragged her to this meeting but she wasn't going to let him set the agenda.

His lips quirked into a smile. 'So much for the pleasantries.'

'This isn't social,' Lydia said. 'And you are putting me in danger by insisting on these meetings.'

'What danger?' He said forward. 'Have there been threats?'

Lydia glared at him. 'I was recently attacked by Maria Silver and her hired help, arrested on suspicion of murder after being set up by the Fox Family, and you have coerced me into passing on information, an activity which carries a health warning in my world. Trust is everything. This,' Lydia waved a hand. 'Could get me killed.'

Mr Smith smiled. 'I think you exaggerate. But please don't think I'm unaware of the sacrifice you are making.'

'Against my will,' Lydia said. 'You blackmailed me.'

'I offered a deal. You took it.'

Annoyingly, he wasn't wrong. Lydia glared at him, anyway. She had taken the deal to get out of the police cell. It didn't mean that she had to play nicely.

'If you follow simple rules, you will stay quite safe. I promise you. What favour?'

'I want to know what Alejandro Silver is up to.'

'What makes you think I know anything about this man? Other than the obvious. He runs Silver and Silver. He is a lawyer. He has extremely deep pockets.'

'The Silvers were looking after JRB. You told me you were working undercover for them both.'

'Oh, yes,' Mr Smith said. 'So I was.'

'You've stopped?' Lydia said. 'You're no longer pretending to be a courier?'

'I wasn't pretending,' Mr Smith said. 'I was an excellent courier.'

'You know what I mean.'

Mr Smith had a rucksack slung over one shoulder and he took it off and put it onto the table between them. 'You requested pastries,' he said, producing a bakery box from within. It was a little squashed, but the pastries inside were intact. Portuguese tarts, Lydia's favourite.

'Pasteis de Nata,' he said. 'Passionfruit and cocoa, blueberry, and classic.'

Lydia picked up the classic version. They were perfection already and didn't need any adornment or adulteration. She could smell the buttery pastry and vanilla custard, but she hesitated before taking a bite.

Mr Smith read her mind. 'Please. Why would I go to this much trouble to poison you? I could just pay Angel to slip something into your coffee.'

Lydia decided to ignore this disturbing idea. She took a large bite, savoured it, and then continued as if nothing had happened. 'I just want to keep an eye on what the Silver Family are up to and it's unwise for me to be seen to be keeping an eye. After the unpleasantness with Maria Silver, I need to let things settle down.'

'I'm more than happy to do you a favour, Lydia,' Mr Smith said. 'But it would be the third one. Are you sure you can pay your debt?'

'Third?'

He counted on his fingers. 'Getting you out of jail, reporting on the Silvers, and healing your wounds.'

'I didn't ask you for the last one. That doesn't count.'

He nodded. 'Quite right. My mistake.'

At least the man was going to be reasonable. Superficially, at any rate. She could tell he had been working closely with the Families as he seemed to know how to conduct himself. The modes of conversation were very familiar, which was alarmingly comforting. It was undoubtedly part of his training to emulate speech patterns to put his subject at ease. Knowing that didn't stop it being effective, though, which was irritating.

'Are you going to ask your questions, then?' Lydia said. 'Collect your debt.'

'There's no rush,' Mr Smith said. 'This is a long-term indenture, you will return your obligation in small pieces, once a week. I thought I had made that clear?'

Lydia finished the pastry instead of replying. She chased it down with some coffee, forgetting that it had gone cold, and stood up. 'Great. See you next time, then.'

Mr Smith sat down and selected a blueberry pastry. 'You've been very busy with Charlie Crow this week. How is your training going?'

'Training?'

'For the Family Business. Or has he started to test you in other ways?'

Lydia gritted her teeth. It went against everything she had ever known. You didn't reveal anything about your Family to an outsider, not even something innocuous. You never knew the importance of the smallest detail, so it was safest to just keep your mouth shut.

'I have accompanied my uncle on visits to local businesses, he likes to keep an eye on people in the community and helps them out when there is trouble.'

'How did it make you feel?'

'What relevance does that have?'

'Indulge me.'

Lydia disliked talking about her feelings almost as much as she hated talking about her Family, but at least it wasn't expressly forbidden. 'I felt proud.' Lydia had selected one of the feelings from the complicated mass. It wasn't a lie, but it wasn't the whole story. Seeing Charlie's reception first-hand had been impressive and unsettling. People were clearly grateful to him, but frightened, too.

Mr Smith smiled, as if guessing the words she was leaving out. He held his hand out to shake. 'Thank you, Lydia. Until next time.'

She clasped his hand and shook it briefly. She was braced for the power surge, but it still made her stumble. Material whipping in the wind, salt on her lips, and the creaking of wood. Gold flashing in the sun, blinding her. Lydia closed her eyes and breathed through her nose until the smell of the sea retreated and she no longer felt as if she was rocking.

'We're going to have so much fun.' Mr Smith looked positively gleeful and Lydia turned away, using all of her energy not to stagger as she made it to the door.

Hell Hawk.

LATER THAT DAY, Lydia was watching the husband of a client. It was her only remaining open case, aside from the background checks, not that she would admit as much to Charlie. She was grateful for the well-placed cafe and its generous window, but her backside was numb from the high stool she had been perched upon for longer than it was designed for. She understood the market and didn't begrudge the cafe their choice of uncomfortable seats which didn't encourage the punter to linger past their welcome, but it was hard on an honest P.I. going about her business.

Outside, the rain had slowed to a drizzle. Lydia had drained her coffee long ago and was just wondering whether to add a sandwich to her next refill, when she caught a familiar gleam. She gripped the table edge and watched Fleet's reflection in the window as he slipped onto the stool next to hers.

'Can we talk?'

'I'm working,' Lydia kept her gaze on the shop opposite. It was just for show, though. Purple elephants could have come tap-dancing out of the front door and she wouldn't have seen them. 'Speaking of, how did I not see you coming?'

'There's an entrance at the back.'

'Thought I would do a runner?'

'Something like that, maybe.'

She caught the flash of his smile in the glass and it was too much. The pain was circling above and she knew it would land at any moment. 'How did you find me?'

'You told me about this place,' Fleet jerked his chin across the road. 'Ongoing job, right?'

Well that was another reason not to be in a relationship. All that caring and sharing was unbecoming to a P.I. 'I'm not ready for this.'

'For what?'

'Friendly chit chat. It's too soon.'

'That's the thing,' Fleet said. 'I'm not either. I don't want to be your friend.'

Lydia pushed her cup away and pulled her jacket from where it was bundled up by the window. She wanted to say 'well, that's all that's on offer' but, suddenly, couldn't trust herself to speak. She slipped from the stool, turning away.

'Lyds,' Fleet's hand was on her arm and the heat of it

was startling. There was the sound of rushing water in her ears.

'No,' Lydia said. Her feet were stuck, her entire body frozen in place. She had to leave, but she couldn't move.

'Look at me,' Fleet said. 'I messed up. I know that. I should have handled things differently. I don't know how... I don't know what, but I know I should have done something. But I'm on your side. I'm always on your side.'

'I can't do this,' Lydia managed. Fleet was on his feet, now, he was pulling her arm, pulling her towards him. For a moment she let herself go, let his arms go around her and her body rest against his. She closed her eyes and tilted her chin upward. It was sheer muscle memory, blind habit, but part of her wanted to do it anyway. It would be so easy to kiss him and for all the thinking to stop.

'What can I do to make it up to you?' His breath was on her face.

She opened her eyes and looked into his, so close and so beautiful. The thinking was loud and insistent. Lydia knew she couldn't trust herself for a moment longer. She moved back a step and his hands released her instantly. He would never try to restrain her against her will. Not unless it was part of his job.

With that thought, the bitterness was back, acrid in her mouth and mind. 'You can't,' she said flatly.

'I can leave my job.'

The words hung in the air between them. Lydia could see that he was serious and that shocked her into silence for a long moment. 'I'm not asking you to do that.'

'I know. But you feel like I chose my job, my position, over you.'

'Because you did.'

'It's not that clear cut and you know it.' Fleet reached for her hand, pulling her back to him. 'I will do it, though. I choose you.'

Lydia was shaking her head before she realised she was saying 'no'. 'You love your work. You can't give up your career for me. It's too much pressure, it would break us.'

'But you're saying we're broken, anyway, so-'

'So it's impossible. Some things can't be fixed. That's just how it is.' Lydia pulled her hand back and turned to leave. Her eyes were prickling with tears and she needed to get away. Blinking, she wrenched the front door open, but Fleet was behind her. 'You're working,' he said. 'I'll leave.'

She didn't trust herself to say anything else, so just nodded and returned to her position by the window. Which gave her the perfect view of DCI Fleet walking away.

CHAPTER SEVEN

A nother day, another cafe. On the Saturday, Lydia found herself sitting in the window of a Costa, waiting for Jayne Davies to leave her position behind the counter at 'Jayne's Floral Delights', the florist opposite. She was discovering that surveillance on behalf of somebody else was nowhere near as satisfying as when she was carrying out work for her own business. The past hour had dragged by, not helped by the fact that she kept half-expecting, half-hoping, Fleet to walk in and try to talk to her, again. She both yearned for it and dreaded it.

She dragged her attention back to the view of the street, people streaming past, intent on their phones. Charlie had indicated that Jayne's contribution to the local welfare fund was way down and he wanted to confirm her story about falling profits. All she needed was a moment alone with Dylan, Jayne Davies' step-son and Saturday helper. Although she hadn't seen anybody walk into the florist in the time she had been watching, which suggested they were telling the truth about hard times in the flower-selling business.

Lydia didn't feel good about doing this job, but she had to show willing in some capacity. This was the tip of the iceberg when it came to the Family business, she knew, and it seemed like a small ask. Besides, it was this or letting him know more about her Crow powers and that was a can of worms she would like to leave closed tight for as long as humanly possible. Plus, the welfare fund was a genuinely good thing for the people of Camberwell, and Lydia was probably a more welcome visitor than Uncle Charlie. She took a hit from her Americano and pushed down the bad feelings. Her situation contained more rocks and hard places than ever before and working out a path between them was giving her a permanent tension headache. She took a flask from the inside pocket of her jacket and added a generous glug to the coffee. That was better.

Finally, Jayne Davies appeared out the front of the shop. She walked down the road at a purposeful pace and Lydia assumed she was going for her usual lunchtime routine - a browse in the Italian deli followed by a filled ciabatta at one of their tiny tables in the back. She watched as Jayne walked past the greengrocers with its inviting displays outside on the pavement. Lydia had gone into the place once, drawn in almost against her will by the Pearl mojo inside. She had avoided that stretch of pavement ever since and she wondered, now, whether Charlie had included the Pearls in his community programme.

Lydia stepped into the florist, past a huge display of

funereal wreaths and up to the counter where a bored-looking boy-man was slouching over his phone. 'Dylan?' Lydia said, making it a question, even though she knew the answer.

'Yeah?' He dragged his eyes from his phone briefly, clocked that Lydia wasn't anybody he knew, and returned his gaze to the screen.

'How's business?' The place was empty on a Saturday lunchtime, so bets were on that it wasn't good, and that Jayne hadn't been lying, but still. Good to be thorough. A good result here might get Charlie off her back for a few days. Maybe.

Dylan took his own sweet time before dragging his attention back to her. Lydia's fingers itched to produce her coin. She would enjoy seeing Dylan's eyes widen in fear as he realised who he was casually ignoring, but she also knew the punishment was too great for the crime. With great power comes great responsibility as Sun Tzu said. Or was it Spiderman?

'What?' He said eventually, a small frown creasing his dozy features. 'Do I know you?'

'No,' Lydia said, forcing a pretend smile. 'Just making conversation. I'm in the market for a wreath. Or a bunch of flowers. I haven't decided.'

'Example wreaths are over there,' Dylan indicated the display, 'or we can create a seasonal spray. What's the occasion?'

'Retirement,' Lydia said. 'And it's a rush job, I need it for Monday morning.'

Dylan shook his head. 'Not likely. We're slammed.'

Lydia looked around at the empty shop. 'Is that a fact?'

'Yeah,' Dylan turned his phone toward Lydia and she saw that he hadn't been chatting with friends or browsing Insta, as she had assumed, but he was looking at a customer management database. He only flashed the screen in her direction so Lydia didn't have time to take in any details. 'Online orders, innit?'

'Right,' Lydia said.

'We could get something for later in the week. Maybe Wednesday?'

'What?' Lydia had momentarily forgotten that she was meant to be in the market for flowers. 'No, that's okay. That'll be too late. I'll pick some up in the supermarket.'

Dylan was already engrossed in his phone again.

'Can I ask you something?'

Dylan looked up, eyes still blank. If his was the face of a criminal mastermind Lydia would be extremely surprised.

'Can you recommend a good accountant? I run my own business and mine is crap.'

'We use Weston's. They're okay, I think.'

Lydia knew the firm, they were on Camberwell Grove. She had run surveillance on one of their staff for a separate case a while back. A personal matter, though, nothing to do with the professionalism of the accountancy practice. She thanked Dylan, who had already dropped his chin, his face bathed in the blue light from his phone.

. . .

BACK AT HER FLAT, Lydia was feeling optimistic. She could do this. She could learn small parts of the Family Business, nothing too serious or very illegal. She could make nice with her Uncle Charlie. She could cope with him ordering her food and she could smile and look attentive. Maybe not all the time and she would have to drink plenty of whisky, but she would manage.

Sitting at her desk, Lydia unscrewed the brand-new bottle of whisky and poured until her Sherlock Holmes mug was more than half full. Then she tipped the bottle again until it was up to the rim. It was medicinal, she told herself. It was cold in the room, the high ceilings working against the single radiator which was clanking and hissing underneath the window. It had been cold in her bed, too. She missed Fleet and she hated that she missed him. She drank from her mug, letting the alcohol warm where her thoughts could not. She would survive this, she knew. She just had to keep her business going, focus on work, keep Mr Smith happy without letting anything important slip, and keep Charlie happy without losing her soul. Simple.

She looked up Jayne's Floral Delights and browsed the website for a few minutes. It certainly offered online ordering and seemed slick enough to be successful. The photographs of the bouquets were modern and arty and looked entirely different to the style of floristry she had seen in the shop. It was no guarantee they were selling, of course, but it might mean Charlie would want further investigation. She made some notes for Charlie, trying not to think about the implications. What if she did confirm that they were doing good business? Would that

63

mean that Jayne was lying to Charlie about her profits? And if so, what would the repercussions be? It couldn't be really bad, surely. This wasn't the Bad Old Days. The Crows were legit, now.

When she had been training in Aberdeen, her mentor had told her that she couldn't think too much about the knock-on effects of her investigations. 'We're paid to do a job and as long as we do it well, we get to sleep at night.' Lydia had never found it that simple, though. She was meddling in lives, she knew, unpicking knots that sometimes would be better left tangled.

Next, she tapped a message to her best friend, Emma, apologising for not being around. She cited work and said she hoped Emma was well. Part of Lydia longed to pitch up at her friend's house, to sit on her comfy sofa and unburden herself. But old habits die hard. Lydia was not the touchy-feely sharing type and never had been. She preferred distraction and pushing those squashy icky emotions down deep inside until they couldn't make her feel anything.

Lydia clicked around in her files, willing herself to get dragged into busy-ness. Anything to stop thoughts of Fleet and everything she had lost. She ought to take on some new clients, phone back some of the possibilities which had come in via email or had left telephone messages, but her mind kept jumping around the Families and the events of the last few months. After a few more minutes, she pushed her chair back from the desk and tilted her head back, shutting her eyes and looking inward. There a tightness in her chest and she wanted, more than anything in this particular moment, to drain the whisky bottle and crawl back to bed. Instead, she made herself take several counted breaths and then turned her mind to the facts. Tristan Fox had seen an opportunity to set her up and had jumped at it. Was that just his dislike of her being friendly with Paul? An old-world concern about mixing their Family blood? Basic prejudice? Or had he been encouraged by somebody else? The old alliance between Crows and Silvers was on shaky ground, Maria Silver's actions had seen to that, and maybe somebody saw that as an opportunity. Break up alliances one by one, isolate each Family... But why? To weaken them? To break the truce? Lydia shivered at the thought.

Despite herself she felt a surge of gratitude toward Paul Fox. She might not be able to trust him, again, but he appeared to be trying to mend their shaky alliance and that had to count for something. She still couldn't quite believe he had sent Tristan to another continent, though. She allowed herself to imagine it was true, just for a moment, and the surge of relief was overwhelming. She hadn't realised how frightened she still was of Tristan and, by extension, Paul's brothers. She ought to include Paul in that group, but the part of her who had fallen for him all those years ago persisted and he was separate in her heart and mind. Which was a different kind of terror.

There was something else on her mind, something which had occurred to her while she had waited for Mr Smith. She went to see her flatmate to discuss the matter.

'How are you doing?' Lydia leaned on the door

frame, watching Jason's hands fly over the laptop keyboard. He was completely absorbed and took a moment before he looked at her.

'I'm learning about encryption and rootkits.'

'You look happier,' Lydia said, choosing not to engage with the tech-speak. The subject she wanted to discuss was a delicate one and she didn't know how best to raise it. Jason had been so content since she had passed on her old laptop, it felt cruel to drag things up.

Jason smiled. 'I am.'

She took a breath. 'I'm sorry I didn't find out about your last day. And about Amy. I told you I would look into it and I didn't get very far.'

'It's okay,' Jason said, his face clouding. 'I appreciate you trying.'

'Thing is,' Lydia crossed the carpet and sat on the bed next to Jason. 'I asked Fleet for help with it before, but I've got a new contact, now. One who works higher up in intelligence. He might be able to find something out for us. If you still want to know.'

Jason's outline was shimmering, very slightly, and Lydia put a hand on his forearm to still him.

'I don't know,' he said after a moment. 'I'm kind of scared. And we've found a way to get me out of the flat, now. With you.'

'That's kind of what I thought,' Lydia said. 'But I just wanted to check. I didn't want you to think I'd forgotten about it.'

He nodded his thanks. 'I'll let you know if I change my mind, but right now it's nice to live in the moment. I can feel a future for the first time since I died.' He laughed. 'That's a weird sentence.'

'It's a wonderful sentence,' Lydia said, meaning every word. 'I'm so happy you are happy.'

And it didn't hurt that he was doing all of her corporate background checks. Money was rolling into the business bank account like never before as she had always limited the number of cases she took like that as they made her want to cry with boredom. 'And I'm so glad we are working together,' she added. 'You are a brilliant partner.'

Jason's smile got even wider and she patted his arm before leaving him to it. Time was money, after all.

BACK IN HER OFFICE, Lydia stood next to the radiator for a moment trying to warm up. She eyed the whisky bottle which was, unaccountably, already half-empty. She hadn't yet eaten lunch but she didn't feel remotely buzzed. Her tolerance for alcohol had always been extremely high, but this was ridiculous. Perhaps it was something she should keep an eye on. Immediately, Lydia dismissed the thought. Bigger fish. Besides, if she never got drunk, she couldn't have a problem. That was the rule, right?

She went into her bedroom to get another pair of socks, hoping that warm feet would make the rest of her feel less icy. The door to the terrace had a thin curtain that was pulled half across. The slice of the outside world was unappealing. Sleety rain was coming down heavily and Lydia grimaced at the thought of leaving the flat for supplies. Since Charlie had revealed his surveillance, Lydia hadn't felt the same way about her outdoor space. It had been bad enough that a hit man had attempted to throw her off the roof, but now she had Charlie and his covert cameras. It didn't matter that she had removed it and checked over the terrace carefully. It felt sullied. Bloody Charlie.

Paul Fox was on her mind. Having admitted to herself that she wanted to believe him, even after everything that had happened, she knew she had to be smart. Animal charm had always gone a long way in the Paul and Lydia show and she had to make sure he wasn't playing her. First off, she could check his facts. She counted back the hours from their meeting and searched for flight times to Tokyo out of London. Having narrowed down the list of most-likely flights, she thought about asking Jason whether his hacker skills were up to accessing the airline's passenger information before realising there was a simpler solution. She made a call to Karen, her old boss in Aberdeen, the woman who had trained her as an investigator. Karen had been in business for over twenty years and had a vast network of useful contacts. For a reasonable fee she could find out most things, and Lydia knew she had helpful friends in every transport sector. You often had to know if someone was doing a flit, especially when a lot of your work involved infidelity, custody battles and acrimonious divorce. One of Lydia's proudest moments as a trainee had been when she had stopped a man from taking his three small children to Central America during his monthly contact-visit. She could still see the pure relief on the mother's face.

In less than an hour, Karen called her back. Paul and Tristan Fox were on the passenger manifest for flight 2102 from Heathrow to Tokyo on Tuesday. They both had the chicken.'

'What about the return journey? Did you manage to find that?'

'Of course,' Karen said. 'Just Paul, as you expected. He had the chicken again.'

'Thank you,' Lydia said. 'Invoice me.'

'Nae bother, hen,' Karen said. 'Anytime.'

LYDIA MET Charlie downstairs in The Fork to give her report on Jayne's Floral Delights. He was in his favourite seat and she slid onto the chair opposite. 'Shop was dead on Saturday.' Lydia didn't know what made her omit her online research, the fancy website with its high-end arrangements, but obeying her instincts was a reflex she hadn't broken. Besides, it might make Charlie think badly of the business without proper proof.

'All right,' Charlie said. 'Check it again next week-end, just to be sure.'

'I have clients I have to get back to, a business to run.'

Charlie sighed. 'Do I have to remind you of our agreement?'

'That Pearl fruit shop seems to be doing a good trade,' Lydia said, keen to change topic. 'As you would expect.'

'What about it?' Charlie sounded defensive.

'Just that it's odd. Right in the heart of Camberwell.'

'High streets are dying, hadn't you noticed? Some nice little business want to move into Camberwell, we're not going to block them.'

'We?'

Charlie frowned. 'Have you heard of the Camberwell Regeneration Plan? Miles Bunyan has been pushing for it.'

Lydia shook her head and said, 'No'.

'Part of the deal, which has subsidies and tax breaks to encourage development in this area, involves encouraging small businesses. I can't go around running people out of Camberwell for being born into a particular Family.'

Put like that and Lydia was shocked. 'That's not what I meant, I'm not trying to keep people out, I just wondered. I didn't know where we stood with the Pearls these days. As a Family, I mean.'

Charlie shrugged. 'Pearls have always been quiet. Useful for supplying you what you need from their nice little stalls and shops, but not too bright.'

'Don't be prejudiced,' Lydia said.

'I misspoke,' Charlie waved a hand. 'I meant not too powerful. They never bothered to conserve their energy, keep it close. They diluted their power all over London and beyond.'

'Now you definitely sound prejudiced. I heard in biology lessons that nature prefers a wide gene pool. Makes for strong babies. Just look at the Royal Family, we want to watch we don't end up with weak chins.'

'Biology,' Charlie smiled indulgently. 'I'm not

talking about that. I'm talking about Family Power. Different rules.'

Lydia wanted to argue further, but she recognised that it was pointless. Charlie was set in his ways and it would take more than a lively debate to shift him out of them. A lot more.

CHAPTER EIGHT

A single magpie was sitting on the wall of Uncle Charlie's house. Lydia greeted it as she entered and it hopped along the path in front of her, as if leading the way. 'I've been here before, you know,' she told the bird and then felt faintly ridiculous when it flew away.

Charlie opened the door in a black tracksuit with a white towel around his neck. 'I didn't think you meant literal training,' Lydia said. 'I'm not dressed for the gym.' And will never set foot in one, she added silently.

'Come and get a coffee,' Charlie was striding back through his house, heading to the kitchen. The energy was flowing off him and Lydia realised something; he was excited. The knot in her stomach tightened. This was not going to be an easy conversation. She accepted a small cup of espresso and a bottle of cold water from the fridge. 'Caffeine and hydration, hot and cold, it's the best combination to really wake you up. And we need to be fully awake today.'

'Right,' Lydia wasn't fully listening as her brain was

busy with trying to formulate the right words. 'I need to talk to you about something,' she managed.

'Fire away,' Charlie said. 'This way.'

'It's about the business side of things,' Lydia spoke to his back as she followed Charlie up the stairs. He was showing no signs of pausing for a chat and Lydia had to get this out. 'I'm not sure I'm a good fit.'

Charlie didn't pause on the stairs but he stopped at the top and turned around to face Lydia. He always towered over her, but with the height advantage of the stairs, he was like a mountain. Lydia curbed the urge to shade her eyes as she looked up. 'You said you were 'in'. You made a deal.'

'I'm still 'in', that's not the issue,' Lydia said. 'I just don't think I've got an aptitude for the business side. And I've got my own business to run. I think it's better left in your capable hands.'

Charlie's eyes narrowed. 'There's something else.'

'I think you should keep the details of the business side quiet. Don't involve me. It's safer if I don't know the nitty gritty.'

'What do you mean 'safer'?'

'I'm 'in'. I would never do anything to harm you or the Family or the business. I need you to trust me when I say it's better if I don't know certain things.' What she didn't know, she couldn't pass onto Mr Smith in a moment of weakness. Or through coercion. He was being very gentlemanly at the moment, but who knew how long that would last?

'Have you got back together with that copper? Is that the problem?'

'I'm not with Fleet.' Lydia swallowed past the sudden lump in her throat. 'That's not the point, anyway. I just think it makes sense. If I'm not running the business side, why tell me about it in detail? The fewer people know about our business the better, right? That includes me. Loose lips and all that.'

Charlie shook his head. 'This sounds a lot like you going back on your word. I want you in the business. Getting to grips with it at every level. Running the books, everything. I won't be around forever.'

'Crows will be lining up for the honour. Pick someone.'

'I already have,' Charlie said, but Lydia could tell he was weakening. Maybe she wasn't his first choice, after all. Maybe he had just wanted her on side as a sign of loyalty to his big brother or for the look of things. Succession had always been important and she was the rightful next in line. Maybe he just had to be seen to be following the line and would be grateful of a way out of working with her.

'I don't think it's where my skills lie,' Lydia said, truthfully enough.

'Drink up,' Charlie said. His voice was neutral and he turned away too quickly for Lydia to get a read on his expression. They were on the third floor of his house. Lydia expected a home office, maybe a spare bedroom, instead Charlie opened the door on a large empty space which spanned the entire footprint of the house. There was a single pillar about a third of the way across the space which must have been put in to replace a load-bearing wall when the rooms were knocked through.

The floor was oak, the walls white and winter light streamed through the large windows which lined the front and back walls. If she didn't know Charlie better, she would have said it was a dance studio.

She walked into the middle and turned slowly, taking it in. This amount of unused space was probably one of the biggest luxuries in London. 'What do you do in here?' There was no gym equipment, no mirror, no plants, furniture, or storage. Nothing. She felt a breeze on her cheek and turned her head, looking for the source.

Charlie was watching her and she stopped. The hairs on the back of her neck lifted and she thought, for a second, that somebody was standing just out of her field of vision. Someone in the corner of her eye. And then they were gone.

'This was where I trained your cousin.'

Maddie.

'She was making great progress until...' He stopped.

Until she had gone off the rails, almost killed a man, crashed a car, run away, hidden with Paul Fox's help. When Lydia had found her (at Charlie's request), Jason had had to save Lydia's life. Then Maddie had invited Lydia to join her in her mad rampaging world, before disappearing. She was the Night Raven in Lydia's mind. A spirit who visited her dreams and reminded her that the myths of her Family were alive and kicking.

'Why are you showing me this?'

'If you're not going to get involved in the Family Business, there are other ways you can demonstrate your loyalty. Other ways you can be useful.' Charlie tilted his head. 'We all have to play our part, Lyds, you know that.'

'I don't have any skills,' Lydia said. 'Except investigating. I'm quite good at that and getting better all the time. Crow Investigations is at your service.'

'Don't insult me,' Charlie said. 'You are Henry Crow's daughter. You have our coin. Show me.'

Lydia felt her coin appear at her fingertips and she folded it into her palm. Not fast enough to evade Charlie's gaze, though, and he nodded at her closed fist. 'You're the rightful heir, don't you want to find out what that means?'

For her whole life, Lydia's parents had told her to stay away from Uncle Charlie, to hide what she could do and that if he so much as sniffed opportunity, he would use her without thinking twice. Given that she felt essentially powerless, her only ability to sense the power in others, it had never seemed like much of an issue. Of course, nothing had seemed like an issue when she was growing up. The Crow Family stories were just that, stories. Her mum and dad had protected her well. Now she had to protect them. She thought fast and said: 'You know what I can do. You think I can refine that? Learn to read my senses better or have a bigger range? That could be overwhelming in a place like London. If I'm sensing people's Family power from further away, I'll get too many at once, they might all just blend together.'

Charlie shook his head. 'That's just the start. Maddie couldn't lift a paperclip when we began, she was able to drive a car after a while.'

'She was able to crash a car,' Lydia amended. 'And I'm not interested in driving with my mind.'

Charlie spread his hands in a gesture which told her he didn't really care what she was interested in and said: 'Why don't we just get started. Sooner we start, sooner we finish. And if you're not going to be hands-on with the business administration...'

'Fine.'

'Close your eyes.'

Lydia did as she was told. Instantly, she felt vulnerable. She was standing alone in the middle of a vast room. Charlie was near the wall by the door and he was her uncle. She was safe, she told herself, but her body didn't agree and felt her heart rate kick up.

'You can feel your coin in your hand. Hold your arm out straight and open your hand so that your coin is lying flat on your palm. You've flipped your coin a million times, but now you're going to float it. Just have it lift up from your palm and hold it in the air a few inches above your hand.'

Lydia obeyed the instruction. She could feel her coin, the slight weight of it and the edges against the shallow cup of her stretched palm. 'I don't see-'

'Concentrate,' Charlie said and his voice brooked no argument.

Lydia realised that she wasn't getting out of the room anytime soon unless she showed willing. She scrunched up her forehead to show she was concentrating.

'Picture your coin floating six inches about your hand. Just steady in the air.'

Lydia didn't bother to picture anything, she just

concentrated on looking like she was trying to do something. She tensed her muscles and scrunched her eyes. After what felt like a decent amount of 'effort' she put her arm down and opened her eyes. 'Sorry-' The words died. Her coin was hanging in mid-air, directly level with her eye line and an arm-span away. It wasn't spinning, just sitting in the air perfectly level as if held by an invisible shelf.

'Good,' Charlie said. His face was flushed and Lydia grabbed her coin, pocketing it. 'Next, we'll try a neutral object.'

'I'm tired,' Lydia said, trying to inject exhaustion into her voice. She let her body slump a little. 'I feel woozy. Like I'm going to faint.'

Charlie crossed the room quickly and put a concerned hand on her forehead. 'You do look a little pale,' he said. 'Don't worry, you'll get stronger with practice. It will get easier.'

All Lydia could think about was getting out of that room and away from Charlie's house. There was a fizzing in her body, like something was going to explode. She didn't think she was going to throw up, it didn't feel like nausea, but it wasn't beyond the realms of possibility.

'Good work, today,' Charlie was saying as he followed her from the room and back down the stairs. 'Get some rest. Get Angel to give you dinner. I've told her to feed you.'

Lydia managed to thank him and get out of the door. There were five magpies on the path and she nodded to acknowledge them, not trusting herself to speak.

Halfway home, Lydia couldn't keep speed-walking and she crouched down on the pavement to take a few breaths. She hung her head low, trying to get oxygen back into her system and to stop the ringing in her ears. Her coin was safely back in her pocket, she knew that, but somehow it was in her hand at the same time. And, when she opened her eyes, it was also hanging in the air about six inches from her nose. That wasn't possible. That wasn't right. Her coin was part of her, like her thumb. It appeared when she wanted it and disappeared when she didn't. She could flip it in the air, make it spin a little more slowly. She had never made it hang in the air like that before, it had never occurred to her that such a thing was possible. And now there were three. But that wasn't right. There was only one, she knew that, as surely as she knew she had two feet. So why could she feel one in her palm and see one in front of her? How was that possible?

'No,' Lydia said, and the coin in her line of sight disappeared. She straightened up and checked her pocket. Nothing. Just one coin, again, heavy and reassuring in the centre of her palm.

CHAPTER NINE

Waking up alone, starfished across a cold bed in a room that felt as if Jason must be somewhere close, leaching the warmth from the air, Lydia's head pounded. It took her a moment to orientate herself. She had dreamed of Maddie but, unlike the run of nightmares she had experienced in the past, Maddie was just a distant figure, silently standing at the edge of her dream activities, not interacting with Lydia, not warning her. It was as if Maddie had given up.

Lydia focused on the almost-empty bottle of whisky which was on the nightstand. She wanted to drink it and, at the same time, registered that this was not a good impulse. The bottle was at her lips and the liquid burning down her throat before she thought any further. Slumped against her pillows, Lydia waited for her head to clear. Booze had always been good at sharpening her up, counter to what most people seemed to experience and, these days, it felt like the only way she could function. All of her senses were screaming that working for Charlie was a bad idea, that meeting Mr Smith was a bad idea, let alone the giant chasm of miserable need which had opened up inside since she had left Fleet. It was too much.

Enough. Lydia had finished her permitted ten-minute pity-party and now she forced herself up and into the shower. As she scrubbed at her scalp and lathered the shampoo, her mind wandered back over her dreams. She had been somewhere dark and filled with dense foliage. Trees creaked and an owl hooted. It had been a fairy tale landscape that she only half-remembered from childhood stories, filled with dangers she couldn't quite see. And Maddie. Somewhere in the dark, just off the twisting path. Watching Lydia fuck up from a safe distance.

Jason was in the kitchen, making tea. He eyed the empty whisky bottles on the counter and then glanced at Lydia.

'Don't say a word,' Lydia said. 'I'm not in the mood.'

Jason held up his hands. 'No judgement. You're missing Fleet. I get it. It's grief.'

'He's not dead,' Lydia said and then regretted it. 'Sorry.'

'That's all right,' Jason said. 'You're grieving for the loss of the relationship. There are five stages-'

'Feathers, don't tell me that,' Lydia tried to smile. 'I can do one. Maybe two stages of this. No more.'

'Seriously,' Jason said. 'If you need to talk...'

'I'm fine,' Lydia lied.

'Drowning your sorrows isn't a long-term solution.'

'Really, I'm fine,' Lydia lied again. 'Let's talk work. If I stay busy, I'll be even better. Honestly.'

'All right,' Jason held up his hands. 'Talk to me about your cases.'

Lydia felt her shoulders sag. 'Not much to say. I'm on my last cheater and I'm not in the mood to take any more. Charlie has got me running over town at his beck and call and now he's added training into the mix.'

'Training?'

'Don't be pleased, I can't bear it. Be on my side.'

'I am on your side. What training? Like kick-boxing? Circuits?'

Lydia picked up the tea that Jason had made and wrapped her hands around the mug, warming them. 'Crow power stuff.'

Jason's eyes widened. 'Holy shit.'

'Yep.'

Jason stretched past Lydia in the small space and picked up the kettle, refilling it at the sink and hitting the switch. Then he got a stack of bowls from the cupboard and began pouring cereal. He compulsively made breakfast food and hot drinks when he was thinking, or upset or concerned which meant, in practice, that they went through a lot of cornflakes and teabags. 'It's okay,' Lydia tried. She put a hand on his arm. 'Jason.'

When he looked at her, his eyes were shining. 'Aren't you a bit excited? To see what you will be able to do? To find out more?'

Jason had always been curious about Lydia's Crow

power, but Lydia had been brought up to hide it, minimise it, stay normal and stay safe. It was a tough habit to shake. Plus, she had never felt powerful. Her Crow whammy amounted to sensing power in others which had only increased her sense of inadequacy. All of these magical Family members strolling around London and Lydia just able to know they were there. It wasn't exactly the stuff of legend.

'I mean, you power me up, right? What if you could access that ability to power yourself? Or do other things? You must have wondered about it.'

'Maybe,' Lydia said. 'I don't like being forced into it, though. I don't trust Charlie.' Saying the words out loud made everything seem worse. Lydia took a sip of her tea and swiped a bowl of cereal. To change the subject, she updated Jason on her surveillance of the florist. 'The website looks slick, but there's no way to know if it's actually doing good business.'

'Oh, there definitely is,' Jason said.

'What?'

'Hack into their site, look around and see if there's a way to access their customer management database. They probably use a separate secure payment system, but the emails with order confirmations should be pretty easy to get into. You want me to try?'

'Could you look without anybody knowing?'

'Yeah,' Jason said. 'I wouldn't change anything and I wouldn't do anything bad. Just look.'

It wasn't ethical, but if it put them in the clear with Charlie it would definitely be in Jayne Davies' best interests. And if it didn't put her in the clear? Well,

Lydia would worry about that when it happened. One problem at a time. She gave Jason the go-ahead to try and he instantly abandoned the cereal in favour of his laptop. Small mercies.

Jason was sitting on the sofa, tapping away, and Lydia made some buttered toast. By the time she carried it through and joined Jason, he was scrolling through an email account. 'This is the email account which handles the customer orders,' he angled the laptop to show Lydia. 'There are lots.' He clicked into one message and Lydia scanned the order confirmation. It was for a hand-tied winter bouquet, delivered to an address in Camberwell, and the customer had apparently paid almost £200. 'Feathers, that must be quite the bouquet.'

Jason resumed scrolling through the messages while Lydia ate her toast.

'Looks like they took around twenty grand in orders last month. I will have to go further, take a look at their accounts to see profit and loss to get a net figure.'

'That's all right,' Lydia said. 'That's enough to let Charlie know they haven't been entirely honest with him.'

Before she could second guess herself, she rang Charlie and gave him an update. She had been commissioned to do a job, just like any other, and she had to see it through. Besides, if she didn't, he would find out another way. There was little that got past Charlie Crow and, for all Lydia knew, this job might have been a test of her loyalty. She was on thin ice in that area already and couldn't afford to fail it.

· · ·

A COUPLE of days later and Lydia hadn't heard anything else from Charlie. She allowed herself to hope that he was getting bored of using her as his pet project. Perhaps her lack of enthusiasm for either the Crow Family business or the training had paid off and he was going to back off. Leave her to run her investigative firm. It wasn't likely, but a few minutes of hope with her morning whisky was the closest thing to happiness she had felt in a while.

The relaxation was short lived as it was Thursday again. Lydia kept a sharp lookout for a tail on her way to her meeting with Mr Smith. She didn't like having a pattern of behaviour and she especially didn't like having one she hadn't chosen. All it would take was for one suspicious Crow, Aiden perhaps, to catch wind of her connection to Mr Smith and all hell would break loose.

Lydia was trying to be just enough of a disappointment for Uncle Charlie to lose interest. She knew that clinging to the hope that everything could go back to the way it was before was probably not realistic, but she wasn't ready to let it go, just yet. If she worked hard enough at being ordinary, perhaps she could make it so. It was like childhood all over again.

That thought reminded her that she hadn't spoken to Emma for a few weeks. She pulled out her phone and pressed the call button. Emma had coped extremely well with the discovery that Lydia lived with a ghost and Lydia had intended, as always, to be a more consistent friend, but her job and her life conspired against her.

And, of course, Emma had her own busy life. Two small children, a husband, family of her own, and a job. While Lydia no longer had to pretend to be normal around her best friend, which was a relief, it was also another thing that had changed, another new world order to navigate. After a few minutes of catching up on Emma's news, Emma asked how work was going for Lydia. 'Fine,' Lydia said, approaching the safe-house building. She walked past it, toward the park, doing a loop back to flush out anybody following.

'I know what that means,' Emma said. 'You sound stressed.'

Lydia rolled her shoulders. She was a Crow. Crows didn't feel stress. 'Nah, I'm all right. Just got a few things going on, you know how it is?'

'I know how you are,' Emma said. 'You don't have to pretend with me.'

'Honestly,' Lydia said. 'I'm not loving working with Charlie, but it's a necessary evil. It won't last forever.'

'You think?' Emma wasn't being unkind. She was honest and straightforward, just two of her excellent qualities.

'It better bloody not,' Lydia said lightly. 'Or we'll end up killing each other.'

'Don't even joke,' Emma said.

As ALWAYS, Lydia had arrived early for her meeting. She swept the flat each time, looking for surveillance equipment but also for anything that might have been left carelessly around, any clue as to the activities of Mr Smith's department. Lydia didn't expect to find anything, but it felt like a small measure of control. Besides, that was par for the course in investigative work. You sifted through a whole lot of nothing in return for the occasional win. It wasn't a profession for the impatient.

Mr Smith, for example, wouldn't have made a good P.I. Not based on his current demeanour. They had spent twenty minutes playing 'Mr Smith asks Lydia a question and Lydia side-steps it', when a tell-tale muscle began jumping in his smooth jawline.

'You don't seem to understand the terms of our deal.' Frustration finally broke through. 'I did you a favour and now you are returning it by giving me updates from your life.'

'You're not asking me about my life,' Lydia said. 'You're asking about my uncle and my father and they are both off limits.'

'You can't answer every question with a question of your own,' Mr Smith said. He was visibly trying to restrain himself and Lydia felt a click of understanding. He wasn't really angry. He was playing it as another gambit. Pretending to lose a little bit of control in order to make Lydia feel powerful. If she felt powerful, she might make a mistake. She couldn't help but admire the man. And maybe she could learn a technique or two. Free training from the spy guy.

'Are you MI5 or MI6? You never clarified.'

Mr Smith flashed a smile, all traces of frustration

and tension instantly gone. 'I told you, that's not how this works.'

'We didn't really hammer out the details,' Lydia said. 'You never expressly forbade questions. Anyway, I'm just making conversation. If I've got to be here, we may as well be friendly.'

'You want to be friends?' His expression was suddenly serious. 'I would like that very much. But I don't think you mean it.'

'What if I did?' Lydia pushed the box of pastries across the table toward Mr Smith. 'You know I've lost my police connection. I need another one.'

'I'm not police.'

'Not exactly, but that doesn't make you useless.'

His lips twitched. 'Thanks. My department works with both security services, but isn't a formal part of either.'

Lydia suppressed a shiver. A department that was too secret to be a formal part of MI5 or MI6. That sounded dangerous. 'So, it would help me to help you if I knew the kind of thing you are interested in. What is your department investigating? Is it the organised crime angle or the weird stuff?'

'Both,' he said, picking up his cardboard coffee cup. 'Which you already know.'

Lydia nodded, trying to hide her discomfort. 'And do they know about you?'

A slight hesitation. 'No. They don't have your ability.'

'My ability?'

'You sense it, right? Power in others?'

It was Lydia's turn to hesitate.

'Don't bother denying it,' Mr Smith said. 'Can we keep the lies between us to a bare minimum. I know you're a Crow. Why quibble on the details.'

He was being disingenuous, details were everything. Still, Lydia made herself smile and made it look easy and relaxed. She forced the tension from her muscles. 'Fine, let's not quibble. What's the end game? What are you hoping to achieve?'

Mr Smith shrugged. 'I'm on a task force. It's very new and very quiet. The stated objective is information only. Observation. Like documentary makers, we're not supposed to interact or affect our subjects. That will change, but I don't know when. Higher ups probably don't even know. It gets political at the top.'

'And you're all right with that?'

'Information is power. And I have a personal interest.'

'Because of your-' Lydia waved her hand. 'Stuff. Have you always been able to heal people?'

'Yes.'

'Tell me about your first time.'

He shook his head. 'I don't think so. We're not friendly enough for that.'

'Okay, tell me about your department. What do they think is going on with the Families? Do they believe the stories?'

'They're not big on belief,' Mr Smith said. 'They're into facts. Science.'

It was interesting that he referred to his department as 'them'. Either he wasn't strongly affiliated, which might work to Lydia's advantage, or he was pretending not to be in order to ingratiate himself. 'I'm not going to be a lab rat,' Lydia said.

Mr Smith shook his head. 'They don't cart people away and do illegal tests. This isn't the seventies.'

'How do they do their science, then?'

'Volunteers.'

'I find that very hard to believe.'

'Aren't you curious? Don't you want to know if there is something in your DNA or a new enzyme or a part of your brain that you are using in a different way to normal people?'

'I am normal,' Lydia lied. 'I grew up in Beckenham. I had a guinea pig. I watched TV on a Saturday morning and had swimming lessons in the afternoon.'

He shook his head. 'You know what I mean.'

'I hope you're not looking for a new volunteer, because that's never going to happen.' She had no intention of becoming somebody's experiment.

Mr Smith held up his hands. 'I want to be your friend, that's all.'

'And for me to inform on the Families,' Lydia said baldly.

He winced delicately as if she had made a faux pas at a tea party. 'I wouldn't put it quite like that.'

'I would,' Lydia said. She stood up. 'And now I'm leaving.'

'You'll come round.'

'I will not,' Lydia said, as she grabbed her jacket from the back of the chair. She was at the door, grabbing the handle when Mr Smith spoke again. She didn't break stride, didn't look around, but the words landed nonetheless.

'You're as curious as I am.'

CHAPTER TEN

Lydia had gone to bed early. She felt tired in a way that wasn't related to exertion. Tired in her soul. She had dozed for an hour and, around midnight, woken stark awake and lay there, looking at the familiar shapes and shadows of her room, lit by the dim glow of street-lights seeping through her curtains. She heard Jason walk down the hall and assumed he was heading for his bedroom, but then he knocked on her door, lightly.

'Come in,' she said, sitting up. The air was cool and she pulled the duvet up, knowing it was about to get even colder.

'You need to see something,' Jason said, hurrying over with his laptop.

'You're glued to that thing,' Lydia said. 'Don't work too hard.'

'I love it,' Jason said, instinctively hugging the computer close. 'But look.' He sat on the bed next to Lydia and opened the screen. 'After I catalogued the order emails, I had a poke around. This is a business email, so not much personal stuff, but I found messages from the online bookkeeping site they use which led me into their accounts.'

'Led you into?' Lydia said, raising an eyebrow,

'Well,' Jason shrugged. 'I went looking. But in there I found a strange pattern of payments. Look.'

Lydia peered at the screen. It showed a list of incoming and outgoing transactions, labelled neatly for the end of year accounts. Lydia used a similar system for her own business. She was just about to ask Jason what was unusual when she saw it. A payment for three thousand pounds from JRB Inc two days ago.

'I couldn't find a corresponding order,' Jason said. 'And there's no payment reference, no invoice in the accounts or the sent folder of the email address.'

'What the hell has a florist in Camberwell got to do with JRB?'

'Yeah,' Jason said. 'I mean, first I thought that an order was made in person and somebody forgot to put all the details into the system. But it's odd they forgot. I mean, that's a lot of flowers.'

'Or the payment was for something else entirely.'

'Several somethings, actually,' Jason said. 'There are matching payments made on same day for the last four months. The first has a note in the 'reference' section, which says 'address withheld as per customer instruction', so I'm guessing it's a recurring payment for a regular order to an address that has been recorded somewhere else.'

'Who on earth are JRB sending three grand's worth

of flowers to every month? And why wouldn't they want the address put into a database? That's pretty paranoid behaviour...' Lydia trailed off as she realised that they were, at that moment, mining the florist's private accounts for information. 'Can you get more on JRB from these transactions? Is there the digital equivalent of a paper trail?'

'I don't know,' Jason said. 'I will ask the collective and see what they advise.'

'The collective?' Lydia couldn't help but ask.

Jason was tapping away, but he nodded. 'They might need payment. Is that okay?'

'Sure,' Lydia said. 'We can pay them for their time. That's fair. I wonder what the going rate is for hacking. I guess it's too much to hope that they're all ghosts, too.'

WATCHING the florist on the following Saturday, Lydia observed the same lack of visible commerce. Again, she waited for Jayne to take her lunch break and paid Dylan a return visit. Once again, he was engrossed in his phone, and he didn't look up as she browsed the shop.

Stepping up to the counter, he dragged his gaze from the screen. Lydia didn't see any recognition in his eyes. 'Do you do deliveries?'

'Sure,' Dylan said. He pulled a hardback notebook from underneath the counter and flipped it open. The page was marked with a tatty ribbon and Lydia saw some scrawled writing and a few doodles of robots. 'What do you want?'

'I'm not sure, yet,' Lydia said. 'I just wanted to check the charges.'

'Free delivery with orders over fifty quid. Within London.'

'Okay,' Lydia nodded. She could see an open door behind Dylan which, she assumed led to the stock room and the place where the bouquets were made. If she knew more about flowers, she might be able to get him to go out there for a moment.

Dylan returned to his phone, saying. 'Retirement, right?'

'Sorry?'

'You were after a wreath. Last week? Sorry we couldn't help.'

'That's okay,' Lydia said. 'I got a bunch from M and S. This order is big, though. And I don't need it until next month.'

'How big?'

'I don't know, what can I get for five hundred?'

Dylan perked up. 'We've got lots of examples on our website. Browse the gallery there.'

'I want to know what they smell like, though. What have you got that smells good? Really strong.' Yep, flower-talk was not Lydia's strong-suit.

'Roses have a scent,' Dylan indicated a bunch of yellow flowers in a bucket to her left.

Lydia shook her head. 'I need something stronger.'

'Hang on,' Dylan said, 'I think we've got some Gardenia in the back.'

The moment he disappeared through the door, Lydia leaned over the counter to get a closer look at the notebook. Figures, messages to 'call Beth' and a prosaic 'to do' list. Lydia took out her phone and flipped the pages, photographing each one. She registered that there were occasional name and address with order numbers and, sometimes, prices, but she didn't try to read anything, just worked as quickly as she could.

She had only done six when she heard Dylan return and she had to flip the pages over and stand back.

Dylan was empty-handed. 'We don't have any out the back, but I'll make a note to get some in, if you want to come back?' He picked up a pen and hovered over the notebook. 'Can I take your name?'

'Shaw,' Lydia said. 'Rebecca Shaw.' She gave him the number of one of her burner phones and thanked him.

BACK AT HER DESK, Lydia went through the pictures. There weren't many addresses, especially given the amount of income Jason had found. Lydia's guess was that only telephone or in-person details were taken in this way and the rest were recorded by the online payment system used by the florist's website.

The addresses were all in affluent areas, which made sense until you stopped to wonder why folk would travel to Camberwell to order a bouquet of flowers when they lived on the other side of the river. Perhaps they were laundering money for JRB and part of the agreement involved sending flowers to JRB's friends? Assuming JRB had any. Could shell corporations have friends?

Lydia hated this type of investigation almost as much as she hated the background checks for corporations and recruitment agencies. It was so bloodless, so technical. Whether it was money laundering or tax evasion or insider trading, you could easily forget that there were real people suffering, somewhere along the line. And the people truly responsible were never the ones who got punished for it. At least, hardly ever.

Lydia didn't like to admit the other reason she was in a bad mood about it. The Crow Family had been involved in schemes not a million miles away from this kind of thing back in the day. Protection rackets, money laundering, and feathers-knew what else. It made her shudder. The Bad Old Days.

On the final page she had managed to capture, there was only one address. It was surrounded with flowers and vines, like someone had been doodling while on the phone, but had decided to take a break from the comical robot which appeared on the other pages. The address was near Hampstead Heath. Lydia recognised it because it had been in the news for being one of the most expensive addresses in London. What really made Lydia's heart race, though, was the name above the address. No first name or title, just the surname. Pearl.

Next to the address, almost obliterated by the doodled foliage was a date and the word 'paid'. Lydia went back to the florist's accounts and found the most recent payments for three grand. The date matched.

THE HOUSES in this part of London were not for ordinary mortals. The street that Lydia was driving down was known as billionaires' row and the address she had been given was on a gated street with a private security guard in a small wooden cabin. Lydia pretended to consult the clipboard she had brought with some mocked-up paperwork to give him the address and explained that she was making a delivery on behalf of Jayne's Floral Delights. She had hired a white van for the day and was hoping that the guard didn't ask to look in the back, as it was entirely empty.

'Where's the usual guy?'

'Sick bug,' Lydia said.

The road led to a row of detached mansions. Each had to be no more than five or ten years old, but they dripped with white columns, leaded windows, mullions and topiary and fountains, like miniature stately homes. They were all similar, clearly built by the same developer, but some were even larger than others. The address on Lydia's phone led her the biggest of all. It had a carriage driveway which swept past the house, and neatly clipped box hedges enclosing an ornamental garden. The heavy wooden gates at the entrance swung inwards as Lydia approached and she could see security cameras on the gateposts pointing both outward and in toward the house. Lydia couldn't see any signs of life, just large leaded windows reflecting the weak January light and an impressive doorway, flanked by white columns.

As she drove around the curving driveway, the front door opened and a small girl with tangled blonde hair adorned with a plastic tiara, muddy jeans, and a checked shirt which reached her knees hopped down the steps and stood, watching.

Lydia got out of the van, trying to smile in a non-threatening manner.

'You're not from the flower shop,' the girl said, tilting her head. Her voice was surprisingly mature. It was the voice of a small child, but the intonation was more adult. It was unsettling.

'I'm Lydia,' Lydia said. 'And I wanted a word with the head of the Pearl Family.'

'You're Lydia Crow,' the girl said. 'And you must mind your tone. Our king doesn't meet with any bird that flutters by.'

'I apologise,' Lydia said. 'May I meet with the king? I would very much like to make his acquaintance.'

'Not his,' the girl said. Baby lips pursed while she thought.

After a moment she turned and opened the door fully, leading Lydia into a huge square entrance hall. Open doorways led off in all directions and a staircase led up to an open gallery which ran across three sides of the hall. The floor was shiny marble, which Lydia imagined came as standard in these homes. What was almost certainly not standard, was the tree growing up through the middle of the room. It had a twisted trunk which looked like several trunks plaited together and the spreading branches reached the gallery railing above, twisting and twining with the wooden railing of the gallery.

Lydia followed the girl through an arched doorway which led to a set of stairs leading down. These stairs were less opulent than the main staircase, but the walls and thick carpet were immaculately clean and glowed with subtle mood lighting. It felt more like a five-star hotel than a private residence and there was the slightest scent of chlorine. 'There's a pool down here?'

The girl didn't answer.

The stairs turned a corner and, at the bottom, there was a space with a console table, small armchair and two closed doors. One was plain oak or another hardwood, polished to a high shine to bring out the woodgrain, the other looked like nothing else in the house so far. It was lacquered black and embedded with hundreds of tiny pieces of mother-of-pearl, like the lid of a jewellery box. There was the faint thump of a bassline through the door, a sound which was suddenly amplified when the girl opened it.

Lydia stepped into a room which could only be described one way, even if that way seemed faintly ridiculous in the twenty-first century. It was a throne room and the person lounging on the throne was both beautiful and sharp like a piece of broken glass. Music pulsed from hidden speakers, coloured lights danced, and throughout the large space, bodies were moving rhythmically. It was a small nightclub underneath a house, the mirrored walls making it difficult to assess its size.

The girl tugged on Lydia's arm until she bent down to the girl's height. 'You may approach,' her companion whispered, her breath hot in Lydia's ear. 'But you may not linger. Make your point quickly.'

'The king,' Lydia whispered back. 'Are they a he or she or should I stick with 'they'?"

The child shot her look of confused offence. 'You say 'your majesty'.'

'Of course,' Lydia said, trying to look reassuringly contrite. The child was frowning, as if rethinking this introduction. Feeling as if she was taking part in a play and a hot sense of self-consciousness creeping up her neck, Lydia stepped forward toward the purple velvet armchair. It had an enormously tall back and shiny-black scrollwork on the frame, stylised and cartoonish like something out of a Disney film. The king wasn't looking at Lydia, they were watching the dancers with half-closed eyes. One hand, draped across the arm rest twirled in lazy circles at the wrist, as if conducting the revelry through a drug-haze.

Lydia didn't know if she should bow or clear her throat or say 'greetings, your majesty' but it was a moot point as, suddenly, she didn't feel as if she was able to do anything at all. A strange sense of being rooted to the spot, along with a sludgy feeling in her veins, like everything had just slowed down. She could hear her heartbeat in her ears, which seemed impossible given the loudness of the music, but there it was, thumping slowly, slower than she expected.

The king was looking at her, now. Out of the corner of their eyes, their head very slightly tilted in her direction. She had never seen any person so beautiful before, Lydia realised. Not in real life. It was overwhelming. Somebody was at her side. It wasn't the child who had led her into this place, it was an older girl. She could have been twelve or twenty, it was difficult to say with the elaborate face paint. A line of sparkling crystals curved along each cheekbone and she had a bright rainbow of eyeshadow and thick black eyelashes and liner. It ought to have looked ridiculous, but somehow (probably because she was young and very beautiful), it didn't. 'The king is too busy to see you today,' the girl said. 'You must follow me.'

Lydia wanted to say that the king didn't look all that busy, but she felt herself unrooted from the floor and had enough sense to follow the girl meekly, after bowing her head in what she hoped was a respectful manner in the direction of the throne.

The teenager led her back up the stairs to the entrance hall. It was shadowed and dark, the enormous tree mysterious and vaguely menacing in the darkness. Lydia blinked, wondering if her eyes were taking time to adjust, the flashing lights from downstairs were still exploding in her vision. Then she realised that the elaborate window coverings had been drawn against the daylight.

'Goodbye,' Lydia said to the teenager who was already walking away. She didn't reply. When Lydia turned back, wondering whether she could get away with a quick look around the rest of the house, she jumped in surprise. The small girl who, Lydia would have sworn couldn't have beaten her upstairs without being seen, was standing at the front door, twisting a strand of blonde hair around her fingers while she waited.

'You made me jump,' Lydia said, hoping that acknowledging it out loud would ease her discomfort. It didn't.

Back outside, Lydia was surprised to find that night had fallen. The street lights were lit and the temperature had dropped another couple of degrees. If pushed she would have said she had been in the house for twenty minutes, tops, but her phone told her it had been closer to two hours.

'You bored us today,' the little girl said. Her voice was far older than her face. Or perhaps that was the confidence in her tone. 'The king says that if you decide to visit again, you must bring two gifts. One to make up for today and one for the visit itself.'

Lydia didn't bother asking how the girl knew what the king thought, even though she hadn't seen them converse. Instead she tried to make her voice deferential, which didn't come naturally. 'What sort of gift?'

The girl shook her head. She inserted a finger into her mouth and tugged on the nail.

'What does the king like?'

The girl had already turned away, and was halfway through the open front door of the house.

'Ah, come on,' Lydia said. 'Just a little hint. If you tell me what you like, I could bring you a gift, too.'

The girl stopped. She turned slowly back to face Lydia. 'Lydia Crow is offering me a gift of her own free will?'

Lydia swallowed. What had she walked into? 'Yes,' she said. She thought quickly. 'A gift that I choose, but given freely.'

The girl nodded. 'That is a very good offer and well put.' She smiled and Lydia felt herself lean forward, wanting to be closer. That was the Pearl she supposed.

The girl could have lifted her foot and Lydia would have kissed it.

'I like colourful things. And glitter.' The girl turned back and moved a few more steps. At the door, just when Lydia thought she was going inside, she looked back over her shoulder. 'The king likes dead things.'

CHAPTER ELEVEN

Lydia tried to keep her pace even, not allow herself to speed up as she walked back to the van and got inside. She itched to move faster, to run, to fly. The sound of beating wings was deafening as she turned the key in the ignition. She forced herself to drive beneath the speed limit on the way home. She was too late to return the van for the daily rental rate and would have to deal with it the following morning. An irritation which barely registered above the pounding in her chest.

Lydia's heart rate didn't slow down until she was safely behind the locked door of her flat. Jason was in his customary position on the sofa, laptop open. He looked up when she walked in and closed the lid immediately. 'What happened? You were ages.'

Lydia sat next to Jason and told him about the Pearls' house, the strange girl and the king. She left her request until last. 'They are big on gifts and the king won't speak to me without a good one.'

'I take it you're not thinking of a bottle of wine,'

Jason said. 'What about some money? You said Pearls like that.'

Lydia sat next to Jason on the sofa. 'You can say no,' she began.

'What?'

'The kid said that the king likes dead things.'

'Well that's not creepy at all.' Jason was trying to smile but it didn't reach his eyes.

Lydia touched his cold arm. 'You don't have to decide now, think about it. But you do fit the bill. And we know we can get you out of the flat, now.'

'You need to find out what the Pearls are up to,' Jason said, after a moment. 'You think they're working with JRB?'

'Maybe. Or they might know something about them. If they've been messed around by JRB, they might consider an alliance with us. That would be pretty handy right about now.'

'Since you pissed off the Silvers.'

'Yes,' Lydia said. 'There is that. But it's completely fine if you don't want to do it. It's a big ask.'

'You think an alliance with the Pearls would be a good idea? For the Crows? For you?' Jason wasn't vibrating but he was looking slightly-more-dead than usual. He was always pale, but his face had a grey-ish pallor. 'There could be safety in numbers.'

'I don't know,' Lydia leaned back, resting her head on the back of the sofa. 'It just feels like the ground is pretty shaky at the moment. Like one more little mistake could snap the truce into pieces. And then feathers-knows what would happen.'

'Maybe nothing,' Jason said, hopefully. 'Maybe it's just all stories. Stuff from history and none of it matters any more. Maybe the truce isn't needed anymore.'

Lydia looked at him. 'You believe that?'

'Sadly, no.' Jason leaned back next to Lydia, his body signalling defeat.

'Me neither.'

A couple of days later, Lydia was due at Charlie's house for another training session but she called to put it off. His demands in that area had been increasing and it was harder and harder to keep control. Part of Lydia was elated that she wasn't as powerless as she had always assumed, but most of her was frightened by it. She didn't like not knowing what was going to happen or what she might inadvertently reveal to Charlie. Every training session was an exhausting charade. 'I'm not feeling well.'

'Is that a fact?'

'Stomach issues,' Lydia said. 'You don't want the details. Trust me.'

'That's a shame.' Charlie managed to make the phrase sound like a threat. 'Feel better soon.'

The light on Lydia's answer machine was flashing and she listened to her messages. A prospective client left a number, but no details. She sounded angry and Lydia guessed it was another infidelity case. Not that it mattered. While juggling Charlie and Mr Smith, Lydia couldn't see how she could effectively do her job. A fact which made her furious. And thirsty. She looked at the whisky and then forced herself to make a mug of coffee, instead.

While she was in the kitchen, the phone rang and she let the machine pick it up.

The voice was agitated and the sentences disjointed. The caller was speaking very fast, but Lydia recognised it as the man who had called a couple of weeks earlier. She crossed back into her office, teaspoon in hand to listen. 'This is Ash. Uh, I've called before. Please call me back. I need help. They extended my hold and I know they mean well, but they can't help. They've got a certain perspective. A medical perspective. I need someone to find out what's really going on. I'm older than I...I'm not... I still don't have the right...' Then something unintelligible. 'I can pay. Call me back.'

Lydia looked at the blinking red light for a moment and then went back to make her coffee. She felt sorry for the man, but she had enough problems.

CHAPTER TWELVE

Christmas Eve was always a big deal in the Crow Family and Henry had kept the traditions he had grown up with. Vikings always counted the new day as beginning when the sun went down on the old one, so Christmas officially began once darkness fell on Christmas Eve. That was when feasting and gift-opening and drinking began in earnest. Christmas Day was for visiting family but, in deference to her mother's wishes and for Lydia's general protection, they had ducked out of the Crow Family Christmas Day gathering, seeing Charlie on Boxing Day when he arrived in the suburbs, hungover and quiet, ready to watch sport with Henry while Lydia played with her new toys.

The insurance money for Lydia's stolen Volvo had come through and, with the money she had saved from Paul's apology-cash, she had just enough to replace the ancient banger with a new rust-bucket. What she hadn't had, though, was the time or energy to do so. Lydia booked an Uber and packed a wheelie case and rucksack with hastily wrapped gifts. Then she checked on Jason. He was reclining on a pile of pillows on his bed, laptop resting on his knees. 'Is it okay if I stay overnight?'

'Course,' Jason said easily. 'My charge seems to last a good twenty-four-hours these days.'

'Still chatting with your hacker pals? Will they go offline for Christmas?'

Jason glanced up, a single eyebrow raised to show her just how stupid a question that was.

'But it's Christmas!' Lydia said, playing on her ignorance. She could see how much Jason enjoyed having an area of expertise. One that was current and not a result of his status as a ghost. It was good for him and he seemed more alive than ever. 'Even SkullFace has to celebrate Christmas!'

Jason shook his head, with a mock-withering look.

'Your present is on my desk. It's not much.' A book of fiendish math and logic problems, set by GCHQ, and a large notebook with squared paper. Lydia had hesitated over the packs of Sharpies, but she didn't want to encourage Jason to start writing on the walls again.

'I haven't got you anything, I'm afraid.'

'You're doing all the background checks for me, that's gift enough.'

'Aren't you giving me a salary?' Jason asked, his face serious. He held it for a couple of seconds, long enough for sweat to break out on the back of Lydia's neck, before grinning. 'Gotcha.'

'Hilarious,' Lydia said. 'Have a good night.'

. . .

THE SUN WAS low in the sky as Lydia travelled to the suburbs where she had grown up. The Uber driver was playing Last Christmas on a loop and Lydia didn't even mind. Christmas Eve had come at a good time, she needed away from Camberwell and Charlie's constant presence. She felt hemmed in, by him and by Mr Smith and by the Families. She had promised to be 'in' and she would keep her word, but that didn't mean she liked it. When her mum opened the door wearing a Santa hat, Lydia felt prickling in her eyes. She couldn't afford to be weak, but this was the one place she ought to be able to let her guard down.

As she followed her mum through to the living room, she vowed to open up about her feelings. Emma was always telling her that she wasn't alone and that she had to stop acting as if that was the case. 'Tea?' Her mum said over her shoulder. 'Say hello to Dad and then come and help me make it.'

Lydia stopped in the middle of the room. Henry Crow was hunched in his favourite chair. The snooker was on the television, but he wasn't looking at it, he was staring down at his lap. A line of drool poured from his slack lower lip. Lydia was stunned with the horror of it, but her mum swooped in with a fresh Kleenex, wiping up the dribble. There was a child's plastic sippy cup on the coffee table, next to the pillar candles and foliage her mother always put out in December.

She turned horrified eyes onto her mother, who was hovering, uncertainly. 'It's okay, darling. Let's make tea.' She scooped the cup off the table and said, in a loud and bright voice, 'Cup of tea, Henry?'

Her dad didn't respond.

In the small kitchen, Lydia could almost imagine everything was as it should be. It looked exactly the same as it always had. There was the blue vase in the window, the souvenir magnets on the fridge, the metal pan rest on the counter and the beige toaster with the faded dial which her parents had had since the early eighties and refused to replace even though it burned one side of the bread.

'Why didn't you tell me?' As soon as the words were out, Lydia knew why. Because she would have come to the house and her presence made her dad worse. Her power-up ability seemed to strengthen whatever was ailing her dad and his Alzheimer's-like symptoms got more intense whenever she was around.

'I didn't want to worry you,' her mum said, turning away to fill the kettle. 'You've had more than enough on your plate. And I don't suppose that's changed now.'

'I had to go in,' Lydia said switching subjects. The thing that had once seemed unthinkable had happened, but it paled into insignificance next to what was happening in this house, right now. 'I made a deal with Charlie when I was in jail. It seemed like the best option at the time. Now, I don't know...'

'I'm proud of you,' her mum said. Lydia was getting the milk from the fridge and she was glad they weren't looking straight at each other. She didn't have to see the conflict and pain in her mother's face, and could pretend that she was okay with her only daughter choosing to go all in with the Crow Family after she had given up her career and spent twenty-five years in the suburbs in order to keep her away from it.

'Don't let him push you around, though.'

Lydia knew she meant Uncle Charlie. 'I won't.' There was the sound of feathers fluttering in her ear and she forced herself not to flinch. 'What is wrong with Dad? Has he been to the doctor?'

'They say vascular dementia. Tiny strokes destroying his brain.'

Lydia sagged against the counter. 'Hell Hawk.'

Susan shrugged. 'I'm not convinced. I've asked for a second opinion, so we're just waiting on the appointment. I don't want them looking at his age and jumping to conclusions.'

Lydia wanted to say 'we both know what's wrong with him' but she wasn't sure whether her mum was ready to hear it. That Henry Crow was ill because he had been repressing his magic, his Crow nature, keeping it under wraps for the sake of his wife, who wanted to give their daughter a normal upbringing. 'When did it get this bad?' Her last coherent conversation with her dad had been when he had used a charm to sharpen his mind. A relic from Grandpa Crow. Had using it done this?

'He had a fit last week,' her mum said, dumping teabags into the food recycling. 'He's not been right since, but it's just a matter of time. He'll be better again, I'm sure of it.'

'Is there anything I can do?' The moment the words were out of her mouth, Lydia regretted them. She knew the best thing she could do was to stay away, her presence always seemed to make her dad worse.'

Her mum put a hand onto her arm and gave a gentle squeeze. 'I don't think so, darling. You spend as much time with him as you want.'

She didn't say 'while you can' but Lydia heard it loud and clear.

WAKING up on Christmas Day in her childhood bedroom, Lydia wanted to have a drink. It was still early, though, and she didn't know if her mum kept whisky in the house. She wanted to take the edge off the world so badly it made her hands shake.

Her mother was in the kitchen, wiping down already-spotless counters and stirring a pot of porridge on the stove. 'You want croissants? I've got some in the freezer I can put in? Or there's toast. I know you won't want any of this,' she indicated the pan of oaty gloop.

'Just a coffee, thanks,' Lydia kissed her mother on the cheek. 'How's Dad?'

'Still asleep,' she replied. 'He won't be up until after lunch, I'm afraid.'

'I have to go to Charlie's,' Lydia said. 'Sorry.'

'That's okay, thank you for coming.'

They were being weirdly formal with each other.

'Are you seeing Emma today? I've got gifts for her little ones.'

And there was the urge to cry, again. This normal world of gifts and her normal best friend and semi-detached houses, where the worst thing was the possibility of hateful porridge. There was a thumping noise from upstairs and her mother hurried up. Lydia stirred the oats. Not the worst thing. Not by a long shot.

Lydia dropped off the gifts at Emma's house on her way back to Camberwell, walking the distance to Emma's house and booking another Uber to get to Charlie's. First on her list after the holiday had to be getting a car.

It was a family day and she didn't want to intrude, but the half an hour of watching Archie and Maisie hyperactively bouncing around the living room while Tom and Emma laughed with each other was the single most precious thing Lydia could imagine. Maisie was so enamoured with the gift she had opened moments before Lydia's arrival that Emma couldn't coax her into opening Lydia's gifts. 'I'm sorry,' Emma said.

'No worries,' Lydia said. 'It's nice that she's enjoying herself.'

When it was time to leave, she hugged Emma tightly and felt the power of friendship flow between them. It wasn't Crow magic, but it was real and solid.

Emma pulled back and looked into her eyes. 'You doing okay? Really?'

Lydia gave her a rare full smile. 'Today was lovely. Thank you.'

Emma accepted the side-step, possibly because Maisie had just come out of the living room and into the hallway. She barrelled into Lydia's legs and wrapped her arms around her knees. 'Not go.'

Lydia couldn't kneel down with Maisie gripping her so she patted Maisie's curly head and promised a trip to the local soft play centre in the near future.

When she looked up, Emma had her eyebrow raised. 'You have to stick to that, you know. Maisie won't forget.'

'I know,' Lydia said, a touch defensively.

'Blimey,' Emma shook her head. 'You are full of Christmas spirit.'

CHARLIE'S HOUSE had two topiary trees in enormous stone planters on either side of his front door. His nod to the season was that they were tastefully lit with white lights and inside the house was ablaze with white candles in pewter holders. He might have looked like a thug in a suit, but Charlie had taste.

Lydia hadn't seen this many Crows in one place since the meeting in The Fork and it was overwhelming. Feathers, claws, and the beating of wings, plus the occasional uncanny sense that she was soaring high above the city, the feeling of a warm thermal current buoying her up as the horizon tilted. If she was completely honest with herself, it was a rush. The way she imagined drugs would feel.

Her Aunt Daisy had been the one to open the door to Lydia. Her face was flushed and Lydia guessed that the alcohol had been flowing for several hours. After they exchanged season's greetings and a slightly stiff hug, Daisy led the way down the hall to the big kitchen diner. Happy chatter, party hats, people wearing tinsel and Christmas jumpers, Bing Crosby on the discreet audio system; everything was the same as no doubt every other house in the street. Except for the real candles flickering on the tree in defiance of the London fire prevention service's best advice and the life-size straw goat which Lydia knew would be waiting outside on the patio, ready to be lit when darkness fell.

'What would you like?' Daisy had led the way to the bar, a table covered in white linen and booze bottles of every kind.

'Whisky,' Lydia said, already reaching for the blessed amber liquid.

'Charlie's in the living room,' Daisy was saying as Lydia poured herself a full tumbler. 'And John's here, somewhere,' she looked around. Without warning she leaned in close, gripping Lydia's arm hard enough to hurt. 'Have you heard from her?'

Never mind Mr Yul Goat, you could have lit Daisy's breath. She shook her head. 'Sorry.'

Daisy's eyes narrowed. 'Don't lie to me.'

Lydia pulled away. 'I've got to pay my respects.'

'Yes.' Daisy said, her voice loud and a little slurred. 'Yes, you do.'

Lydia wove through the crowd, nodding and exchanging greetings as she went. She needed to be seen by as many as possible, be visible and smiling for a half an hour or so and then she could slip away. Go back to her flat and drink one of her Christmas presents with Jason and his hacker collective for company. She felt bad about side-stepping Daisy, for telling a half-truth, but she could hardly tell her the full version. That she saw Maddie in her dreams. That sometimes she felt she was hovering just to the left of her shoulder, but when she turned, she was nowhere to be seen. That sometimes, when she was walking down the street or sitting at the metal table on her roof terrace or conducting surveillance in her old Volvo, she felt eyes upon her and would have laid money that Maddie was somewhere nearby, watching.

In between the large kitchen diner, there was what had been a dining room when the house had first been built and was now a kind of entertainment space. Low leather sofas, a wall of books, and a flat screen fixed above the fireplace. Aiden was slumped on one of the sofas, squished with a couple of similarly-aged, similarly-boneless-looking Crows. They all wore loose woolly hats and low-ride skinny jeans, and Lydia stood in front of them just long enough for them to notice her. 'Aiden,' she said, keeping her voice chilled. 'Good Yule.' After a moment, the youths struggled to their feet and offered handshakes and season's greetings.

In the living room, which had an impressive bay window shielded with both white blinds and wooden shutters, an enormous log was burning in the fireplace, kicking out more heat than was necessary with the press of bodies.

Charlie was standing in front of the fireplace, holding court to a circle of Crows. When he spotted Lydia, he threw his arms wide and shouted her name in a booming voice. Everybody stopped talking and looked, which was exactly the point. Charlie loved a bit of theatre and this was his moment. The prodigal child had returned to the fold and Charlie was going to make sure everybody knew where the credit should lie. It was also no mistake that she was now approaching him in his palace, like an acolyte hoping for benevolence. She walked into his embrace, the whisky she had just downed helping her to smile at the crowd once Charlie had released her from his hug and slung an arm around her shoulders. She looked around at the Crow Family and felt the smile begin to hurt the muscles of her face. It was going to be a long afternoon.

CHAPTER THIRTEEN

L ydia had downed another two tumblers and was ready to leave. She had paid her respects and, more importantly, had been seen to do so. 'I'm heading off,' Lydia said quietly to Charlie. 'Need an early night.'

'Nonsense,' Charlie said. 'You've got to stay for the goat.'

When Lydia had been small, she had dreamed of being at Charlie's famous Christmas party, of getting to watch the Yule goat, a life-size straw animal adorned with red ribbons, go up in flames. Now, standing in Charlie's house with her wider family all around and her mother's blessing to be there, she only wanted to run away. Fast.

'You'll stay,' Charlie was saying, now, certainty in his voice.

Then another cousin or great-uncle or somebody-removed, joined them, red-faced and grinning. 'Game's starting. You two in?'

Charlie shook his head and the man opened his

mouth, maybe about to cajole or tease and then clearly thought better of it. He dipped his head at them both, suddenly deferent.

'What game?' Lydia said, feeling sorry for him.

'Poker. In the kitchen. Low stakes, just for fun.'

'Maybe,' she said. 'I'll be through in a minute.'

After the man had moved away, Charlie spoke mildly. 'I wouldn't. Not unless you're very good. Philip will rob you blind.'

Lydia had been thinking she could join a hand or two to shake Charlie and his intense tete-a-tete and then melt away. She wanted to tell Jason about her dad. Never having been much of a sharer, there was something about Jason's undead status which seemed to loosen her natural reticence. Some of the time, anyway. Maybe it was because he was a ghost, maybe it was because it was Christmas or maybe it was the sixth tumbler of whisky, but she felt like some caring-sharing time in her PJs.

'Besides,' Charlie said. 'We've got some business to attend to.'

'Today?' Lydia asked, surprised.

She followed Charlie through the packed house, hoping he didn't mean a bit of training. With everything swirling around inside, she felt like it wouldn't take much to bring up her lunch. He led the way out of the front door and onto the street. The cold was a slap in the face and Lydia felt her nausea clear. 'Where are we going?'

Charlie opened the passenger door and waited while

she got inside before walking around and getting into the driving seat.

'Won't take long,' he said, flashing her his shark smile. 'Then it's goat-burning time.'

'Home-time for me,' Lydia said. 'You can drop me off. I told you, I'm knackered.'

Charlie ignored this and pulled out into the quiet street. Camberwell was subdued, but there were still plenty of people around. London didn't stop, not even for Christmas Day. As they approached the Thames, the roads got even busier, although there was definitely less crawling and waiting than usual.

Charlie chatted as he drove, talking about different people at the party and anecdotes from parties past. Lydia recognised it for what it was – a wall of conversation to stop her from asking questions. She settled into the leather seat and looked out of the window, biding her time.

A hotel carpark sign came into view and Charlie steered down into it. After they had parked, he led the way to a door marked 'reception' which opened into a stairwell and lift. He punched the button for the top floor and stood very still and quiet, arms crossed like a bouncer. Lydia sensed him putting on a cloak and she tensed herself, wondering what the hell was so important that Charlie would revert to work-mode in the middle of his Christmas. Having promised herself she wouldn't beg Charlie for information, reasoning that if he wanted her to know where they were going, he would have told her, she could feel her resolve weakening.

Before it broke, the lift doors dinged and slid open and Lydia was hit by a wave of Silver.

It was a party. Lydia heard elegant background music – something classical. Men in black tie and women in jewel-coloured gowns and high heels were drinking from champagne flutes, standing in little groups and talking and laughing. Picture windows filled one wall, with the lights of the city twinkling and a view of the river.

Charlie's hand was on the small of her back, steering her forward, when every part of Lydia wanted to fly away. 'What in the name of...' she began.

'This way,' Charlie said. 'And play nicely.'

A few people nearest the lift doors looked at them curiously as they passed, but there had been too much drink taken to raise anything other than a few eyebrows. Lydia expected screaming and, perhaps, violence, glasses thrown and the cry of 'intruders!' but they moved through the throng with minimum fuss. Charlie seemed to know exactly where he was going and, before Lydia had managed to get her breathing under control or adjust to the sense-overwhelm of so many Silvers in one place, they were through the main room and out into a short corridor before the door to a hotel suite was opened for them by a woman in a hotel uniform. 'Would you like anything to drink?' The employee asked. Lydia saw that she wasn't in hotel uniform, after all. The clothes were too expensive, even for a nice gaff like this. The white blouse was silk and she was wearing spike heels with red soles under perfectly-cut narrow black trousers. And she was a Silver. Lydia hadn't realised immediately because everything tasted of the cool sharp metal.

'No thanks, love,' Charlie was saying. He walked over to the window and looked out. 'Nice view.'

Lydia was looking around. They were in a living room area twice the size of The Fork and when an inner door opened, she caught sight of a bedroom with a bed that looked like two king-size divans put together. A bed that could sleep a football team.

Alejandro Silver was wearing a suit which looked more casual than the sea of tuxedos in the main room, but still managed to look sharper and smarter than all of them put together. That was bespoke tailoring, Lydia assumed, with a good helping of excellent genetics. And natural power.

'Charlie,' Alejandro said, shaking his hand and barely glancing at Lydia. 'Thank you for coming.'

'Best to get this sorted,' Charlie said. 'You're looking well.'

'And you,' Alejandro said. 'I trust the holiday season has been good to you?'

Charlie nodded. 'And to you.' He nodded in the direction of the party. 'Celebrating a good year for the firm?'

'The firm and the Family,' Alejandro said. He spread his arms. 'We've been blessed.'

'Glad to hear it,' Charlie said. 'Now, the matter of the children.'

Alejandro nodded. The woman who had let them into the suite, went to another door and opened it, producing from within the unwelcome sight of Maria

Silver. She was wearing a blood-red floor-length gown and a silver tiara that made her look like royalty.

'What's going on?' Lydia asked Charlie, who looked completely unperturbed. She felt her hands curl into fists, nails digging into palms. She forced herself to unclench. Produced her coin instead and held it there, secret and comforting.

'Maria, my dear,' Charlie stepped forward.

Maria's expression might have appeared neutral to a casual glance, but Lydia could see the suppressed fury in her eyes. She was feeling the same and a bolt of unexpected kinship shot through her. They were both here under duress, she realised, wayward children dragged to account by disappointed elders.

'Mr Crow,' Maria said, leaning in to air kiss Charlie on each side.

'Charlie,' Charlie said. 'I am such an old friend of your father.'

Maria's eyes half-closed and Lydia could see a muscle jumping in her cheek. There was a pained silence before Maria managed to say 'Charlie'.

Alejandro and Charlie nodded in unison. Satisfied.

'You don't have a drink,' Alejandro said. 'Were you offered one?'

It wasn't a serious question, Lydia could see. Alejandro knew the woman who had let them in, whoever she was, hadn't forgotten her duty. It was something else. A reminder that he was the host? That they were visitors in his world? What had it taken to bring Charlie Crow to the Silvers on Christmas day? Lydia screwing up, she supposed. Big time. But she was the wronged party. She was the woman who had been set up by the police. Yes, she had put Maria in jail a few months earlier, but that had been different. Maria had been guilty of murder.

The murderess herself was staring at the floor like she wanted to die herself.

'I think we should get this sorted,' Charlie said. 'It's always good to see you, of course, but we need to get back.'

'Of course,' Alejandro said. 'Maria will be your point of contact from now on.' He didn't glance at his daughter as he spoke. It was like she wasn't there.

'You'll be busy with your parliamentary duties. Congratulations.'

Alejandro held up his hands, mock humble. 'Too soon to say, but I am daring to hope. Yes.'

Charlie snapped his fingers at Lydia and she wondered what he wanted her to do. Beg? Roll over? Fetch a newspaper?

'It will be a great honour to serve the city I love and its people,' Alejandro continued. He sounded like a politician, that was for sure. Duck to water.

'We wish you every success,' Charlie said. 'You have the support of the Crow Family.'

The Silvers had had people killed. Maria had attempted to kidnap Lydia to do Feathers-knew-what, but Lydia could see the logic in Charlie's move. The truce had to hold. It was good sense to make nice with the Silver Family and to keep the alliances strong. Especially if Alejandro was going to add political power to his arsenal. Still. It didn't mean she had to like it. Or that she hated Charlie for blindsiding her with this meeting, rather than talking to her about it first. He was treating her like a naughty child dragged in front of the grown-ups to apologise. Sod that.

She stepped forward to Maria, hand out. 'Congratulations on your new position as head of the firm. They are lucky to have you.'

Maria blinked. Then she touched Lydia's hand in the briefest, weakest handshake the world had ever seen.

The bolt of Silver travelled up Lydia's arm but she plastered on a smile and offered her hand to Alejandro next. 'To new beginnings.'

THE DRIVE back to Camberwell was quiet. Lydia could sense that Charlie wasn't finished, so she wasn't entirely surprised when he refused to drop her at The Fork. 'Day's not over, Lyds,' he said. 'Duty calls.'

She wasn't going to give him the satisfaction of complaining about the surprise meeting, wasn't going to act like the shamed teenager even if he was treating her that way. Head up, game face on and don't show them you care. Advice from Henry Crow when Lydia started secondary school. Lydia looked into her own reflection in the window, staring into her eyes until they felt like a stranger's. A stranger who didn't care about anything.

Back at Charlie's house, the party was continuing as if they hadn't been away. Lydia plastered on a festive smile and knocked back a whisky at her earliest opportunity. She had been given the perfect chance to tell Charlie about finding the Pearl King while they were alone in the car, but the Silver meeting had thrown her. Lydia had always known that Charlie had very rigid views on how things ought to be done, but she was beginning to realise exactly what that meant.

A red-faced couple stumbled past Lydia in the hall as she headed to the kitchen. She was just pouring another drink when a ripple of excitement went through the party. She heard somebody say 'it's time!' and the phrase was taken up, repeated.

Charlie appeared, carrying a bundle of twigs, bound into a torch. There were cheers and hoots, people stamping and clapping and pulling on outer layers. Charlie led the way out of the glass doors and into the garden. The burning of the straw yule goat was one of the oldest Crow traditions, brought over from Scandinavia when they first landed on the British shores. 'As you all know, it is a great honour to light the midwinter fire. We burn the old year to usher in the new and we cleanse our world of our enemies.'

More cheers, glasses raised and clinked together, applause. Lydia was near the back of the throng and, being on the short side, didn't have a good view.

'This year, I am pleased to announce that my niece, Henry Crow's very own Lydia, is to have that honour. Step forward, Lydia.'

The crowd parted and Lydia could see Charlie, the torch now lit and held aloft in front of him. The fire was bright in the darkness and she blinked, trying to clear her vision. The faces of her family were strangely lit, glowing from below as many people had picked up candles on their way out of the house. She walked through the crowd, which was now eerily quiet. Halfway to Charlie, she realised something important about the straw shape. It wasn't the usual Yule Goat. It was a creature with pointed ears and a long brush tail. Its face was comically elongated making it look both more ridiculous and menacing at once. A fox.

'Nobody messes with this family.' Charlie's voice carried clear and strong. 'And we will show no mercy to those that dare.'

He passed the torch to Lydia, the heat coming from it was fierce and she had to blink away sudden tears from the smoke. He nodded at her. 'Go on.'

Lydia knew what he was doing. A final bit of theatre for the Family. He was in control, he was the leader and he had brought Lydia in from the cold. Now she had to show the Family where her loyalties lay by burning an effigy which represented Paul Fox and his Family. Show him and everybody else that she wasn't stepping out of line, that the old ways and the old alliances were holding firm and that she, Lydia Crow, was ready to follow them.

She was a Crow and Crows didn't flinch.

Hating Charlie in that moment, she stepped forward and thrust the torch into the body of the fox. It caught instantly, the fire ripping through the straw, consuming the body and the head of the creature almost immediately.

Lydia barely registered the whoops and cheers. She watched the blazing figure and tried not to feel as if her freedom was burning up along with it.

CHAPTER FOURTEEN

Once Lydia was finally released from Charlie's house, she walked home. She needed the air and movement to clear her head and to release some of the tension which had built up. Her thoughts chased each other, looping in circles with no resolution. Perhaps she should have told Charlie about her contact with the Pearls, her suspicions that they might be working with JRB. His little performance had put her out of the sharing mood, but it was more than that. He was clearly still all-in with the Silvers and that didn't sit right in Lydia's gut. She thought he was making a mistake.

Jason was watching The Princess Bride on his laptop, and there were several mugs lined up across Lydia's desk. 'Merry Christmas,' he said, hitting pause on the film.

'It's Boxing Day, officially,' Lydia said, flopping next to him on the sofa. 'Sorry I'm so late. Charlie was in a weird mood.'

'I forgot you weren't here,' Jason said, indicating the mugs. 'I was working.'

'Christmas, Jason,' Lydia said, mock-scolding him. 'All work and no play...'

He shrugged. 'It's not my favourite time of year.'

Lydia instantly felt awful. Of course it wasn't a fun day for the bereaved ghost. 'Sorry.'

'I like my book, thanks.'

Lydia accepted the change of subject. 'Shall we finish the film?' She went and got herself a drink and a blanket from her bedroom and curled up next to Jason to watch Westley and Buttercup and to try, very hard, not to think about Fleet.

A COUPLE OF DAYS LATER, and Lydia found herself making an odd decision. She didn't know if it was because Charlie had not-so-subtly forbidden fraternisation with the Fox Family and it had ignited her inner rebel, or whether she was just being diligent and thorough because it made sense to investigate who had been whispering in Tristan Fox's ear, suggesting that he set Lydia up for murder. Either way, she called the most recent mobile number she had for Paul Fox, the one he had used to call her, and was both disappointed and a little disgusted at her weakness when it was out of service.

It made sense that Paul would have ditched his phone, but it did mean that Lydia had to head over to the Foxes' den to find him. A thought that made her skin break out in goosepimples, but strengthened her resolve.

She couldn't walk around jumping at Fox-shaped shadows. She couldn't do her job or live her life if she was afraid. So, she wouldn't be afraid. She produced her coin and made it spin in mid-air about six inches above her outstretched palm. Watching it was like a meditation and, within minutes, the fear had drained away. She could do this.

Still. There was no point being foolhardy. She might be willing to believe that Paul didn't want her dead, but that didn't account for the rest of his Family. She wrote a note and called her preferred bike courier, arranging for immediate pick-up. She met the courier at a Turkish cafe a couple of streets away, having given a false address as her office. She wasn't paranoid enough to believe that every courier in London was a front for the secret services, but there was no need to let everybody know her business. She had an account with the company under the business name 'Magpie Holdings'. Couriers were only human and the temptation might be too strong to take a peek at the correspondence of a P.I. Curiosity was a powerful motivator, after all, and there was always the chance of a little opportunist thievery.

The courier, who had no idea of Lydia's suspicious ruminations, removed her bike helmet before walking into the cafe, revealing highlighted blonde hair in beach-girl waves and a tan which must have come from a bottle, unless being a bike courier paid better than Lydia imagined. She took the sealed jiffy bag and Lydia signed with a fingertip squiggle on the proffered screen. 'Guaranteed within two hours, right?'

The courier nodded. 'Your receipt will be emailed.'

. . .

AN HOUR AND A HALF LATER, during which Lydia had read a book borrowed from the stack of Angel's cast offs, which she had taken to leaving on a free library shelf at the back of the cafe, and eaten a plate of crispy fried potato rosti and eggs, Lydia's phone rang with the number of the phone she had sent to Paul.

'Very cloak and dagger,' Paul said, approvingly. 'What are you wearing?'

'Excuse me?'

'I'm imagining a trench coat and a monocle. Maybe one of those old-fashioned hats. Trilby?'

'Sorry to disappoint you,' Lydia said.

'Never,' Paul's Fox charm was effective even at this distance and Lydia concentrated on breathing evenly and telling her weak physical body not to respond to him. It wasn't entirely successful.

'Stop it,' she said, irritation breaking through. 'This was just a courtesy. To let you know that I formally acknowledge the great sacrifice made by your Family in banishing Tristan Fox. I didn't appear entirely trusting when you told me and I wanted to make sure it had been properly...' Lydia paused for a moment, the correct word evading her. Finally, she finished with 'noted'. Which wasn't really impressive enough, but would have to do.

'You checked it out, then.' Paul said.

Lydia kept quiet.

'We should meet,' he said, after a moment. 'To celebrate our continued alliance. Swap notes in these troubled times.'

'I don't think that's necessary,' Lydia said, ignoring the spurt of excitement. She did not need to see Paul Fox.

'I might have important information.'

'Do you?'

'I will tell you when we meet.'

'I'm too busy for games,' Lydia said.

'We both know that's not true,' Paul said. 'See you in an hour.'

After he hung up, a text came through with the words Imperial War Museum. Lydia hoped it wasn't a sign.

It was too cold to be standing around and Lydia circled the green space in front of the museum while she waited for Paul. She couldn't help thinking about the first time she had met him after returning to London, in this same place. Realising that she had reached the exit back onto the street, she turned back and saw Paul on the path behind her. The full force of 'fox' hit her and she realised that she must have been truly preoccupied not to sense it before she had turned. Sloppy. She truly had decided to trust him again, that much was clear. That much was alarming. Her heart leapt a little at the sight of him, too. It was an old reflex from when they had been an item. Which was history. Ancient history.

In a concession to the cold weather, Paul was wearing a black beanie hat and a khaki green bomber jacket over his standard uniform of close-fitting black t-shirt and jeans. It was something of a relief to see that he had a small amount of human weakness.

'Little bird,' he said, stopping a respectable distance. 'You don't look well.'

'I'm fine,' Lydia said. As soon as the words were out she could taste the lie. She felt shaky. And she wanted to sip at the flask that was stashed inside her jacket.

Paul tilted his head. 'Gotta look after yourself. I didn't just banish my father to have you drop down dead of your own accord.'

'Was that a joke? Are we joking about this already?'

Paul smiled. 'Just trying to ease the tension. I want you to relax.'

Lydia shook her head. 'Not going to happen. Not now, not ever. What information did you want to share? I assume it doesn't come free?'

'I spoke to Jack and the rest of them. They said that Tristan was very unhappy about us reconnecting.'

Lydia was going to ask why but she wasn't sure she wanted to hear the answer. Besides, this was old news. If Paul had dragged her across town to hear the same apology, the same explanation, she was going to lose it. She didn't have time for games or powerplays from Paul, she had her hands full with Charlie and her own personal spy master.

'Then, some Russian told him that the Crows were planning to move against our Family.'

'I remember. And I've already told you that wasn't true.'

'As far as you know,' Paul said. 'Don't know how forthcoming your uncle is with you.'

'Very,' Lydia said. She felt her coin in her hand and gripped it tightly. 'Especially now. I'm his right-hand.'

'And do you know what the left hand is doing?'

'Of course,' Lydia said.

Paul waved a hand. 'But I've been looking into the Russian and have found out something interesting. He picks up payments in cash from an office off Chancery Lane. It's registered to-'

'JRB,' Lydia interrupted. '*Feathers.*'

BACK IN CAMBERWELL and on foot, Lydia was trying to walk off the nervous energy which was fizzing through her. Seeing Paul was always a little disturbing. He reminded her of her past lust and their ill-advised relationship. She was in no state to deal with it, not with the aching emptiness Fleet had left in her middle. Her phone was in her hand and her fingertip hovering over his number, before she was conscious of the movement. She forced herself to switch the device off and put it back in her pocket.

As Lydia approached Well Street, a black cloud of smoke appeared above the roofline and there was a smell of burned plastic. Turning the corner, she sped up automatically, ready to step into the road to avoid the Pearl-owned grocers, when something made her stop moving altogether. The space which had held the sickly-pastel frontage of Jayne's Floral Delights was no longer there. Or, more accurately, the space was there, but it now held a burned-out shell, illuminated by the flashing lights from a police car and fire engine. The emergency services looked like they were packing up.

Lydia turned and moved down the nearest side street. Her phone was in her hand and she called Charlie. 'What the hell?'

'Not on the phone,' Charlie said and cut the connection.

Lydia headed for Grove Lane and Charlie's house. The front garden was filled with birds, mainly corvids, and Lydia greeted them as she marched up to the front door. She banged on the wood with the side of her fist, trying to release some of the adrenaline. She had to play this right. Be calm. Not antagonise Charlie. Get answers.

Her uncle opened the door, eyebrows raised. 'You're in a hurry.'

Lydia pushed past him and into the house. 'What did you do?'

Charlie's brow furrowed in an excellent impression of gentle confusion. 'What are you talking about?'

'The florist. Jayne Davies' place. It's been torched.'

Charlie shook his head. 'Very unfortunate. Such a shame they weren't up to date on their business insurance payments.'

'You did this.'

'We did this,' Charlie said, all pretence at gentility gone. 'You can't run Camberwell without being firm. Otherwise we couldn't keep control. If I let one business screw with me, what's to stop everybody else doing the same? You have to toughen up, Lyds. This is the real world.'

Lydia didn't answer him for a moment. She allowed herself a beat to modulate her breath and to let the first flurry of possible replies run through her mind.

'I know it seems harsh,' Charlie said, his voice a little softer. 'But I made sure there wasn't anybody in the building. They are closed this week for Christmas.'

Lydia felt her insides liquify. It hadn't even occurred to her that somebody might have been hurt. It was a place of business, but that didn't guarantee nobody had been inside when the fire was started. She forced herself to nod. 'Okay. Good.'

'Late night start, checked the place out thoroughly in case of surprises. It could have been so much worse.'

'Good,' Lydia said. 'Smart.' She didn't even really know what she was saying, just that every particle in her body wanted to be out of the house and away from the man standing in the hallway. He looked like the uncle Charlie she had known her whole life, but he wasn't the same man. That man was someone who ran a family with a dodgy past, someone who commanded respect and kept the worst of the drug gangs out of Camberwell, but someone who was part of the modern world. The man stood in front of her at this moment was something else. He wasn't acknowledging the past or honouring their traditions, he had one foot planted firmly in the 'bad old days'. No, more than that. The bad old days were the bad current days.

'I'm glad you popped round, as it happens. Here,' Charlie said, reaching behind Lydia to a small console table just inside the front door. 'Your payment.'

'I don't want payment,' Lydia said. She wanted to get

out before she threw up. Karen might have insisted that they couldn't think about the consequences when they did their job, but Lydia didn't agree. Besides, she had known something bad would happen. She had known and she had told Charlie about Jayne Davies' business anyway. The guilt was a hammer to her stomach and it took her breath away.

'Take it,' Charlie pressed a set of car keys into her hand and then closed her fingers over them, using both of his hands. He held them like that for a moment, looking her dead in the eye with his shark's gaze. 'You're with us, now, Lyds. And you need a motor.'

CHAPTER FIFTEEN

C harlie waited, watching as Lydia walked down the path to the main road. Lydia pressed the key fob and a gunmetal grey Audi which was parked directly outside the house responded. Lydia glanced back and Charlie raised a hand before retreating behind his door. The satisfied expression on his face made her stomach hurt. The car wasn't a flashy or brand-new model, but it was in excellent condition and far beyond anything she could have afforded to buy with her insurance pay out. Inside it had been expertly valeted and there was a branded air freshener hanging from the rear-view mirror. She drove it back to The Fork, finding her usual parking space a street away. Lydia tried not to admire how perfect the vehicle was for her needs and how quiet the engine, how deft the handling and definite the brakes. Any trace of enjoyment in the car felt like a betrayal of her independence and her moral code. Charlie had burned down a business like it was just another day at the office.

She had barely set foot inside her flat when her phone rang. She stared at the screen, frozen. She had been expecting an unknown number, which would be Paul calling from his new phone. Maybe to tell her again that she didn't know what her own flesh and blood was up to. Which, unfortunately, had just been proven to be perfectly accurate. But instead it was DCI Fleet and it took every ounce of her willpower not to slide the green icon to the side to hear his voice. He had respected her request to stay out of her life up until now and she wondered if there was an emergency. Something really important. As she wrestled with her emotions, the seconds ticked away until the phone stopped ringing. It had gone to voicemail and she waited to see if he would leave a message.

He didn't.

The disappointment was a punch to her stomach. Lydia tried to get back to work, but her concentration was shattered. She kept looking at her phone as if willing it to ring again, even as she was aware that she still wouldn't allow herself to answer. She couldn't speak to him, couldn't trust herself to stay strong and separate.

After ten minutes of torture, she picked up her jacket from the sofa and left the flat. She would go for a brisk walk, do some food shopping for dinner and maybe some comfort food for right now. Outside the air was like a slap in the face. London never usually got that cold, especially in comparison to Aberdeen, but this winter was the exception. Or Lydia was less robust than usual. She zipped up her jacket and stuffed her hands into her pockets.

Lydia turned left outside The Fork but had only taken a couple of steps when a familiar car pulled up alongside the kerb. Fleet got out, his hand resting on the roof. 'Can we talk?'

Lydia couldn't answer for a second. The sight of Fleet, tall and beautiful and wearing one of his delicious suits with the familiar grey wool coat over the top was too much to take in all at once. He was both known and unknown, this man. She knew every inch of his naked skin, had whispered and laughed with him in the dark, had spent hours staring into his eyes, and now those same eyes were roving around the scene, skittering from her feet to her shoulders to her face and then bouncing away, as if burned. Lydia thought she had prepared herself for the pain of seeing Fleet as a separate person, no longer her better half, but she had not.

'Just for a few minutes?' He said. 'In the car, if you like, it's freezing today.'

'Okay,' Lydia managed. She opened the passenger side door and got into the car, moving on autopilot. She could do this. The moment Fleet closed his door, she realised her error. They were too close and in an enclosed space. She could smell the Fleet bouquet and she was lost, hurtling backward in time to his bed, to her bed, to her sofa, desk, kitchen worktop and every floor in the flat.

'What do you need?' She was proud of that. It was business-like. Calm and contained. Efficient.

Fleet still couldn't meet her eye. He looked out of the windscreen as he spoke. 'A case that might be your kind of thing.' Then he described the man who had telephoned Lydia from the Maudsley hospital a few weeks earlier.

For a moment Lydia regrouped. She had been expecting Fleet to ask her about the arson attack on the florist, that he must have somehow subliminally divined that a Crow was involved. 'He's an in-patient in the psychiatric unit, right? He requested my services and I told him 'no'.'

'He said. He keeps phoning the station, though, and there's nothing we can do. I thought you might reconsider.'

'To stop him bothering you?'

Fleet flashed a sheepish smile. 'Partly. But mainly I think it's your kind of thing. It sounds a bit-'

'Odd?' Lydia supplied. 'Weird? Unreal?' She stopped herself before she said 'magic'. She wasn't with Fleet. Which meant she had to make sure those walls went back up. She remembered the feeling of being in the police cell. How had he not come to see her, there? Not reassured her? He said he had been trying to help her and, logically, she believed him and understood the difficult situation he had been in. Illogically, though, her body was tensed for flight and there was a bitter taste in her mouth.

'You know what I mean. I can't help him, but maybe you can.' Fleet shrugged. 'I feel sorry for the guy. He sounds really distressed. And we're really stretched at the moment.'

Lydia narrowed her eyes. She felt manipulated. And she had enough of that from Charlie. 'Isn't it below your pay grade? Why do you know about a random phone call to the station?'

'He told the sergeant that he had tried to engage your services so it got passed to me. Now I'm trying to pass it back.' He gave a small, regretful smile. 'Thought I would try, anyway. I'm slammed at the moment.'

Lydia ignored the fact that Fleet still had anything related to her passed straight to him. She thought, instead, about asking him about his current cases, but she stopped herself. She wasn't his girlfriend, his support, his confidante. 'I'm too busy. I told him that.'

'Fair enough,' Fleet said. 'Sorry to have bothered you.'

Lydia reached for the door handle, ready to leave. What had been so weird that Fleet would contact her, though? She ran over the story from when Ash had telephoned. It hadn't struck her as out of the ordinary in a magical sense. She turned back. 'What was weird? I get that the man is unwell, but he's being looked after by mental health professionals. If he has been wrongfully sectioned, then that's a civil matter surely? Something for a solicitor.'

Fleet looked at her, then, a deep crease across his brow. 'Ash believes that he has lost his true identity due to amnesia, and he wants help tracking down the details of his life. He wants help to track down his parents so that they can clear up the mix-up and bring him home.'

'He said his name wasn't his real name,' Lydia said. 'When he called me, he said that the people around him were imposters and that they had given him a false name or something. It definitely sounds like a mental health issue, so he's in the right place getting help from trained professionals. I don't see how me getting involved is going to help him. It might make him worse, confirm his delusions.'

Fleet nodded. 'Makes sense. Sorry. I got taken in. He sounded quite reasonable.'

Lydia was battling her senses. Not just her normal animal ones, the ones which were twisting her guts in a mix of anguish and desire, but her Crow sense. The one which told her when a person was packing power. She had caught an unusual gleam from Fleet in the past, but had become used to it with repeated exposure. It had been just part of him, the general 'Fleet' feeling. Now, having had no contact for almost a month, it was more distinct. It wasn't recognisable as Crow, Fox, Pearl or Silver. It was closer, if anything, to the flavour she got from Mr Smith. Which was disturbing.

'There's something else,' Fleet was saying.

'What?'

'I'm worried about you.'

'Don't,' Lydia said. 'My welfare is not your concern.'

'You're in touch with Paul Fox. After everything. You can't trust him.'

'And how would you know that? Am I under police surveillance, officer?'

Fleet winced. 'It's not like that.'

'If you are watching me in your own time, that's called stalking. So, which is it? Professional or personal invasion of privacy?'

Fleet's face went blank. 'Just be careful,' he said. 'Please.'

Lydia opened the door and got out of the car as quickly as she could. It had been a mistake to get into it in the first place. Standing on the pavement, sucking in lungfuls of Fleet-free air, she knew that she couldn't make that mistake again. She wasn't strong enough.

CHAPTER SIXTEEN

D espite the fact that it was the week between Christmas and New Year, traditionally a time for lounging about in PJs or taking it extremely easy while pretending to work and eating the leftover chocolate, Lydia knew that Mr Smith would still expect her to keep their standing appointment. On the plus side, Lydia had something she wanted to ask him.

Lydia knew that she shouldn't confirm Mr Smith's suspicions about her own power, but she also knew that she had to show willing in some way, soften him up. Since going home she hadn't been able to stop thinking about her dad and what would come next. Her mum would look after him at home as long as possible but, at some point, it would end with Henry Crow in a care home or hospice. Sitting in a chair or bed, staring into the distance and seeing nothing. It was the kind of thing you knew might happen to your parents one day. One day far in the future. But now, all Lydia could see was his face and the horrible blankness where his eyes used to be.

She pushed the pastry box away, the association with these enforced meetings spoiling her enjoyment forever more, and took a long sip of her coffee. She itched to add a nip from her hip flask, but resisted the urge. She needed a clear head. 'I've been thinking about you.'

Mr Smith licked sugar from his fingers and then wiped his hands on a paper napkin. 'That's nice.'

Lydia took a deep breath. 'You have an unusual signature.'

Mr Smith looked interested for the first time. 'Is that so?'

'How did you heal me?'

His expression closed down immediately. 'We're not here to talk about me.'

'I wondered if it was something you could do again. On somebody else. And whether it would work on a brain condition.'

Mr Smith tilted his head, appraising. 'Who are we talking about?'

This was a big disclosure. Henry Crow was officially out, but he was still the rightful head of the Crow Family and weakness of any kind was not something the Crows advertised. Still. If there was a chance Mr Smith could fix her dad, it was a risk she had to take. 'My father,' she said, her throat closing up as she spoke. 'He's got Alzheimer's or something similar.' She didn't add that it might be a magical disease, brought on by suppressing his own power. Firstly, that was just a guess on her part and secondly, the habit to disclose the bare minimum in any given situation ran deep.

'I don't wish to cause offence,' Mr Smith said, 'but the Crow Family are not considered to be generally a good thing. You must be aware that the NCA have been investigating them for years for organised crime. Making Henry Crow stronger isn't high up our list of priorities.'

Lydia didn't betray her surprise. Her understanding was that the Crows had been borderline legit for years, and that Charlie's recent foray into arson had been an aberration. She had assumed that the National Crime Agency would have lost interest decades ago. Either Mr Smith was lying or she was seriously naïve when it came to her family's activities. She had a horrible feeling it was the latter. Pushing that aside, she leaned forward, planting her elbows on the table. 'I'm Crow Family,' Lydia said. 'You healed me.'

'You're different.'

Lydia looked Mr Smith square in the eye. 'I'm also difficult to motivate.'

After a moment, he nodded. 'It might be possible. And I suppose I could leave it out of my report. I can't promise it will work, though.'

'Noted.'

'And I would need a gesture of goodwill. And payment up front.'

'I am happy to demonstrate my motivation, and I can do a part-payment first, but full payment only after my father is cured.'

'Not cured. After I've attempted a full cure.'

'No. Part payment for the attempt. Full for the cure.'

'But I might not be able to do it, why should I even try if I won't get the full payment?'

Lydia thought for a moment. She had to be sure that he was going to give it his full effort. She had seen the drained look on his face after he had healed her of a few bruises and a broken rib. He was playing her for all he could, doing his job, but it was possible there was more to it. If she had learned one thing from her father and Uncle Charlie's attempts at training it was that magic was tricksy. It never gave without taking away. 'Fine,' she said. 'Full payment for full effort, regardless of results. But how will I know you are giving your full effort?'

'I give you my word,' Mr Smith said.

Lydia was about to tell him that she wasn't a small child and that she would need more, when she realised he meant it. 'We would shake on it?'

He nodded. 'Coin to coin. Binding.'

Lydia remembered the chink sound of metal on metal when she had shaken his hand in the police station. Was she really about to make another deal with the mystery man? She thought of her father's slackened face and the line of drool hanging from his mouth and held out her hand.

After they had shaken, Mr Smith sat back in his chair. 'Now, that gesture of goodwill.'

'What do you want?'

'I want to hear about your life. How is working for your uncle going? Have you had any further trouble from the Silvers?'

'No more trouble,' Lydia said, ignoring the question about her uncle. She thought for a few seconds, calcu-

lating the least-worst piece of information she could give
Mr Smith. He would need breadcrumbs if she was going
to lead him toward healing her father.

'I've got something for you,' Lydia said.

Mr Smith inclined his head, but didn't say anything.

'You're familiar with the truce, I assume?'

'Set in 1943, when the four Families agreed to put
an end to the fighting in light of the losses incurred.'

'Good,' Lydia said, glad she didn't have to give a
history lesson. 'Well, someone has been trying to
break it.'

'Who?'

'I don't know, but every lead points to your old pals,
JRB. You know they were clients of the Silver Family,
maybe still are, but finding information on them has
been difficult.'

'This sounds like the lead up to another request for
my help, rather than you offering me something of value.
Your debt is growing.'

'I've found evidence that JRB are linked to the Pearl
Family. They might even be one and the same, I don't
know. That means the Pearls are in some way complicit,
if not active, in trying to destabilise the Families.'

'Not necessarily,' Mr Smith said. 'How strong is this
link you've found?'

'What do you know about the Pearls? I thought they
were quiet shopkeepers, not very powerful, not very
interested in politics and power-play.'

'Unlike the Crows and the Silvers.'

'Yes,' Lydia said impatiently, 'which is why our
alliance with the Silvers was always so important. If we

were on the same side, we were less likely to tear each other apart in the race to the top. At least, that was the theory. And it's all dust now as far as I'm concerned.'

He raised an eyebrow.

'Maria Silver has been named the new head of the Silver Family. And she's not my biggest fan.'

Mr Smith nodded. 'This is a reaction to Alejandro setting his sights on politics, I assume?'

Of course he knew about that. 'So, the Pearls?'

He leaned back in his chair and regarded Lydia for a long moment. When he spoke, it was in the tones of someone recounting an often-told story. 'Once upon a time, a woman went through a door in a chalk hillside and married a prince. When she came back, three hundred years had passed, and all of her human family were long dead. She wasn't alone, though. Growing inside her belly was a child. Half-fae, half-mortal, and that baby girl was the first Pearl.'

'I don't believe in fairies,' Lydia said.

'Nobody sane does,' Mr Smith said. 'That doesn't mean they don't exist.'

On New Year's Day, Lydia woke up late, a foul taste in her mouth. She had finished another bottle of whisky the night before and the evidence was on her nightstand. She had slumped down, shoving her laptop to the bottom of the bed, sometime after two. She retrieved it, and pushed her pillows up against the headboard. Once she was sitting up and had swilled her mouth out with a stale can of cola, Lydia felt her mind clearing.

She fired up the computer and checked her email. Jason had sent her a neat list of work completed with a hyperlink to their new shared folder. Feeling ridiculous, she emailed the ghost back to say 'thank you'.

Fleet had reminded Lydia about the phone call and with the need to do something which felt like a positive act, she called the Maudsley and asked for the ward that Ash had given. 'This is going to sound a bit odd,' Lydia said, 'but I received a call from one of your patients. He said his name was Ash. No surname. And that might be a nickname. He didn't seem completely sure.'

'How can I help?' The nurse on the line sounded genuinely sympathetic and Lydia wondered what it took to do that job and still be gracious to randoms interrupting your busy work day.

'He sounded distressed and, I don't know, I felt like I should check on him. Or alert you or something. I don't know...'

'This ward is for inpatients receiving psychiatric treatment. Unfortunately, many of our clients are often distressed. You're not family?'

'No,' Lydia said. 'I don't know him at all. I know you can't give me details and I'm not asking for any information, I just wanted to pass on what he told me in case it's medically relevant, I guess. If just felt wrong to completely ignore it.'

'I understand,' the nurse said. 'I'll make a note. When did he call?'

Lydia gave the details she could remember.

'And what did Ash say to you? Did he give a reason for contacting you?'

'He wanted to book me. I'm an investigator, and he wanted me to find his parents. He said his name wasn't his real name and that everything had changed. He said there were imposters everywhere, that nothing was real.'

'I see,' the nurse said. 'That sounds distressing. I'm sorry.'

'No, it's fine,' Lydia said. 'I was just thinking about it and I felt bad that I hadn't tried to help him, I guess. Can you just tell him that I called to check up on him?'

'Of course. May I take your name?'

'Lydia Crow.'

There was a pause. 'That's interesting,' the nurse said. 'I'm looking at his file right now and you are down as his emergency contact and on his approved list of visitors.'

'How is that possible? I've never met him.'

'He gave us those details, actually. We haven't been able to track down his family. We've actually passed his details onto the police in case he comes up on the missing person database.'

'Wait. He was right? His name isn't Ash? You don't have his actual identity?'

'It might be. We haven't been able to confirm that. He had no ID on him when he arrived. He was transferred from A and E to us for emergency assessment.'

'So you haven't been in touch with his family?'

'Unfortunately not.'

'Can I speak to him, now?'

'I'm afraid he's in group at the moment. I will tell him you called, though, and you can always visit. Open visits are allowed between two and four every day and ten until twelve on Saturdays. You will need to bring some ID and there is a list of items you may not bring with you or gift to a patient on our website.'

After hanging up, Lydia spent a few seconds hoping that she hadn't inadvertently got Ash into any kind of trouble or contravened her own rules for privacy for clients. He wasn't a client, of course, but he had come to her for help. She had the feeling she had done the wrong thing, but couldn't work out what the right action would be and, after a minute more of fretting, she let it go.

THE FORK HAD BEEN CLOSED over Christmas and New Year, but it opened on the third of January and seemed as busy as normal. Life in London never paused for long. Lydia had ordered a coffee and a bacon roll and, as a nod to health, a glass of orange juice. Angel wasn't serving, she was leaning on the counter scrolling through her phone while a new employee fumbled with the coffee machine. He had a slight build, light brown hair, and an intensely worried expression, but that was probably because he was new. Lydia didn't imagine that Angel was a very patient teacher.

'Thanks,' Lydia paid the new guy and took a sip of her coffee while he went into the kitchen to retrieve her breakfast.

'You seen this?' Angel straightened up.

'What?'

She passed her phone to Lydia, clicking her tongue on the roof of her mouth as she did so. 'Aren't you supposed to be a detective?'

'Investigator,' Lydia corrected. 'For hire. Doesn't mean I spend my days scanning the news for jobs.' She trailed off as her attention was caught by the video playing. It was from the BBC website and Angel had subtitles on. A high-ranking police officer was giving a press briefing in front of a cordoned-area, her face serious, but Lydia wasn't reading the words. She had caught sight of a familiar figure behind the yellow tape, amongst the crowd of people. Fleet.

'It's local, though,' Angel was saying and Lydia forced herself to focus on the words being spoken by the reporter. The fifteen-year-old daughter of local councillor Miles Bunyan had been missing for three days and police were appealing for witnesses. Lydia knew that meant the team were scraping the barrel for leads, and would now have to contend with a stream of time-wasting phone calls, most innocent, some intentional, and some downright psychotic.

She squinted at the screen, trying to work out where the film had been shot and what the cordon was protecting but the clip ended and another one started, a climate change report this time. Rolling news. An onslaught of misery and fear.

'Bunyan,' she said out loud. 'That name rings a bell.'

'Head of Southwark Council,' Angel said, sniffing. 'Always banging on about the Camberwell Regeneration Plan.'

Lydia didn't reply, she was replaying the glimpse of Fleet, waiting for the spike of adrenaline to fade. Had he looked tired? Happy? Worried? It was pointless to speculate and it was, she reminded herself, none of her business, but the thoughts kept looping.

Her breakfast appeared and she took it to a table in the window. Her appetite had gone, but she forced herself to eat, scrolling on her own phone while she chewed. She found the news story and followed the various reports. There wasn't much information, but that didn't mean much. Fleet's team would be careful about what they released to the press, especially when launching an appeal. The more they kept quiet, the easier it would be to spot the genuine tips. She put her phone face down. She felt bad that a girl was missing, but it wasn't her job. The name Bunyan was very familiar, though. Then she realised why – Charlie had mentioned him. He counted Bunyan as an ally in the continual fight to keep Camberwell afloat.

Draining her orange juice like the glass of medicine it was, Lydia stood up to leave. There was something else tickling at the back of her mind. Something important. It wasn't until she had walked back upstairs to her flat and sat at her desk for ten minutes that the thought finally sidled out from the shadows and into the light.

She leaned back and examined it for a few moments, cross that it hadn't struck her before. It had been when Angel had handed her the phone, it had reminded her of when Angel had pointed out the man hanging from Blackfriars Bridge. Kicking herself, she went downstairs to confront a certain dreadlocked person.

Angel was sitting at one of the cafe tables, reading a paperback while the new kid swept the floor.

'Give us a minute,' Lydia said to him. He looked at Angel who nodded.

Lydia stood by Angel's table, trying to marshal her thoughts. Charlie hadn't just been watching her through his camera or turning up to ask her things. He had been pushing her around without her even knowing it.

'You work for Charlie,' Lydia said flatly.

'Yeah,' Angel put the book face down on the Formica. 'What of it?'

'You showed me that news article. The hanged guy on Blackfriars Bridge.'

Angel shrugged. 'You would have seen it, anyway. The story was everywhere.'

'You've been reporting to Charlie, I assume?' Lydia forced herself to unclench her fists, to let her arms hang by her sides and her face to relax. Angel was an unknown quantity and she moved quickly. Lydia had seen her wielding a giant cast iron pan over a burner and had no desire for things to get physical.

Angel shrugged. 'He pays my wages. He asks, I answer.'

'Did he tell you to nudge me toward certain jobs?'

Angel sighed, looking bored rather than anything else. 'Sometimes. He seemed to think that the direct approach wouldn't be most effective.'

'Why does he want me to look into this?' Lydia tapped the phone screen to reawaken it, revealing a picture of Miles Bunyan and his wife looking tearful.

'I think you're misunderstanding the nature of our agreement. He asks, I answer. Not the other way around.'

'And that's okay with you?'

'He's Charlie Crow. And I work at The Fork.' This was spoken like Lydia was a functional idiot.

She smiled, producing her coin and spinning it in the air. She had been trying not to use her mojo on people, not wanting to walk too far down the path of coercive control, but Angel was pissing her off. 'I'm Lydia Crow,' she said. 'And I think we should have a little agreement of our own.'

Angel gave her a look which was both vaguely annoyed and very tired. 'You gonna pay?'

'I'm going to let you keep your job,' Lydia said. 'Which is pretty reasonable from where I'm standing.'

BACK UPSTAIRS, Lydia sat at her desk and poured the last of the whisky into her mug. She didn't know why she was so thrown by the news from Angel. She had been aware that Charlie had been trying to control her from the moment she stepped foot back in London, but it was unsettling that she hadn't suspected Angel. It made her wonder what else she was missing.

CHAPTER SEVENTEEN

Lydia paced her floor until Jason asked her to stop because she was making him nervous, and then called her uncle. 'Are you near the cafe? I need to speak to you.'

'And a happy new year to you, too, Lyds.'

Lydia didn't reply. After a moment, Charlie said. 'I could go for some more breakfast.'

Angel looked alarmed when Lydia arrived back downstairs and even more worried when Charlie pushed open the door.

'Coffee,' Lydia said. 'Make that two.'

She steered Charlie to their usual table.

'I might want to eat,' he said.

'No time,' Lydia said. 'I saw the news.'

She watched Charlie's eyes, expecting him to flick toward Angel. They didn't and, once again, Lydia marvelled at how good her uncle was at concealment. He was wasted in Camberwell. 'Did you ever think about joining the secret service?' Lydia said.

'What?'

'Nothing,' Lydia sipped her coffee. 'Shame about that missing girl.'

Charlie lifted his cup. 'I wanted to talk to you about that, as it happens.'

'Oh, right?' Lydia kept her voice light.

'It's something we should get involved with. See what we can dig up.'

'By "we" I assume you mean "me".'

He shrugged. 'You're the expert. You found Maddie.'

'I'm a bit busy at the moment,' Lydia said. What she didn't say was that she didn't like being manipulated and she *really* didn't like casual arson. If she investigated something on Charlie's behalf, what would the repercussions be this time?

'Not too busy for this,' Charlie said and his eyes were flat. He flashed his shark's smile and his eyes didn't change. It was a warning and Lydia didn't even need to glance down to know that the tattoos just visible beneath the folded cuffs of his black shirt were writhing.

'Why do you care so much?'

'Miles Bunyan is an old friend. He has been very good to this area.'

'The Camberwell Regeneration Plan?'

'Amongst other things,' Charlie waved a hand. 'Miles Bunyan has cared about Camberwell when his colleagues would happily see all funds diverted to Bermondsey.'

'Is he a good father, too?'

Charlie paused. 'What are you insinuating? That

he's the reason Lucy has run off? He has done every-thing for that girl. He has been mother as well as father ever since Caroline passed, held down his job, been head of the council, active with charity work-'

'Okay, okay,' Lydia held up her hands. 'Got it. Father of the year.'

'It'll be that boy of hers. Unsuitable outside influ-ence. Happens all the time, some good-looking kid turns a young girl's head, makes her forget her sense.'

Lydia decided to pretend that Charlie wasn't having a go at her. Tensions were already high between them and didn't need any more stress applied. 'I'll see what I can do,' Lydia said, placating. Then, because she couldn't help herself, she added 'it would help if I was still friendly with Fleet.'

Charlie bared his teeth. 'You don't have to be friendly to get information.'

'I can't promise anything,' Lydia said. She made to leave and Charlie stopped her with a hand on her arm.

'Not yet. We need to pay our respects.'

MILES BUNYAN WAS SITTING on the brown leather sofa in the narrow living room of his Victorian end terrace. It wasn't a big room, but there were the original sashes in the bay window and the house was close to Burgess Park. Lydia wondered how much council leaders got paid.

'It's good of you to come,' Miles was saying. 'I don't... I don't know what I'm doing at the moment.' He started to stand up. 'Would you like tea?'

'Lydia will make some,' Charlie said.

Lydia was glad to escape to the kitchen, away from the heavy sadness in the living room. She found mugs and teabags and filled the kettle, then took the opportunity to have a good look around the room. It had a dining area which led to doors and out to the garden. The conversion was nicely done and fairly new-looking. There were a few takeaway menus pinned to the fridge with magnets and a pile of post on the counter.

She went upstairs and found Lucy's room. The last time she had been snooping in a missing girl's bedroom it had been Maddie, her cousin, who was missing. Maddie had turned out to be alive and well, well enough to attempt to kill Lydia, in fact. Lydia hoped that history would only half-repeat itself in this instance. The room was very clean and tidy and looked like the 'after' in a Marie Kondo clip. Either Lucy had been that way, or her father had taken the opportunity of her absence to have a clear out. There was a white desk with an angle-poise lamp and a single succulent in a teal pot. Before Lydia could get started on the bedside drawers, she heard the living room door open and Miles's voice. She slipped out of the room and into the bathroom across the landing. She flushed, washed her hands and headed back down the stairs, smiling at Miles who was standing at the bottom, looking lost.

'I thought you might need... A hand. Directions.'

'I'm fine,' Lydia said. 'You can help me carry, though.'

In the kitchen, Lydia concentrated on finishing making the tea. Miles stood stock still, like a clockwork toy that needed winding. 'We are really close. She wouldn't go off without telling me. She knows how worried I would be. How worried I am. She would never... I know what you think. What the police think, but you're wrong. She was happy. She had no reason to leave.'

And then, the awful sound of him crying.

Lydia turned, a mug in each hand. She ought to put them down, comfort the broken man, but she didn't know him and was trespassing on his grief and fear.

He wiped his face with his hands. 'Sorry. Sorry, it's just... I can't help think something bad has happened. Otherwise she would be in touch.'

'Not necessarily,' Lydia said, hating herself for offering hope when it might not be warranted. 'She's fifteen. She might not be thinking straight or be worried that she's in trouble with you.'

'No,' Miles shook his head violently. 'We are more like friends. And she's very sensible. Very grown-up. She just wouldn't.'

'Okay,' Lydia put the mugs down on the counter and squared her shoulders. 'What have the police said?'

'They asked a lot about Josh. That's her boyfriend,' Miles's lip curled. 'He was with her on the night she went missing. He's a bit older than her, just passed his driving test although I won't let her get in the car with him. Too risky. Statistics show...' Miles trailed off. He wiped his face, again. 'You do everything you can to protect them, you know? Everything. And then... This.'

'What is he like?'

'Joshua?' Miles shrugged. 'Seventeen-year-old boy.

Polite, at least. Speaks to me which is more than I can say about the last one. He was bad news. I told the police, I told them they should be looking at her ex. They keep saying they are following all enquiries, standard language.'

Lydia nodded. 'They will be, though. They will do everything possible. What does Josh say about Lucy? I assume they've asked him about that night?'

'He's claiming amnesia. Says he doesn't remember anything before he was found wandering around Highgate the next morning. He must have taken something. Drugs. What if he gave Lucy something? She could be ill... Lying somewhere.'

Miles moved suddenly, picked up a mug and turned away. There was a deeply snotty noise as he cleared his throat. Lydia followed him back to the living room but he paused right outside the door, speaking quietly and quickly. 'They suspect me. I know they do. I don't mind, I understand, I know it's usually,' his voice caught and he took a ragged breath, 'it's usually someone they know, I know that. But I don't want them to waste their time. I want them to find her.'

SITTING in Charlie's car afterward, Lydia recounted the conversation. Charlie nodded. 'That's pretty much what he's been saying to me. I told him we will do everything we can. He has been good to us, good to Camberwell, we owe him.'

'What happened to Lucy's mother?'

'Cancer,' Charlie said. 'When Lucy was three. It's

been her and Miles ever since. He's not so much as looked at another woman. His daughter and his work are his world.'

'What is his work?'

'Apart from leader of the council? He's got a directorship, I believe.' Charlie looked away and Lydia didn't know if he was being evasive or whether he was embarrassed by not having more specific information.

'You want me to use my contacts? See if I can get an update on the investigation?'

Charlie nodded, not looking at her.

'You could have just asked me, you know,' Lydia said. 'You don't need to go the long way round.' She wondered if he would acknowledge his use of Angel.

Charlie started the engine and checked his wing mirror before pulling out into the traffic. He didn't answer and Lydia could see the tattoos on his forearms writhing. She added another piece of information about her uncle Charlie. He didn't like being confronted.

When they arrived at The Fork, Charlie stopped outside and made no move to get out of the car. 'Right then,' Lydia said. 'Thanks for the lift. I'll be in touch.'

Charlie didn't look at her when he spoke. 'This is bad, Lyds.'

'I know, she's just a kid.'

He shook his head sharply. 'Everyone knows Miles is a friend of mine. He should be protected.'

'You can't be held responsible for everything,' Lydia said, wondering if Charlie had always been this cavalier about other lives. *There was a kid missing.*

He glanced at her then and Lydia saw that his eyes

were bloodshot. 'I'm the head of the Crow Family. If people think I can't protect my close friends, what are they going to say about my ability to protect the community? Their families? Livelihoods?'

Taking a deep breath, Lydia texted Fleet. She headed it 'work enquiry' to head off any suggestion that this was a personal request. The mug on her desk had the dregs of whisky in the bottom and she swirled it out in the sink before adding a fresh shot. Her phone rang five minutes later.

'What can I do for you?' His tone was calm and professional, and Lydia could hear phones ringing and other office sounds. The sound of his voice still punched her in the gut, though. A spike of longing so strong it made her hunch over in her chair.

'Lucy Bunyan. I was hoping you could talk to me about it.'

'Why?'

'Family connection,' Lydia said, standing up and pacing the floor. She had to let out the excess energy coursing through her body or she would crack open like an egg. 'Charlie is pals with Miles Bunyan. He asked me to help. If I could.'

'I can't tell you anything that hasn't been given to the press. This is a sensitive operation with a high profile.'

'You getting pressure?'

'Nothing I can't handle,' Fleet said, there was the sound of a door closing and the office sounds disappeared. 'I can't do this.'

172

'Fair enough,' Lydia said. 'I said I would try and I've tried.'

'No,' Fleet said. 'Not on the phone. You want to talk, meet me for a drink tonight.'

LYDIA HESITATED OUTSIDE THE HARE. She cursed Charlie and his demands and the world at large for putting kids in danger. There wasn't anything she could do that an entire police department couldn't, but now that she had met Miles Bunyan and could put a grieving, frightened father to the story, she couldn't help but try. Damn Charlie and his intuition. He had known the best way to get Lydia onside.

Fleet was at the bar, waiting for his pint. He nodded at Lydia. 'Usual?'

'Red wine,' Lydia said. 'What? It's bloody freezing.'

Sitting in the corner of the pub with her back to the wall and a large glass of red within grasping distance, Lydia reminded herself to breathe. She might not be romantically involved with Fleet now, but he was a good person. She could trust him. Not the way she had, perhaps, but enough for this particular job.

'I'm going for a slash,' Fleet slid out from his seat almost as soon as he had sat down.

It took Lydia a moment to realise what he had done on his way - unlock his iPad and leave it on the table. She didn't hesitate, scrolling through the images.

When he returned, she didn't put it down and angled it to show him exactly what she was looking at. She had enough spy-shit mind games with Mr Smith.

'CCTV places her and her boyfriend partying in Highgate Cemetery.'

Fleet nodded. 'We've had a witness come forward to say that they saw a couple matching their description heading into the woods just after half eleven.'

'Highgate Woods? Which entrance?'

'The one nearest Highgate tube station. Gypsy Gate.'

'Credible witness?'

'Yes.'

'And what is this?' Lydia pointed at the evidence photograph. It showed a blazer jacket which was either old and originally black, or new and dark grey.

'Boyfriend's jacket. Complete with blood stains. Also belonging to boyfriend.'

'How much blood?'

'More than a shaving cut, less than an arterial bleed.'

'Lovely. Does that mean he isn't a suspect anymore?'

'Could have been defence wounds, if he was attacking her, but no. No other blood found and we haven't found any motive. By all accounts they were a golden couple. We're looking into her ex, apparently he was the jealous sort.'

'Good,' Lydia said. 'Miles mentioned the ex.'

Lydia tapped for the next image. The previous image had shown the jacket laid out on a table in the forensics department, but this was it in situ, where it had been found by an officer during the mass search of the woods.

'It was off the path, but otherwise not hidden. Just sitting there,' Fleet said. The jacket was on top of a large tree stump, folded, as if its owner had intended to come back for it.

'It must have been freezing that night. Why would he take a layer off?'

'Teenage love keeping him warm?'

Lydia nodded to concede the point. 'And alcohol. They were partying in the cemetery, right? Just drinks?'

'CCTV shows them drinking from cans of Marks and Spencer's ready-mixed gin and tonic before things get a bit heated. Then they move out of shot. There are only cameras around Karl Marx's grave because of the vandalism there. And those were only installed relatively recently. We're lucky we got anything.'

'Gin and tonic?' Lydia screwed up her face. 'What the hell is going on with today's teens?'

'Swiped from home, most likely. Opportunity rather than taste. Although, who knows? People can surprise you.'

'He's seventeen. Can't he buy whatever he wants? Or does he look young?'

'Maybe he's not a big drinker. Maybe they thought it was romantic. When I said they were getting heated, I didn't mean they were arguing...'

'Got it. Has the search finished?'

'Yes, last night. Nothing else found, sorry.'

'Better than finding something,' Lydia said, thinking about decomposing remains and shallow graves in the frozen mulch. She could hear birds calling as they wheeled high in the sky and shook her head to clear it.

Fleet was looking at her and Lydia could practically hear him thinking.

'What?' She said, her patience snapping.

'There's something else. We're keeping it out of the press.'

'My lips are sealed,' Lydia said.

'We've interviewed the boyfriend. He was found by a dog walker early on the first. He was confused and hypothermic and still seems to have total amnesia for the whole evening.'

'Seems to,' Lydia repeated. 'What does the hospital say?'

Fleet shrugged. 'Just that it's perfectly possible and that there's no way to tell if its genuine or not. He says that the last thing he remembers is heading out to meet Lucy just after seven on the thirty-first. He claims he was at home until then, sleeping in until midday and then revising in the afternoon. He's doing A Levels at Peckham College, which is where he and Lucy Bunyan met, and they've got mocks next week.'

'You believe him?'

'About the amnesia or his claim that he was studying?'

'Any of it.'

'Amnesia is convenient, but he doesn't have anything resembling defence wounds. If anything, he looks like a victim. And he appears genuinely distressed that Lucy is missing.'

'What do you reckon?'

Fleet paused. 'That he's telling the truth. He seems like a traumatised kid. You want to see for yourself?'

'Is that allowed?'

Fleet shook his head. 'When has that stopped me?

Besides, I value your opinion.' He slid his iPad across the table and Lydia took her ear buds from her pocket and put them in. The video of Joshua's initial interview was queued up and she hit the arrow to start it playing.

Fleet was right, Lucy Bunyan's boyfriend looked like a frightened child. Yes, he had scruffy sideburns and a proto-goatee which he had probably been proudly growing for months and the muscles of a sporty young man, but the expression behind his eyes was that of a nine-year-old lost in a crowd. Lydia had the urge to comfort him. His right leg bounced up and down throughout the questions and he kept rubbing his eyes like a tired toddler. As well as his female legal representative, there was a man from social services there for safe-guarding. At seventeen, Joshua didn't fall under the rules for children, but he wasn't legally an adult either. The two police officers interviewing him did an excellent job of radiating calm concern for his welfare, while also subtly questioning every aspect of his story. Just as Fleet had said, there wasn't much of a story. Joshua didn't remember anything from the time he left his house to meet Lucy.

'Joshua's father has confirmed that he was home all afternoon, in his room.' Fleet said.

One of the officers on the video was asking Joshua about his A 'Levels, trying to put him at ease. Then, the other one chimed in with a different question. 'Do you remember where you were going to meet Lucy?'

'I don't know,' his hands were fists, rubbing at his eyes.

'What do you usually do when you meet up with Lucy? Do you have favourite hang outs, activities?'

'Depends. Sometimes we go to each other's houses. Or we do something, go to Nando's or whatever. I don't remember what we did that day. We'd talked about doing something for New Year's Eve, but I'm not sure we'd chosen. Some mates were having a house party, maybe we went there?' When he moved his hands away, the skin around his eyes was red from the repeated action. He blinked back tears. 'I swear I don't remember. Did anybody else see me? They can tell you what we did.'

'Your dad hasn't seen you since you left the house on the thirty-first. He agrees that you had plans to see Lucy.'

Joshua's shoulders sagged. 'You see, I'm telling the truth. I'm trying to help, I swear. I don't know why I can't remember. Do you know where she is? How long has it been? I want her to be okay. She's got to be okay. She's my... She's...' He struggled for breath, doubling over.

'Can we take a break?' The legal rep said.

'No,' Joshua sat up. 'I'm okay. I want to help. You've got to find her. I love her.'

The simple way he said the last words had the ring of truth. Lydia could feel it in her teeth, her blood. This kid wasn't lying.

'All right, Joshua. Let's skip to the woods. You were found walking in Queen's Woods. Do you remember how you got there?'

He shook his head. 'No.'

'What is the last thing you remember?'

'I was really cold. I think I had been asleep. But I wasn't lying down. I was just walking. There were loads of trees and my throat hurt. Like I'd been shouting or I'd smoked a lot. It still hurts.'

'That's really good,' the officer nodded, encouraging him. 'Do you remember seeing anyone?'

'The lady with the dog. She was walking her dog and she asked if I was all right.'

'That's the last thing? What about just before you met the dogwalker? Can you think back?'

He closed his eyes, was silent. After a minute, he opened his eyes and shook his head. 'No. Sorry. I can't. I don't know why. I don't think I hit my head or anything. Why can't I remember?'

'Why do you say you didn't hit your head?'

'It doesn't hurt,' he said, running his hands over his skull. 'It would hurt if I had, wouldn't it? Wouldn't I have a lump or something? My chest hurts, though. And my arms.' He stretched them out and stared at the bandages. 'What happened?'

'You had a series of superficial wounds. Not serious but there were a lot of them and they were quite open. They put antibiotic spray and then covered them over to keep them clean while they heal. Do you remember that.'

He nodded. 'Yeah. I forgot. I just thought it was something else for a moment.'

'I think we should leave it there.'

The recording stopped and Lydia took her ear buds out. 'What were the injuries on his arms?'

'Little cuts. Done with something sharp.'

'Razor blade?' Lydia said, immediately thinking of self-harm. 'Does he have a history of hurting himself?'

'Not as far as we know. And he says he didn't do it.'

'How does he know? He says he can't remember anything.'

'There is that,' Fleet said, acceding the point. 'He says he didn't intend to hurt himself and wasn't carrying a blade of any kind, to the best of his memory.'

'Do you have pictures?'

Fleet tapped the screen and turned the iPad back to Lydia. The cuts chased any thoughts of self-harm straight out of Lydia's mind. They were intricate patterns, visible despite the blood which was seeping, even though Lydia knew the picture would have been taken immediately after the wounds had been cleaned. Her stomach turned over. Someone had taken care when carving these images into the boy's arms. She couldn't imagine anybody managing to do this to themselves, particularly with no prior experience. It had to have hurt like hell. And then there was the clincher – the design spanned the tops of each arm up and reached well above the elbow onto the biceps, each arm matching and equally neat. The kid would have to be an ambidextrous contortionist to have done it to himself.

'What do you think?' Fleet asked, watching Lydia carefully.

'That it's all a bit weird.'

Fleet nodded.

'I believe the kid, though,' Lydia said, indicating the iPad. 'What's your gut say?'

'I'm trying not to go with that so much these days.'

Lydia felt like she had been slapped, although she wasn't sure exactly why. She was probably being sensitive. Fleet was talking about work, that was all. He ruined that theory by softening his gaze and leaning a little closer.

'How are you doing?'

Lydia picked up her wine and drained half the glass before answering. 'This isn't a social visit.'

'I'm doing badly.' Fleet picked up his pint and then put it down without drinking. 'Very badly.'

Lydia avoided his eye and pretended that her heart wasn't trying to leap out of her chest. 'Any other lines of enquiry? Will you let me know if there are any developments?'

'I shouldn't,' Fleet said. 'But I will. Because I choose you. I choose you every time.'

'Not every time,' Lydia said, feeling suddenly heavy. She stood up to leave.

Fleet leaned back in his chair, looking up at Lydia with his steady brown eyes. 'You want me to show you where the jacket was found?'

Lydia had picked up her own jacket but she hesitated. *Feathers.* 'Yes. Let's go.'

CHAPTER EIGHTEEN

Lydia agreed to go in Fleet's car for simplicity. Plus, he had immunity to parking fines. They were cutting it close time-wise as the park shut at sunset and at this time of year that would be half four. The sky was a flat grey, cloud covering the low sun. 'We can always jump the gate if we get locked in,' Fleet said.

Lydia kept her window open a crack, letting in a steady stream of cold air. She scrolled through her phone and tried to pretend that the silence between them wasn't awkward. Fleet got the last space in the small car park behind Highgate Underground. There was a disused train station above the tube line and two exits. They took the most direct route to Muswell Hill Road, assuming that the kids would have done the same. They passed The Woodman pub on the corner and up the road running between Highgate Woods and Queen's Woods. It was unsettling to see this many trees in London, it was even worse than the suburbs where she had grown up.

Fleet voiced the same thought. 'Feels different around here, doesn't it?'

'It's not Camberwell,' Lydia agreed. And it was about to get worse. They took the Gypsy Gate into the woodland, with its information maps and green metal sign, Fleet leading the way. They hadn't walked for very long when the trees became more dense and the sounds of the traffic faded away. There were bare branches, mixed in with the shiny dark green of the holly and some of the big trees still had brown-ish looking leaves clinging on. 'Is that climate change?' Lydia said, pointing at them.

'Hornbeams,' Fleets said. 'Tend to keep their leaves in winter, apparently.'

'Mr Nature,' Lydia said. 'I had no idea.'

Fleet gave her a brief smile. 'I read up on the woods. You never know what will turn out to be significant.'

Lydia was about to launch into some weapons-grade teasing about the likelihood of tree knowledge pertaining to a crime investigation, but then she stopped herself. She had to remember that this wasn't social and that laughing together was no longer on the cards. One day, maybe, but not yet. It was too soon. Would they ever be actual, real 'just friends'? She had no idea. Taking covert glances at him was like sips of water after a week crossing a desert. Both unbelievably sweet and nowhere close to quenching her thirst.

The trees were getting closer and a few minutes later, the sky disappeared behind a ceiling of branches. 'I think it's this way,' Fleet said.

'You think?' Lydia replied, stepping over a tree root. They had left the wide main path almost immediately, and the well-trodden informal trail they had taken seemed to have disappeared, too. Now, they were walking over the dry mulch of fallen wood and bark and leaves. Drifts of brown leaves which remained from autumn, rotting down and hiding who-knew-what. Lydia shivered. *Feathers.* It was cold.

They kept moving, not speaking. Lydia no longer felt the silence between them was awkward, it felt like a held breath. Like they were both listening to the creak of the trees, the rustle of dry leaves. Then Lydia realised what she wasn't hearing. Birds. She stopped moving and thought. She had heard calls when they had started out. Blackbirds definitely, and something trilling and small, maybe a chaffinch. Now there was nothing.

Fleet was a few feet away, looking down at the ground. Lydia wanted to say something, get him to walk back to her, but she didn't know what and, suddenly, she felt her throat close up. It was fear. Primeval fear. She was on the balls of her feet, ready to lift, and could feel the muscles of her back and shoulders flex, as if they could sprout wings. There was a rushing in her ears and Lydia felt time slow as she scanned the trees, trying to find the danger.

There was a movement in the distance, hard to say how far as the closely packed trunks and undergrowth formed an optical illusion. Lydia tracked it, keeping perfectly still and waiting for the figure to reveal itself. A flash of red-brown caught the breath in Lydia's throat. For a moment she thought it was a fox, but it was too high up. Something much larger. A deer? It didn't seem likely.

Fleet wasn't looking at the ground, now, he was staring in the same direction. 'You see that?'

The sound of his voice released Lydia's feet and she moved toward him, not taking her gaze away from the animal, whatever it was. When she was in touching distance of Fleet she said 'what is it?' very quietly.

'Something doesn't feel...' Fleet began, but stopped. His words were falling on dead air, like it was muffled. It was more than just the effect of the woods; it was aggressively deadened. A creepy, unnatural effect that made Lydia feel as if they had walked into a trap box with invisible walls. And now something was happening to the trees. They were growing. Quickly and smoothly, branches extended, twigs appeared, and leaves uncurled. Green leaves in every shade from pale grey to deep emerald, red, white and shining black berries, sprays of white blossom, every possible state of every tree and bush burst into life. Lydia would have doubted her eyes, but the silence was broken by the sounds of cracking wood and the rustling friction of leaves, the damp sound of berries ripening all at once.

'What the -?' Fleet had grabbed her hand, pulled her against his side.

'I don't know,' Lydia's throat was dry. She squeezed his hand. 'We should move.'

The ground was shifting, the drifts of brown leaves whipped by a wind Lydia couldn't feel. She could taste green in her mouth, pollen and leaves, and her nose and eyes were itching. *Children holding hands in the dark wood*. That wasn't a helpful thought and she pushed it away. She had to think. She had to work out how to get them out.

She couldn't see which way to go, but instinctively turned around, pulling Fleet by the hand. They could go back the way they had come. Toward the main path and sanity. Fleet swore as a branch crashed to the ground, just to their left. The wind was stronger, now, and the air was filled with small twigs, leaves, and bark. Something heavy landed on Lydia's lip and she brushed it away with instinctive revulsion. It was a large beetle, which had presumably been minding its own business underneath the leaf mould until a few seconds ago.

And then, as quickly as it had begun, the wind died. The vegetation which had been whipping around their faces, poking their eyes and invading their mouths, dropped back to the forest floor. A shaft of sunlight pierced the tree canopy and illuminated the scene. Lydia was shaking, adrenaline coursing through her system. The greenery had gone and the trees were back to their winter state. Bark on the hornbeams glinted silver in the sunlight and the oak trees stood solid and still, as if they would never dream of shaking their branches.

'Did that just happen?' Fleet was looking around, dazed.

'Has it stopped?' Lydia said.

'Yeah,' Fleet pulled Lydia into a quick hug which she didn't resist. He dipped his head. 'You okay?'

His face was too close, the movements felt too natural. Lydia stepped away, swallowing hard. 'Fine. That was weird, though.'

'Understatement,' Fleet said, straightening up.

His expression was hard to read and Lydia wondered why he wasn't more freaked out. The truth of this hit her like a blow. He had always been exceedingly calm with weirdness. Too calm. Was it linked to the strange gleam he carried? And if so, what did he know about that? What hadn't he told her?

'Look,' Fleet was moving away, his attention focused back on the ground.

The eerie, muffled silence had dissipated and Fleet's steps sounded normal. Small twigs were snapping under his feet and, somewhere up above, there was the sound of birds calling. 'Someone was here.'

Next to the thick trunk of an oak tree there was an area of compressed undergrowth. It was flattened in a shape that would suggests a body had sat there. Plus, there was a pile of cigarette butts. At least ten, maybe more. In addition to those physical signs, Lydia's senses were giving her further information. She closed her eyes to better identify the signature. Pearl. Very faint, just the residue, but unmistakable.

Fleet was snapping on gloves and Lydia did the same. He took photographs of the area, the remains of the cigarettes and the flattened patch of ground before picking up two of the cigarette ends and sealing them in a plastic evidence bag.

Lydia crouched down next to the tree, scanning the ground carefully. She worked methodically, breaking up the ground into quadrants and studying each section left to right, like reading lines on a page. Once she had done the first area, she moved out a little way and repeated the exercise, ignoring the crick in her neck.

'I'll call it into the team, they will get SOC out here and go over the area. We should leave.'

'In a minute,' Lydia said. The greys and browns and greens of the ground had revealed themselves in all their variation. The decaying leaves, fraying pieces of bark, tiny white fungi peeking from between patches of rich green moss. Even in December, there was life, if you were prepared to look hard enough. The smudge was tiny. A little iridescent turquoise glitter on a well-preserved oak leaf. She bagged it.

'What's that?'

Lydia straightened up and gave him the bag. 'Could be make up, or a fleck from clothing. What was Lucy wearing?'

'Nothing sparkly, but I don't know about accessories, make up. Can we get out of here, now? This place gives me the creeps.'

'Too many trees,' Lydia agreed. 'It's not natural.'

CHAPTER NINETEEN

Back in the car with Fleet, Lydia was thinking hard. Fleet stayed quiet, driving back to Camberwell. 'That wasn't normal,' Lydia said, breaking the silence. 'You saw it.'

'Yes.'

Just one word, but a huge admission. 'Does that happen often to you? Seeing things which aren't normal?'

Fleet kept his eyes on the road and Lydia did, too. It was easier to talk about something like this side-by-side. 'Not often. Something out of the corner of my eye, sometimes. A gut feeling which feels stronger than normal.' After a pause he said, 'I saw a man at your flat once. Just standing there.'

'What did he look like?'

Fleet glanced at her, then, a frown creasing his forehead. 'A weird loose suit with the sleeves rolled up.'

Lydia realised something about being finished with Fleet. Her worst fear had come true, already, so it didn't matter if she was open with him. She couldn't break the relationship because that had already happened. What difference could it possibly make if he decided she was a lunatic or a freak? 'That's Jason,' she said. 'He's a ghost. He died in the eighties, that's why he's dressed like that.'

A beat. 'If ghosts exist, why is this my first?'

'Good question. I think I power people up. Any latent ability gets stronger when you are in contact with me. Which explains why your most intense experiences of seeing unusual things have been when we're together.'

'Makes sense.'

'Does it? That's good.'

'And when you say ability...'

'Magic.' Lydia said the word flatly. 'Or Crow power. I don't know what to call it. An extra sense?'

'Could be a brain wiring thing. Like people who smell colours or have ADHD. Neurodiversity.'

'Or you could be having a psychotic break and I'm enabling you.'

'No,' Fleet said. 'I don't think that. I have never thought that. And if I accept that you have different abilities, I must also accept that they are a possibility in other people. Even me.'

The seriousness of his tone made tears spring to Lydia's eyes. Hell Hawk. She was a mess and she needed to get her mind back on the case. 'Which hospital is Joshua Williams in?'

'He's at home, now,' Fleet said. 'Why? You planning to visit?'

'I want to see if he has remembered anything else from that night.'

'He hasn't said so far. We've got a FLO staying with the family and he says Joshua hasn't been chatty on the subject.'

'Can I have his address?'

'His mother won't let you in to question her traumatised son,' Fleet said. 'Even if I were to give you the address which I absolutely should not.'

'Let's go together, then,' Lydia said. 'You want to speak to him again, anyway, don't you? Just let me tag along. I won't say a word.'

Fleet let out a short laugh. It seemed to surprise him. He glanced at her and sighed. 'I can't say no to you, Lydia Crow.'

'Good to know,' Lydia said. She ignored the traitorous flutter in her heart and looked out of the window.

Joshua Williams lived with his parents in the 1930s modernist Ruskin Park House, which had well-tended gardens, and three five-storey blocks with an art deco feel to its curved lines. They made their way up a remarkably clean stairwell with pale yellow tiles on the walls to a second-floor apartment. The FLO opened the door and, after checking Fleet's ID card carefully, invited them in for tea.

Joshua was sitting on the sofa in the small, neat living room, eyes fixed on the television screen where a first-person shooter PlayStation game was displayed. He was gripping the controller so hard that his knuckles were white, but Lydia didn't know if that was his usual intensity when shooting digital zombies in the head. It was warm in the flat and he was wearing a grey T-shirt, the bandages on his arms reaching from his wrist and disappearing up inside the sleeves. Lydia had seen it on the video but Fleet was absolutely right – there was no way Joshua had inflicted those wounds by himself.

Fleet introduced himself and Lydia.

'Hi.' Joshua didn't look away from the screen or pause in his movements.

'How are you feeling?'

'Have you found Lucy yet?'

'No,' Fleet said. 'We will tell you as soon as we have any news.'

'Right,' his eyes flicked at them, just once. 'Sure.'

'I'm not police,' Lydia said, deliberately not looking at Fleet. 'When DCI Fleet introduced me just now, he didn't mention my rank and that's because I don't have one. I'm a private investigator and I'm going to do everything I can to find Lucy.'

Joshua looked at her for a longer moment. 'Why? Did my dad hire you?'

Before Lydia could ask him why he thought his father might be so keen to find Lucy Bunyan, he elaborated. 'He's worried I'm going to be taken in again for questioning, that you will keep me as a suspect unless Lucy comes home and explains to everybody that I didn't do anything to her, that I could never hurt her.'

'Yeah, they kind of jumped on you, didn't they? Don't take it personally. You were the last person to see her and you're romantically-involved. It's just statistics.'

Joshua widened his eyes, then looked at Fleet.

'I'll go help with the tea,' Fleet said, and headed out of the room

'Can I sit?' Lydia moved toward the sofa. It was a four-seater and Joshua was at one end, leaving plenty of space.

'Okay,' Joshua stabbed a button and froze the action on screen.

'No,' Lydia said, glancing at the door, 'leave it playing.'

Joshua frowned.

'Privacy,' Lydia said quietly, cutting her eyes at the living room door, which Fleet had left ajar.

Joshua nodded and turned his body toward her.

'I've just been at the woods.'

Joshua visibly flinched.

'And I know you have nothing to do with Lucy's disappearance. You are as much a victim as she is and I'm really sorry this has happened to you.'

He blinked. 'Thank you.'

'This is going to sound weird, but I don't have much time,' Lydia glanced, again, at the door, estimating how fast she would have to cut to the chase. 'There is something not right in those woods. I could feel it. And then the trees changed. They sprouted leaves and berries all at once, but it wasn't pretty, it was really sinister.' Lydia fixed him with a long look. 'Believe me, I don't scare easily and I couldn't wait to get away.'

'That's... I don't know why you're saying that.'

'Yes you do,' Lydia leaned forward a little. 'Because you and Lucy saw the same thing.' That was a guess, of course. She produced her coin and gripped it in her right hand, for luck.

Joshua was shaking his head but his eyes were wide. 'It wasn't like that. It was really dark. I didn't realise it would be that dark and we were using our phones to see so we didn't trip over.'

'You were pointing it at the ground? Looking down?'

'There were leaves and roots and little mounds of, like, moss. We were well off the path and Lucy was going really fast. She had my hand and was pulling on it, trying to make me go faster, but it didn't feel right. It was like there was someone watching us and that was freaking me out. I thought maybe there was a pervert around or that we were about to disturb a drug deal or something.'

Ah, growing up in London.

'Then it started moving.'

'What did?'

'The ground. It was writhing like it had come alive. Like there were tentacles or snakes or something.'

'What did you do?'

'Shouted to Lucy, tried to get her to stop, but she let go of my hand. She ran off.'

'Which direction?'

'I don't know, she had switched off her phone flash-light. I was looking at the floor, trying to move out the way of that stuff, whatever it was, trying not to fall over, and when I looked up, I couldn't see her.'

'She had disappeared?'

'No, I could hear her running. It was really quiet, like there was no other sound at all, not even traffic, so I could hear her really clearly. Getting quieter though as she got further away... I called out to her, I told her to stop messing around and to come back, but she didn't.'

'Did you try to go after her?'

'I couldn't. The stuff on the ground was up around my legs and I couldn't move. Then there was this feeling like something was running over my body.' Joshua shuddered. 'That's it. I can't... I don't remember anything else.'

'Thank you for telling me,' Lydia said. 'That's really helpful.'

'Really?' Joshua shook his head. 'You're going to have me committed.'

'No I'm not,' Lydia said, keeping eye contact. 'You're not crazy. That really happened. Something bad took your girlfriend and cut your arms and I'm going to find out what and how and, if I can, bring Lucy home safely.'

Joshua put his hands over his face and his shoulders shook. Lydia didn't know if she ought to pat his arm or say something comforting. She could hear Fleet's voice, chatting to the FLO and, a moment later, they appeared in the room. Fleet was carrying a tray filled with mugs. He looked from Joshua's shaking form to Lydia, an eyebrow raised.

Joshua sniffed deeply and dropped his hands. 'One other thing,' he said, ignoring Fleet and the FLO completely. 'Lucy was laughing as she ran.'

'Manic or genuinely happy, do you think?' Lydia asked quickly.

'The happiest I have ever heard her.'

. . .

197

OUTSIDE JOSHUA'S HOUSE, Lydia leaned against Fleet's car rather than getting in. She crossed her arms to try to stay warm. Two children walked into a dark wood... Only one came out. Lydia shook her head to clear it. She didn't need more bedtime stories, she needed to focus on the facts. 'You haven't found her phone, I assume?'

'Nothing from the scene. Just Joshua's jacket. And we've checked her number and her phone has been switched off or out of action since just past midnight. Triangulation with the towers shows Lucy's last known location was the woods. It corroborates Joshua's story, but doesn't give us any further information.'

'Are you going to tell me what Joshua said to you?' Fleet had his hands in his coat pockets. 'Or shall we get going? It's cold out here.'

'I'll walk home from here,' Lydia said. 'Thanks, anyway.'

Fleet held her gaze, not saying anything. At one time, Lydia had felt that she could tell what he was thinking. Now she wasn't so sure. 'He saw the tree roots moving. And he said he felt like something was crawling over him. He might have taken his jacket off then, if he felt like something had got inside.'

Fleet nodded. 'Okay.'

'Thanks for today,' Lydia said, pushing away from the car, ready to leave.

'That's it?'

'What do you mean?'

Fleet looked away, his jaw tensed. 'I thought we were being honest with each other? You told me things you haven't said before. I'm glad you're being open with me. It will put us in a stronger position this time.'

Lydia stepped back, her heart racing. 'That's not what I meant... I'm sorry. I think I'm finally able to be honest with you about my... stuff,' she indicated herself, 'because we're not together anymore.'

'I don't understand,' Fleet said, his brow creasing. 'That makes no sense.'

'I was always so worried about getting too close, showing you too much of my life and the Crow stuff. Now it doesn't matter.'

'What doesn't matter? You're not making any sense.'

Lydia took a breath. 'What you think of me. It doesn't matter anymore.'

Fleet looked like she had punched him.

Lydia could feel tears gathering and she wanted to get away before they fell. She turned and walked toward Denmark Hill.

CHAPTER TWENTY

Lydia's route from Ruskin Park House to Camberwell took her past the Maudsley Hospital. It had a handsome red-brick and stuccoed façade with creamy white columns and an engraved stone pedestal above the entrance. She checked her watch. It was past visiting hours, but she could try.

The reception area was bleak. Not because it was dirty or bare, although the wire mesh screen and safety glass which separated the staff from the rest of the room didn't inspire warm feelings, but because of something in the air. Something beyond the institutional bouquet of pine disinfectant with a whiff of cooked cabbage. After a few minutes waiting, Lydia realised what she could sense. Despair. Terror. Confusion.

The woman behind the screen smiled and her tone was friendly. Lydia explained that she knew she was out with the regular visiting hours but that she had been passing and wondered if she could see Ash.

'Let me see what I can do.'

Lydia waited, scrolling through her phone and making a few notes.

When the woman returned, she was smiling. 'He hasn't had any visitors before, so we're making an exception. This way.'

While Lydia wanted nothing less than to walk into yet another institution, she followed obediently through doors which clicked locked behind her and down bland corridors. 'I'm glad you're here. Ash is a lovely guy and it breaks my heart that he hasn't had any visitors. He's very gentle, very calm, but I can sit in on the meeting if you would be more comfortable?'

'No, that's fine,' Lydia said as they arrived at a plain door. Unlike some of the others they had passed, this was ordinary ply and didn't have a keypad next to it or a viewing panel. The woman fiddled with the lanyard around her neck and lowered her voice. 'Honestly, I'm not sure how much longer Ash will be with us. He would have been treated as an outpatient by now if we had somewhere stable for him to go. Few more days and we'll probably have to turf him.'

'To sheltered housing?'

'Eventually. Probably a hostel first. His key worker has been doing his best to find something suitable, but,' the woman shrugged. 'We're stretched.'

She opened the door to reveal a small square sitting room. There was a varnished pine coffee table and four armchairs with wipe-clean fabric. Two bland art prints of boats were on one wall, off-set by the laminated no-smoking sign.

A man wearing grey joggers and a black hoodie got

up from one of the chairs when they walked in. He was somewhere in his early thirties and was exceptionally good-looking. Lydia knew it was exceptional because he was attractive despite the harsh fluorescent lighting, the ill-fitting clothes and the dark circles under his eyes.

'Ash?'

'Nice to meet you,' Ash said holding out his hand.

'I'll leave you to it,' the woman said. To Ash she said, 'Twenty minutes, okay?' He nodded, not taking his eyes off Lydia's face, his hand was in mid-air and Lydia reached out and shook it over the scuffed table. A powerful shot of Pearl magic ran up her arm and through her body and it took every ounce of Lydia's self-possession not to gasp out loud. As soon as their contact was broken, the sensation disappeared.

'Shall we sit?' Ash was gesturing to the chair nearest Lydia and waited until she had sat down until he did. Polite. Part of Lydia's brain was dissecting what had just happened. She hadn't sensed Pearl at all walking into the room, which was seriously odd. The Pearl signature which had run off Ash didn't feel quite right, either. It wasn't something natural and easy, sitting on him like the colour of his eyes. It was borrowed. Or maybe left. The remains of something left where it had no business being in the first place.

'I'm glad you're here,' Ash said, clasping his hands loosely between his knees.

'How are you doing?' Lydia was leaning forward, trying to get a sense of the Pearl magic, again. There was nothing. If she hadn't felt that single bolt of magic, she would have laid money on him having entirely Family-free blood.

'I've been trying to get my head around what has happened. The computers they have here, the phones. It's all new. Like something from the future.'

'The hospital passed on your details to the police. They will check through the missing person's database and, with a bit of luck, you'll be on there. You have to trust that they will do their job and just concentrate on getting better.'

'I thought you might've changed your mind. About taking my case.'

'No,' Lydia said. 'But I will chase up that police enquiry with my contact. Make sure it's at the top of somebody's to do list.'

There was a pause. 'I can pay.'

'You're not my client which means I'm not billing you. Don't get your hopes up, I really don't think there's much I can do.' Lydia took out her phone. 'Do you mind if I take your picture, though? It might help.'

'Okay.'

Lydia held up her phone and snapped a few shots. He had the sharp cheekbones and wide, shapely mouth of a model. The kind of person who wouldn't need Pearl magic to make people fall in love, want to be with him. 'It might be helpful if you can tell me what you remember about your old life. Before this happened and everything seemed wrong. I'm guessing your name and address hasn't popped back into your mind, by any chance?'

'You think I'm lying?' Ash looked thunderstruck.

'No,' Lydia said. 'I was making a joke. Sorry.'

He shook his head. 'That's okay. People don't joke much in here. I'm a bit out of practice.'

Lydia blinked. Ash no longer sounded unhinged. He sounded sad and very lost. She wanted to ask him if the name 'Pearl' meant anything to him, but had the vague idea that she might plant ideas in his mind. Wasn't there something called 'false memory' syndrome? What if she put back his recovery in her eagerness?

Ash closed his eyes. 'Millennium playing on the radio, everyone worrying about the Y2K bug. That's what I remember. I guess that wasn't a problem, after all.'

'That's a long bout of amnesia,' Lydia said.

'That's what my doctor says.' Ash opened his eyes and looked directly at Lydia. 'I've accepted that the world is real. I don't think everyone is lying anymore. I've used Google. I've looked in a mirror. It would be too elaborate a charade. It must all be real. Which means I've travelled in time. I was sixteen years old and now I'm clearly not. Which is also insane. I do know that. I'm not so crazy that I don't know that.'

'Do you remember anything at all from the last few years?'

'Partying,' Ash said. 'I've been at a party. Lots of music and dancing and drugs. Or I assume drugs, because it's been like I've been tripping, seeing things. Impossible things.'

'What sort of things.'

'I can't say,' Ash said, suddenly sounding panicky, more like he did in their first conversation. He pushed the sleeves of his over-size hoodie up his arms and Lydia caught sight of pale scars, swirling over his skin. 'I'm not allowed. I know that much. They wouldn't like me talking about them.'

'Okay, forget that. What's the last thing you remember before the party?'

There was a pause so long that Lydia started to think that Ash had gone catatonic. He was entirely motionless, staring at his clasped hands. Lydia was just wondering what she ought to do, when he spoke.

'I was meeting my mates, I think. I was excited about New Year's Eve. Everyone had big plans.'

'Right. And this was 1999?'

'Yes. We were too young to get into the clubs, so we went somewhere. We had our own party planned...' Ash trailed off. 'I wish I could remember. We definitely had something special planned. Not at someone's house or anything.'

'It's all right,' Lydia said. 'That's really good. You can call me if you remember anything else.'

'The woods,' Ash said suddenly. 'We were going to party in the woods.'

CHAPTER TWENTY-ONE

L ydia slept heavily, her dreams filled with twisting trees and strange wet, black foliage, which threatened to suffocate. Once she surfaced, fighting the imaginary branches which turned into the twists of her duvet, she showered to slough off the night sweat and went downstairs to the cafe to get a late breakfast. If there was one advantage to discovering that Angel had been working for Charlie, steering her towards cases and reporting back to her uncle, it was that now she felt no compunction whatsoever over cadging food. Angel was clearing tables after the morning rush. 'Where's the new kid?' Lydia said, surprised.

'Scrubbing. He burned my favourite pan.'

'I didn't think he did any cooking,' Lydia said.

'And he won't be again,' Angel said. 'That's what I get for trying a bit of training.'

Lydia stood in front of the counter and contemplated the menu. 'I'll have the full breakfast with toast. And hash browns.'

Angel raised an eyebrow. 'Is that a fact?'

Lydia smiled. 'Quick as you like, I'm starving.'

Angel's expression went nuclear, which was fun. 'Anything else for her ladyship?'

Lydia widened her smile. 'Just some tea. And orange juice. Thanks, Angel. You're the best.' Then. Before Angel could launch across the counter and smack her, Lydia retreated to her favourite seat. It was in the back corner, facing the counter and the entrance with her back against the wall and the big window to her right. Best sight lines, and quick access to the door which led back up to her flat. The food helped to wake Lydia up, but it was still hard to shake the dregs of her dream. Seeing Ash in the hospital had been unnerving. He wasn't crazy and something very odd had clearly happened. It was also weird that the last thing he remembered involved woodland. Lydia didn't believe in coincidences, and she was planning to search the news reports from 1999 for a missing sixteen-year-old, when something else happened to push all thoughts of Ash from her mind.

Charlie was outside on the street, heading for the cafe, but there was something in his gait. He was moving very quickly and Lydia felt her heart rate kick up. Having hesitated too long to get upstairs and avoid him, she watched as he headed to her table with a dark feeling of foreboding. He hadn't so much as nodded at Angel, which meant something serious was definitely up. You could say a lot of things about Charlie Crow, but he was extremely courteous. Lydia put down her cutlery and pushed her plate away. 'What's wrong? Have they found Lucy Bunyan?' She tried to push away the sudden image of a dead girl, hidden under a pile of rotting leaves.

Charlie sat next to Lydia, not opposite her the way he usually did. He put a hand on her arm. 'Your Uncle Terrence is dead.'

Lydia frowned, trying to place the name.

Charlie glowered, removing his hand. 'Don't tell me you don't know Terrence. What was Henry thinking? Feathers, we're your family. You should know their names at least.'

'There are a lot of Crows,' Lydia said defensively. Henry had told her plenty of stories and she hadn't been separated from the family at large. She had been to parties for naming days, Christmas, and New Year. She didn't remember an Uncle Terrence.

'Terrence is banged up in Wandsworth,' he paused. 'Was. He was found dead in his cell yesterday morning. I only just heard.' Charlie looked outraged at this, as if the delay in communication was the worst of it.

Lydia didn't know which question to start with. Who was Terrence and why was he in prison? How did he die? Luckily, Charlie ploughed on. He scanned the cafe as he spoke, seemingly unable or unwilling to look at her. 'You know the old days? Doing time was something of an occupational hazard. It's not like that now, of course, but our old-timers are still doing their stretches. We look after them as best we can, executive cells, cushty jobs, plenty of money flowing in for sundries, all that.'

Lydia nodded as if Charlie hadn't just started

speaking a completely different language. Not for the first time, Lydia appreciated why her parents had warned her against Charlie and the Family business. 'What happened?'

'He was seventy-five,' Charlie said. 'Found with a noose. You don't do that at seventy-five. He'd been inside for over thirty years. They're making out he couldn't hack it. Why would he do thirty years and then decide to check out? Makes no sense. Someone did for him.'

Charlie's phone buzzed and he pulled it from his pocket, glancing at the screen. He answered it, still not looking at Lydia. She had never seen him so agitated. His mood worsened over the course of the short call. 'No,' he said, flatly at one point. His entire body had gone dangerously still and Lydia pushed her plate further to the other side of the table, her appetite truly gone.

'What?' She said, once he had put his phone face-down on the Formica.

'Terrence's friend, Richard, has gone, too. Shanked. He was in intensive care overnight and he just passed.'

'Is Richard one of us?'

Charlie nodded. 'He was on his toes back in the seventies but he came home when we had a spot of bother with the law. Took the stretch to protect the rest of us. He's a bloody hero. Him and Terrence were the last from that era. They sacrificed their lives so that we could fly free.'

'I can't imagine,' Lydia began, the terror of being locked up still very fresh. She couldn't imagine the strength it took to choose that.

'Yeah, not really your style.' Charlie was angry and Lydia could see she was just the nearest target. She compressed her lips to make sure she didn't retaliate.

Charlie blew air out of his nose, closing his eyes for a moment. When he opened them again, he twisted to face Lydia. 'You don't know what it was like, then. I'm guessing Henry didn't include any of it in your bedtime stories. Police had been bought off for years, everything was in harmony. They knew that we were keeping order in Camberwell, that things could be so much worse. It left them free to allocate resources to Peckham. If things weren't strictly legit, they knew we had a code and that there was a fairness to our operation. We were getting paid, but nobody works for free, right?'

Lydia nodded.

'Then there were changes. New blood in at the top, but mainly political reform. A spotlight got turned on police corruption, pressure was applied and, all the time, the drug problems were multiplying, homelessness, over-crowding, racist attacks. Some bright spark decided that some serious crime arrests, a nice package for the organised crime hard-ons, would smooth the way.' Charlie shook his head. 'Probably someone was looking to climb the greasy pole, thought it would look good on their CV. That's all it takes, you know?' He eyeballed her. 'You think individuals don't have power in something like the police, but they do. That's why I was so against you getting friendly with your copper. An avalanche can start with one little rock.'

'I get it,' Lydia said. 'Really.'

'I don't think you do,' Charlie said, but he sounded

calmer. 'Lyds, you're just a kid, still. You're brand new to all this and I'm sorry it's not a better time. I wanted to hand you the keys to a palace, you've got to believe that.'

Lydia nodded to show she did, even though she wasn't entirely sure what he was talking about.

'Anyhow, Terrence and Richard and a couple of old boys, long since passed, swallowed all the charges. And that was that. We went back to business, nice and quiet, the regime changed a few more times at the Met and the political focus shifted to immigration and, eventually, the war on terror.'

'And business changed, too, right?' Lydia said. 'It's not like it used to be.'

'Right, right,' Charlie said. 'We're very professional these days. Everything looks neat and tidy.'

That wasn't exactly reassuring.

'The Silvers have helped us with that over the years. Which is a worrying loose end.'

'They'll keep quiet,' Lydia said. 'They've got as much to lose as we have. Especially now Alejandro is in Westminster.'

'I think you're underestimating how much you pissed off Maria Silver. And now she's in charge-'

'I know, I know,' Lydia closed her own eyes. Just for a few seconds. When she opened them, she didn't want to ask the obvious question. She lowered her voice. 'Do we know who did it?'

Charlie shook his head. 'But I'm going to find out.'

CHARLIE TOLD her he was handling it, but Lydia knew

she had to help. Partly because it was what she did, but also because it was important that the Family saw her take action. Lydia wasn't naïve enough to think that only Aiden had his doubts about her loyalty. Finally, if it turned out that another Family was responsible for the deaths of two Crows, then it would be better if she found out before Charlie. Hopefully it was a random in prison, some internal squabble over the in-jail pecking order. Not a sign of something bigger. And definitely not something triggered by her nosing around the Pearl residence. Or Maria taking the reins of the Silver Family.

Getting access was not going to be easy. She did have a card to play, but it wasn't one she wanted to flip. Every time she thought she was closing the door on Fleet, it swung open again. Still. Two Crows were dead and so there was no real choice. She dialled the number. When Fleet answered she just said, 'I need a favour.'

WALKING into Wandsworth Prison was like stepping back in time. The building was Victorian and the ambience in the reception room was straight out of the seventies. Lydia wouldn't have been surprised to see a Playboy calendar on the wall. Fleet spoke to the prison officers and Lydia kept her mouth shut. After they signed the paperwork which had carbon copies – the officer passed across the yellow portion to Fleet – they were given a thorough pat down which was, according to Fleet, the bare minimum security, and then they were led through an innocuous door and down a short corridor to a set of bars with a locked gate. Instantly, the atmosphere changed and Lydia could feel the ceiling pressing down on her head. There were shouts and screams, echoing off the walls, and a rhythmic banging sound. Part of Lydia was curious to see the main prison. Fleet had described the landings filled with cells, radiating from a central area, but mostly she was just relieved that they were heading to a different place. Once through the first set of bars, they took a side door and crossed a small open yard and into a separate building.

'Visitor suite,' Fleet whispered.

'Suite' was entirely the wrong word. The room the officer led them into was covered in fag burns and paint was peeling from the top of the walls, revealing swathes of damp. A table was bolted to the floor and there were a few mismatched chairs. It smelled of disinfectant and something far worse; the remains of whatever the disinfectant was meant to clean up.

'This is the visiting room?' Lydia was trying to imagine more than a dozen prisoners and their families in the room. Even that small number would be a squeeze and there were nowhere near enough places for them to sit or have any measure of privacy.

'No, miss,' the officer said. 'This is for private meetings. Legal counsel, police interviews,' he nodded at Fleet as he said this. 'General visits are in the main block.'

'Right,' Lydia felt stupid and vowed to keep her mouth shut and just take it all in. Her senses were buzzing but not with any particular 'Family' or power sense, more just a heightened feeling of danger. All those bars between her and freedom. All the badness – and misery – of the incarcerated. She tried, again, to imagine the loyalty it had taken to voluntarily walk into a place like this, knowing you were signing away the rest of your life to it.

Fleet had warned Lydia that their contact was unlikely to talk to them. He was serving eight years for aggravated assault, possession with intent to supply, and three breaking and entering charges. It seemed like a long sentence to Lydia but Fleet said he would 'only serve four'. Besides, when he walked in, Lydia saw that he was also paying the skin tax. Black offenders routinely got handed longer sentences than their white comrades.

'Got any burn, bruv?' Azi strutted to the table and sprawled onto the chair, legs wide and one hand on his inner thigh, practically cupping himself. 'What's up, sweet thing?' He jerked his head up in Lydia's direction, giving her a smouldering look.

Lydia had expected incarceration to humble or beat down a person and that had to be the case for many. It didn't seem to have affected Azi that way, however. Unless his confidence levels pre-prison had been truly stratospheric and she was witnessing him at fifty-per cent ego.

'Don't smoke, sorry,' Fleet said.

Azi ignored him, keeping his gaze on Lydia. His tongue darted out and licked dry lips.

'We're here to talk to you about Terrence.'

Azi looked at Fleet, then. 'What's that to you? Nobody cares in here, innit? He was buzzing all day.'

'Buzzing?' Fleet said. 'He was on something?'

'Nah, bruv. Red light, you get me?'

'He was in bang up?' Fleet asked, understanding dawning in his eyes.

Lydia was still having difficulty following the conversation. 'He was locked in his cell?' She clarified. 'Or isolation?'

Azi shifted his gaze again, taking his time to lick his lips suggestively and move his hand to slip inside his baggy prison-issue joggers. Lydia held his gaze, willing herself not to blush or look away.

'We're banged up all day, innit. Not enough staff to let us out for our rehab classes. I'm supposed to be learning how to dry wall.' The officer by the door shifted. 'You should write *that* down.'

'Terrence was using his emergency bell before he died? Was that unusual? For him, I mean?' Fleet had his notebook out and Azi looked at it hungrily. 'You give me one of them, fam. I tell you what you want to know.'

'You want a notebook?' Fleet raised an eyebrow. 'Give over, Azi. You can't write for shit.'

Lydia hid her shock, but Azi let out a barking laugh. It was the most genuine sound she had heard from him so far.

He nodded at Fleet. 'He hardly never used that bell. Had no need. Was hardly in bang up. He was executive, you get me? Big pad on the ones with a PlayStation and all that.'

Fleet had explained to Lydia that white-collar criminals often held positions of responsibility in the prison and the nicer cells on the ground floor were perks of the jobs they did for the prison staff. High-ups like

Terrence walked straight into the best prison jobs and cells, running complex systems of barter and favours with inmates and staff alike, using their skills and power from the outside world and transferring it to the inside.

'How was he before? Did you speak to him? Did he seem his usual self?'

Azi flicked a look at the officer and said. 'He won at snap. Same as.'

Fleet nodded as if this cryptic phrase made perfect sense.

'No problems with anyone recently? Nothing brewing?'

Azi shook his head.

'I find that hard to believe,' Fleet said. 'There's always trouble. And Terrence is dead.'

Azi shrugged.

Lydia produced her coin, flipping it over the knuckles of her hand. She didn't care that Fleet would see, was past that. He had showed her the scope of his commitment to his job and she wasn't going to hide hers. She was a Crow. She was all in. And it wasn't any of his damn business, any more.

'Look at me,' she said. 'You know who Terrence was?'

Azi flicked his eyes in Lydia's direction and they widened, just a small amount. He was hard, but he wasn't impervious.

'Gangster, innit.'

'That's right,' Lydia said, making her tone the sing-song of a nursery school teacher speaking to a recalcitrant toddler. 'But he wasn't just any good old boy, he was a Crow.'

'I know his name,' Azi said, after a moment. He was watching the coin, no longer looking at Lydia's face.

'Terrence was my blood,' Lydia said. 'I'm keen to find out who is responsible for his death.'

'I dunno,' Azi said. 'He wasn't no bother. You would have to be cracked to take a pop...' He trailed off before suddenly leaning forward, elbows on knees, and whispering. 'Unless it was a screw.'

'That's not going to fly,' Lydia shook her head briskly. 'One of the inmates did this, probably under orders from somebody outside. I need a name.'

'I dunno,' Azi said again. His eyes went to the guard at the door.

'I'm not going after the man who pulled the trigger, I want the person who pointed the gun.'

Azi's eyes flickered with confusion and Lydia wondered if she should rephrase the question.

Fleet stood up and went to speak to the officer at the door. Lydia didn't know if he was going to try to talk him into leaving them for a few minutes or just to ask for a cup of tea, but she took the opportunity to lean in closely to Azi. She could smell body odour, cigarette smoke, and a strange sweet chemical top note. Her senses picked up fear and she flipped her coin, suspending it right in front of Azi's face. She knew he wanted to rear back, to get away, and his eyes were all white, but she wouldn't let him. She put a hand on his knee and stared into his eyes, pushing a little harder than she had ever tried on a person before. She only had a few seconds. 'Who stabbed Richard?'

'Malc.' Azi looked confused that the words had popped out.

'And did he do Terrence, too?'

Azi started to shrug, but it didn't quite take. 'I swear I dunno. Could be. Or one of the same crew.'

'Best guess?'

'I can't,' Azi said, and Lydia saw tears in his eyes. 'They'll kill me.'

'Just tell me who leads the crew. Who pointed Malc at Terrence and Richard?'

Fleet was back, standing behind Lydia's chair, blocking the guard's view. 'Thank you for your cooperation, Azi,' he said loudly. 'You've been very helpful.'

'I haven't!' Azi said, pure panic now. All traces of swagger had drained away and his skin was ashy and damp with sweat.

'This has been so productive, DCI Fleet,' Lydia said. 'I reckon we should stay awhile. Make this a nice long chat. Forget speaking to anybody else on our list, waste of time when we've got Azi, here.'

He looked confused. 'I'm not saying anything.'

'It's been very illuminating,' Fleet said. 'The police would like to recognise your cooperation. I wonder if there is something we can do? Officially.'

'You can't,' Azi whispered. 'You can't do that.'

'I can do whatever I like, son.'

'Malc did it.' Azi said. 'He's the one. Just got the idea on his own. Just did it.'

'And how has Malc been recently?' Lydia said.

'What do you mean?'

'Happy? Depressed? Worried? Anything unusual? Has he come into money?'

'Been living it large? Had more spice and burn than usual? Buying in bulk from the commissary?'

Azi's eyes were rolling, now, he was close to passing out from fear. Lydia pushed away her concern and empathy. There was a job to do and they had to do it. 'Answer the DCI,' she said, shoving a little more Crow into her voice.

Azi licked his lips. 'He's been flush. Like he got a payday.'

'Since Terrance and Richard died?' Fleet confirmed.

Azi nodded, mute.

WALKING AWAY FROM WANDSWORTH, Lydia had to stop herself from running. The urge to fly was running through every bone in her body. All of those doors and locks and bars. They made something primeval in her brain go blank with panic, same as when she had been locked in the Camberwell nick. Crows did not like cages.

She got into the car with Fleet and accepted a lift back to Camberwell. It was going to be hard to be in the enclosed space with Fleet, but the rain was cold and falling with enough force to bounce up off the ground. Besides, she still had some questions.

'So, Malc took a contract in return for cash or favours.'

'Looks that way,' Fleet was watching the road which meant Lydia could watch him. The line of his jaw, the creases around his eyes, the scar on his chin from when he came off a swing set as a kid.

'But how did the order get in? Don't they monitor correspondence?'

'Yeah, all calls are recorded and written communications are read, whether emails or letters. Plus, inmates aren't supposed to have mobiles.'

Lydia didn't miss the phrasing. 'But they do?'

'Yup.'

'Your standard gang-banger pay-as-you-go untraceable phone is another form of currency inside. Payments are made to and from outside payment systems, bank accounts of friends or family members, all sorts of things. You can't have a load of cash change hands or money wired into the inmates prison account, naturally, so the big deals are all done via a third party.'

'So unless we have the burner in question, we can't trace the person who gave the order.'

'Correct,' Fleet said. 'Which is why we're going to have his cell tossed. If he's smart, he doesn't keep it there, but you know most of the boys in there aren't criminal masterminds. We might get lucky.'

Good as his word, Fleet used his police clout and got Malc's cell searched that afternoon. He called Lydia straight after. 'Text with Terrence and Richard's names came through last week. Idiot didn't even delete it.'

'Number?'

'Switched off. Probably already been dumped.'

Lydia blew out a sigh of frustration. 'Why can't they all be stupid?'

'I've turned phone over to tech bods and they'll see what else they can find. Don't hold your breath, though.'

'Right. Thank you.' Lydia was sitting in her office chair, facing her overflowing desk. From this vantage point she could see her laptop half-buried in papers, three old coffee mugs and two empty whisky bottles. She really ought to tidy up before she had a client in here.

'You still there?' Fleet said.

'Yes,' Lydia straightened up. 'Sorry. Just tired. What will happen to Malc? Can we talk to him?'

Fleet paused. 'I will push for a conviction, but I have to warn you the chances are low.'

'Azi named him,' Lydia said.

'Yeah, but he won't do that again. Not in an official capacity. Put that kid in front of a judge and he'll forget his own name let alone anyone else's.'

Lydia knew that she had used her Crow whammy on Azi to make him talk. And she knew he would be in fear of his life if he gave evidence in court against another prisoner. Still. It seemed unlikely that it was that easy to get away with murder when you were already a convicted criminal and in a closed unit like Wandsworth. 'Won't the guards have seen something? Be able to coordinate evidence and with the mobile phone, too-'

'It's not in their interests,' Fleet said. 'Management will want an outcome that doesn't point to negligence on their watch. It looks bad if people can order hits within a highly secure prison.'

Lydia swore quietly.

'I'm sorry. I know they were your family.'

'I never knew them,' Lydia shrugged off his sympathy. 'It's not that. I'm angry.' And worried. If the law was going to let them down, what would Charlie do in retaliation? 'Can you get me in to interview Malc?'

'I'll see what I can do.'

'Thanks.' Lydia was still distracted, rehearsing the conversation with Charlie, wondering if there was any way she could keep this bit of information from him, for Malc's safety. It wasn't like Charlie was just going to drop the matter, decide not to bother to look into it. If Lydia didn't get results, he would get them another way.

Fleet broke into her thoughts, echoing them exactly. 'I guess you're going to tell your uncle about Malc?'

Lydia nodded. 'No choice.'

'I get that,' Fleet said. 'I will warn the prison to put him into protective custody. If they've got the resources.'

Lydia couldn't feel much sympathy for the man who had murdered a couple of old-age-pensioners, even knowing that Terrence and Richard Crow had undoubtedly been no angels. 'You do what you have to do.'

CHAPTER TWENTY-TWO

Charlie texted Lydia, demanding an update. She drove to Grove Lane, trying not to think about what Charlie was going to arrange once she had given him Malc's name. There was no way out of it, though. It wasn't as if Charlie was just going to drop the matter. And if she didn't tell him, somebody else would. Eventually. And then he might guess that she had held out on him.

When Charlie opened the door, he looked drawn. His olive-toned skin was yellow-ish and the lines on his face were deeper than usual. He ushered Lydia inside. 'Quickly,' he said. 'We're not safe.'

'Has something else happened?' Lydia said, feeling sick.

'No. No. Not yet. Only a matter of time. Getting you arrested was a warning shot. This is the real deal. If our alliance with Alejandro is over-' He shook his head. 'I don't even want to think about it.'

It had certainly occurred to Lydia that if JRB were

225

intent on destabilising the Families into breaking the truce, then killing a couple of Crows would be an excellent way to do so. They would have to pin the murders on one of the other Families, though. 'It's not necessarily the Silvers.' She told him about her visit to Azi and the person he named.

Charlie went still. 'That's good work, Lyds.'

'I'll find the person who ordered the attack. That's who we want.'

Charlie nodded, his mind clearly working.

'We shouldn't do anything rash. Not until we've got all the information.' Lydia was watching Charlie carefully. He had gone dangerously still.

'Naturally,' Charlie said. He clapped his hands together, the action loud and sudden after the quiet pause which had come before. He turned on a humourless smile. 'You need to train.'

'I was going to work my contacts, find out who ordered the hit.'

'Training isn't optional,' Charlie said. 'Especially now. You need to be strong. For your own safety.'

Lydia could recognise when it wasn't worth arguing with Charlie so she followed him upstairs to the training room.

It was a grey day but what little light was available streamed through the large windows, illuminating the room. Charlie was in a strange mood. Intense and distracted and Lydia spent the next hour regulating herself, making sure that nothing unexpected happened. She spun her coin, held it in mid-air and produced multiple coins, just ephemeral copies but they looked real enough, and sent them clattering to the floor in a shower of flashing metal. It was tiring, but Lydia felt like the true exhaustion came from continually holding onto her self-control, trying to make sure that only a little happened. She could feel a larger power, hovering, just above her as she obeyed Charlie's instructions. The thing was, it was drawn from somewhere. She was a battery, powering up other people, at least that was her working theory. But that powering-up had to be drawn from somewhere else. She didn't understand it, which meant she didn't like it.

'Okay, that'll do,' Charlie said. 'I can see you're tired.'

'Thanks,' Lydia said, injecting exhaustion into her voice.

'Unless,' Charlie had been leaning against the far wall and he straightened up, now. 'You're putting it on.'

'Sorry?' Lydia tensed.

Charlie was staring intently, his small eyes flat and unreadable and Lydia felt a prickle of fear. She pushed it down. He didn't know. He couldn't know.

'I just wonder if you're trying hard enough,' Charlie said. He glanced away, though, his body seeming to relax.

Lydia felt her own fear slip down a notch and she forced herself to walk near him, to pick up her water bottle and take a casual swig.

The bottle fell from her hand as Charlie looped an arm around her neck, pulling her back so that she was off balance. His forearm was hard against her neck, compressing her windpipe and making it impossible to breathe, and she scrambled for her footing, feeling Charlie behind her like a solid wall. She grabbed his arm, trying to pull it away, dragged her foot down and stamped on his instep as hard as she could, but he was too big and too strong.

Her mind was white with panic. A man had grabbed her like this on the street, tried to bundle her into a van, seconds before the Fox brothers had shown up. She had been strangled by Maddie, too, and Jason had saved her life. Jason wasn't here, though. And the chances of the Fox brothers arriving to save the day and then beat her to a pulp, were slim. Little black speckles were all over the whiteness, now, and Lydia knew she was going to pass out very soon. She had done self-defence training back in Aberdeen and knew that she should have stepped back and to the side, ducking and twisting out of the lock but she had missed the moment in her shock and Charlie had her up against his body, with no room to manoeuvre.

'Come on,' she heard Charlie's voice. 'Fight back.'

Lydia couldn't feel her body anymore. She had retreated to the place on the knife edge of consciousness. Any second and she would be gone. Killed by her own uncle. She supposed it would be handy for him. He had always said he wanted her in the Family, proper, but she had proved a disappointment. And she was a loose cannon, fraternising with Foxes, baiting the Silvers, not showing him the deference he felt he deserved.

A wave of tiredness washed over Lydia and she thought about going to sleep. She was exhausted by it all. 'Oh, for fuck's sake.' It was a woman's voice. Familiar. Not overly welcome. It took Lydia what felt like a long time, but must have been a split second, to realise who had spoken. It was Maddie. Maddie wasn't here, so it had to be a delusion. She had a lot of those. And she was passing out. Or passed out and on her way to being dead.

That did it. She didn't want to be dead. Especially not at the hands of Uncle Charlie. Her mother had warned her to watch out for him and she didn't want her to say 'I told you so'. Teenage petulance wasn't the most noble reason for fighting, but it was better than nothing. Lydia pulled the power which had been waiting in the wings onto centre stage. It felt difficult, like every thought was slow, but she pictured her coin and that helped. She couldn't feel it, couldn't see anything except flashes and speckles and was pretty sure her eyes were rolled up back in her head, but picturing it helped her to focus.

She pulled the power around her, like a cloak. It was warm and comforting and with that comfort came a little more mental clarity. Her coin was in her mind's eye, clear and bright. She saw the room she was in, Charlie behind her, the grey winter light casting pale shapes on the wooden floor, her water bottle rolling away. Her coin in front of her was more real than reality. In that moment, Lydia knew it came from somewhere else. Or it belonged in a slice of reality that was different to the water bottle and the floor and her own body. All she had to do was to join it. At once, she was outside of her body, looking down. She could see her own face, pale and desperate, Charlie's meaty arm across her neck, his tattoos moving. His tattoos had a touch of the hyperreal, too, but they were nowhere near as crisp as her coin.

This vantage point should have been scary, the last moments of hallucination before death, but Lydia no longer felt afraid. She took her time, looking around the room, ignoring her own struggling form below, and seeing the vaguest outline of a second Lydia suspended in mid-air reflected in the multiple mirrors. She looked a bit like Jason when he was at his most insubstantial, a thought which made her smile. She reached out a ghostly hand and passed it over Charlie's arm, feeling a tingling in physical body as she did so.

Instantly the pressure on her neck disappeared and she sucked in lungfuls of painful air. She was back in her body, doubled over and dragging in ragged breaths while every part of her screamed with sensation. She had forgotten, even in those small moments of being incorporeal just how much *activity* a body experienced. She could feel blood moving in veins, muscles stretching and contracting, air moving over tiny hairs in her middle ear, the squeezing of peristalsis in her guts, and the electric crackle of her neurons firing. As her oxygen levels improved with several more breaths, the intense awareness faded and she was able to think about other things. Like the slumped form of her uncle, who was leaning against the wall, hands on his knees. His breathing was coming in gasps, too, like he had been sprinting.

She moved toward the door, keeping her eyes on Charlie in case he made a miraculous recovery and sprang for her. Out of the corner of her eye, she thought she saw a black shape moving. She whipped her head around to see, but the corner of the room was empty. For a second, she thought she saw a black winged shape reflected in the mirrors, but she blinked and it disappeared. It was probably the after-effects of the oxygen deprivation or the adrenaline that was still coursing through her body, making time move differently and colours appear saturated. She couldn't trust her own eyes or her senses. She needed to get away and rest somewhere dark and safe.

'What the feathers was that?' Charlie managed, bringing his head up to look at Lydia.

She felt a spurt of confused anger. 'You tried to kill me.'

'No!' Charlie's voice was different, but Lydia couldn't work out how.

She backed up a few more steps, getting closer to the door while keeping her eyes on Charlie.

'I was,' he paused to suck in some more air. 'Training.'

It didn't bloody feel like it, Lydia thought. Charlie was still bent over and was showing no signs of moving, but Lydia didn't want to wait for him to recover his strength. She was at the door and ready to turn and open it, to flee down the stairs and out of the house. She didn't know what to do after that point and realised that she had to make sure Charlie wasn't coming for her. Otherwise she would have to leave London altogether. She hesitated. 'And did I pass your little test?'

Charlie's shark eyes were moist, like he was actually going to cry. 'What did you do?'

'I don't...' Lydia stopped. Tried again. 'You shouldn't have done that. You really scared me.'

'I got that,' Charlie said, a spark of his old self igniting.

Lydia took another step back, her hand on the door. And that's when she saw what was different about Charlie. His tattoos weren't moving.

CHAPTER TWENTY-THREE

Lydia knew she couldn't go back to The Fork, not at that moment. She would have to eventually, she had to collect Jason or see him to make sure he didn't start fading, but right at that moment she had to get away. Somewhere safe. Somewhere Charlie wouldn't think to look. She drove while she thought, putting distance between her and Charlie. He had attacked her. That had just happened.

Lydia arrived at her destination without fully acknowledging to herself that she had decided to go there. She dialled the number before she could lose her will. 'Are you home?'

Fleet had answered the phone after the second ring. 'What's wrong?'

'I'm fine,' Lydia said, aware that the last time she had called about his flat, she had just taken a beating. 'I can't go home right now, though.'

'I'm on my way there. I'll meet you outside.'

Lydia stayed in the car on the quiet street, counting

breaths in and out. She saw Fleet's car in her rear-view mirror and watched him park. He unfolded himself from the driving seat and she felt herself sag with relief.

Inside the flat looked exactly the same. Extremely neat, warm and comfortable. 'Tea?'

'Thanks,' Lydia said. She sat on the sofa and stared at the wall, trying to gather her wits. She had tried in the car on the way over, but the panic had still been keeping them on a loop. Now that she was off the street and hidden, she made more progress. Charlie didn't know this place. He didn't think she was with Fleet and if he decided to check, he would have to find Fleet's home address which wasn't easy. Not impossible, though. Not for a man like Charlie Crow. The fear gripped her, again, and she was on her feet.

'I need to go,' she called. 'Sorry.' This had been a mistake. She should keep moving.

'Wait,' Fleet came out of the kitchen and crossed the room. He put his hands onto Lydia's shoulders and dipped his head to look into her eyes. 'What's happened. Talk to me.'

'Can't,' Lydia said. 'I need to hide out.' Her mind flashed to Maddie, hiding on the narrow boat courtesy of Paul Fox. She had thought Maddie was the bad one, the wild card, but now she had a glimpse as to why she had wanted to run away. Had Charlie trained her in the same way? Maybe Maddie hadn't started out as socio-pathic. Maybe Charlie had created that particular monster.

'Lyds, you're shaking. I've never seen you like this.

And when I first met you, someone had just tried to kill you.' He tried a small smile. 'You're alarming me.'

Lydia focused on Fleet's eyes. Warm, steady, and full of genuine concern. Hell Hawk, she was not going to cry. She refused. She dug her finger nails into her palms and straightened her spine. 'Charlie. He attacked me.'

Fleet frowned. 'What do you mean?'

'Just that,' Lydia broke from his grasp, it was too intense to look into his face for a second longer. She sat back on the sofa and let her head fall back. The tiredness was lapping at the edges, threatening to pull her under.

'Are you hurt?'

Lydia shook her head. 'A few bruises, that's all. He scared me though.'

'I'll kill him,' Fleet's jaw was clenched. 'Say the word.'

'It was training,' she said. 'It wasn't... He said it was for my own good. Well, not my own good specifically, the good of the Family.'

'Training?'

Lydia let her eyes drift closed. 'You know what I am. Crows can do certain things. Apparently those abilities can be trained to make them stronger, more effective. It's Charlie's obsession. He says we need to be strong, that a war is coming. He doesn't think the treaty is going to hold for much longer. Not now somebody is having Crows killed in prison.'

'Is that why Alejandro has left?'

Lydia's eyes opened and she straightened to look at Fleet. 'What do you know about the Silvers?'

'Just that Maria is the new head of the Family.'

'Is that official intelligence or copper gossip?'

Fleet shrugged. 'You know how it is. Half the people don't believe in the Families and the other half tell tall tales just to make themselves sound interesting. My great aunt was married to a Fox and we all had to give teeth as a wedding present, that kind of thing.'

'Well, it's not wrong. Alejandro is following his political ambitions.'

'That's ominous,' Fleet said.

'I'm not sure it's relevant, though. Charlie is fixated on the Families because he knows them, but JRB are the Silvers' clients and they seem to have connections to the Pearls, too.'

'The prison killings could be more random than you think. We can't jump to conclusions. A list of people pissed off with your family would be handy, though.'

Lydia tilted her head. 'How long have you got?'

Fleet smiled sadly. 'And now Charlie has lost his mind. You want to press charges?'

Lydia almost laughed. 'No, thank you.'

'This is serious.'

The urge to laugh disappeared. 'I know. He's freaking out about the murders. It's a warning. No, more than a warning, it's an act of war. And I'm not strong. He wants me to be strong.' As Lydia spoke, she could feel her thoughts swirling and looping, circling to find an order that made sense.

'You're not defending him?' Fleet said.

'I don't know. I need to think.' Lydia pulled out her phone and texted Paul. She told him she had gone to Fleet's flat and asked if he needed the address.

No need. On my way.

'Paul Fox is coming here. He won't be long. I just need to speak to him and I don't want to do it on the phone.'

'I don't understand, why him? Why now?'

'I can meet him outside if you want.'

'No, that's not what I'm saying.'

'I need to see him. I need all the help I can get.' Lydia was acting on instinct. Something had ignited when Charlie had grabbed her. She had never trusted her uncle and she had been proved right. Maybe the old lines of Family weren't set in stone, maybe there was a better way of deciding who was a friend and who was a foe. Maybe it didn't have to start and end with blood.

Fleet went out to the kitchen to finish making tea and Lydia paced the room, looking out of the window every few minutes.

Paul Fox must have broken the speed limit, unless he had been fortuitously close to Camberwell. He also managed to park and get to the flats without Lydia seeing him from the window. She buzzed him upstairs and opened the door.

'What's happened, Little Bird?' Paul's look of concern was genuine and Lydia realised something as Paul walked into Fleet's flat. The tang of Fox was no longer a warning.

'Trouble at home,' Lydia said shortly. 'I might need to hide.'

Paul nodded. 'Easy.'

'Come to the station,' Fleet said, walking into the room. 'We can protect you.'

'No,' Lydia said. 'I will not willingly set foot in that place as long as I draw breath in this city.'

Fleet's eyes widened and he nodded. 'Fair enough. I can provide police protection, though. Short-term at least. And I've got some holiday accrued. I could take that and be your own personal guard.'

'Don't need it, mate,' Paul said. 'Got all the man-power we need.' To Lydia he said, 'We've got this. Nobody will get near you.'

'You're trusting him, now?' Fleet said. 'This is the man who sold you out. That police station you hate? He's the man who put you there.'

'I seem to remember you were there, too,' Lydia said mildly. 'And Paul didn't set me up.'

'I suppose he told you that?'

Lydia's patience snapped. 'Don't question my judge-ment on who I trust or I will reassess all of my connec-tions, starting with you. If you want to help me, you're going to have to accept that Paul is on my side. I need your help. I need both your help. But I can't spend all my time refereeing. I'm tired and I'm scared and I need all my attention on fixing this. Are you in or are you out? Decide now.'

'I'm in,' Fleet said immediately.

Paul nodded, his lips tight.

'Good.' Lydia wanted to sit down. Truthfully, she wanted to lie down and sleep for twelve hours straight, but above the exhaustion was terror. And that made her jumpy with adrenaline. She paced up and down, trying to think. 'Charlie doesn't know this place so I'm safe here for the time being. Long term, I don't know. I don't know what to do.'

'You want us to move on him?' Paul said.

'No. Don't do anything. I just need to work out how to play this.' Lydia took a breath. 'Malcolm Ferris, goes by "Malc". Know him?'

'Nope.'

Paul was an excellent liar, Lydia had no doubt, but she also thought he looked genuinely blank. She was studying him for any flicker of recognition and caught none. 'Someone commissioned him to kill a couple of Crows,' Lydia said, deciding to just come out with it. 'They were all in the same block in Wandsworth. Emphasis on the word 'were'.'

'I'm sorry,' Paul said. 'That was not a sensible move.'

Lydia caught something else in his tone. Relief. 'What did you think I was going to say? You sound almost happy.'

'No, no. It's just...' He took an audible breath. 'I'm glad my father is in Japan. Otherwise I would have put him top of the list of suspects and that would cause more problems for you and me.'

Lydia ignored the romantic connotations of 'you and me', deciding he intended the phrase to indicate professional friendship. Family alliance. Wholesome stuff. 'Can you ask around?'

'I can send people out and about, see what we can dig up. There might be some whispers.'

'Thank you,' Lydia said.

'Take this,' Paul reached inside his jacket and

produced a burner phone. 'Use this if you need me. I can hide you.'

'I seem to remember Lydia found Maddie when you were hiding her,' Fleet said. 'What makes you so sure Lydia will be safe with you?'

Paul flashed Fleet a dead-eye look. 'I wasn't trying to hide Maddie. I wanted shot of the psycho.'

'Did Maddie know that?' Fleet asked pointedly.

'Stop it,' Lydia said. 'Charlie Crow is unstable and my neck hurts and I need you both to stop bickering.'

Paul and Fleet called a halt to their staring match and Paul looked, instead, at Lydia's neck. 'I'll kill him,' he said. 'Say the word.'

'I'm trying to avoid war, not set it off,' Lydia said. 'But I appreciate the offer. What I really need is information. Charlie isn't wrong to be worried. Someone is gunning for us.'

Paul nodded. 'I'll do the rounds. Someone has got to know who commissioned the hits.'

'Thank you,' Lydia said, opening the door.

When Lydia turned back to Fleet, his face had a strained look and she knew he was trying, very hard, not to comment. After a moment more of silent struggle, he offered to run her a bath.

'Shower would be great, actually,' Lydia said, suddenly viscerally wanting to sluice the last few hours from her skin. And to have some privacy.

LYDIA HAD a long hot shower in which she allowed herself a good cry. She could still feel Charlie's hands grasping, his breath on her neck, and she lathered and scrubbed her skin. When she emerged from the warm steam, wrapped in one of Fleet's soft and fresh-smelling towels, she felt halfway human again.

Fleet had made pasta and poured two large glasses of red wine. The smell of garlic and basil made her mouth water instantly and Lydia realised that she hadn't eaten all day. Fleet sat at his table, work spread out around him. He had passed Lydia the remote control and a bowl of pasta and left her to consume carbohydrate and some mindless television. Lydia was grateful for his understanding. She wasn't up to any more talking and definitely not big questions.

When it got late, Fleet began to set up a makeshift bed on the sofa. 'You take my room,' he said. 'I've put clean sheets on the bed.'

Lydia hovered in the doorway. 'I know it's a lot to ask, but can we put pause on our personal situation and be friends? Just for tonight.'

Fleet stopped moving. He abandoned the sheets and straightened to look at her. 'What does that involve?'

Lydia thought he was making a comment on the fact that he had already given her a place of safety and fed her dinner. She tried to explain. 'This distance between us. I asked for it and I know it's the right thing in the long run, but tonight... I can't...' She took a breath. 'I need you with me.'

Fleet crossed the room and folded her into a hug. Lydia leaned against his chest, breathing in the smell of Fleet, which had always meant safety and, as she did so, she realised that it still did. Something small and hard she had been holding onto dissolved and she wrapped her arms around Fleet's back, letting one hand drift up to the nape of his neck.

He looked down just as Lydia looked up, their mouths meeting in an easy movement. The relief to be kissing Fleet again was like the first taste of whisky and, despite everything, her heavy heart soared.

When they broke for a moment, breathing heavily, hands everywhere, and Fleet's bed miraculously closer than before, having stumbled their way into the bedroom, Fleet smiled and the sweet joy in it almost made Lydia cry. He had his hands on his T-shirt, ready to rip it over his head, when he hesitated. 'I thought maybe you and Paul...'

'Paul?' Lydia tried to shake the emotion and lust from her head long enough to formulate a proper response. Instead she opted to peel off her jeans and socks and step forward to help Fleet with his clothes-removal. 'No,' she said and kissed him. 'Just you.'

CHAPTER TWENTY-FOUR

The next day, Lydia woke up in Fleet's comfortable bed. Fleet was asleep on his front, his head turned to one side on the pillow. She looked at his beautiful face for a moment before quietly getting up. He stirred as she was putting her jeans on.

'Don't get up,' Lydia said. 'It's still early.'

Fleet blinked and rolled over, pushing himself up on one elbow. 'You're leaving?'

'I'm going home,' Lydia said, ignoring the sudden spurt of fear. 'I was wrong last night. I can't run away from Charlie. And I won't run away from my home.' Or desert Jason.

'What if he attacks you again?'

Lydia shrugged, feigning nonchalance. 'He can try. He won't catch me off guard again.'

Fleet pressed his lips together and Lydia could tell he was trying, very hard, not to say something.

'What?' Lydia sat on the bed to lace up her boots.

'I'm just worried.'

'Look. He's still my uncle. He crossed a line yesterday but I'm sure he regrets it. He's under a lot of stress.' As she heard the words, Lydia felt sick. They were the kinds of excuses abused spouses made.

'What can I do?'

Lydia leaned over and kissed him lightly on the lips. 'I'll check in with you every few hours. And I'll call if there's trouble.'

'What if you can't speak?'

'If I say everything is 'hunky dory' then you know I'm in trouble.'

'I'm being serious,' Fleet said.

'I'll leave the GPS working on my phone, and if I go more than six hours without texting or phoning, you can call the cavalry.'

'Four hours.'

'Five. And you text first.'

Stepping back into The Fork, Lydia half-expected Charlie to be waiting for her and was both relieved and a little disappointed to find that he wasn't. She was tensed and ready for a confrontation and it felt like a waste of adrenaline to not see him right away. And, if she was honest, there was a small part of her that had hoped he might be waiting for her to apologise in person. It would make things so much easier if he was contrite. The whole incident could be put away in a box marked 'one off' and they could both pretend it had never happened at all.

It wouldn't work, of course. Charlie Crow would

find it difficult to pull off contrite convincingly, and nothing could erase the image of the real man that Lydia had glimpsed. She just wanted to know what the next move would be. In his mind, Charlie was undoubtedly the injured party, and she was the ungrateful child. The only question was, how was he going to deal with her insubordination? And did he still view her as a potential weapon that he could control or a personal threat?

When Lydia had finished updating Jason on the previous day's activity, she finished by asking him if there was a way of finding the person who had sent the text instructing Malc to murder Terrence and Richard. She didn't have any particular hope, but since Jason's new hacking skills seemed close to magic she thought it was worth asking.

'Not without the other phone,' Jason said. 'I don't think, anyway. I will ask around, though, see if we're missing something.'

'Thank you,' Lydia said.

'But what are you going to do about Charlie? That's... Bad. I can't believe he attacked you.'

'He probably thought it was for my own good,' Lydia said, keeping her voice steady with a force of will. 'But, yes. It's a problem.'

'Stop downplaying it,' Jason was shimmering a little at the edges. 'You don't have to pretend to be okay. What if he does it again? And what does it mean that his tattoos stopped moving? Did you hurt him?'

'Sorry,' Lydia said, blinking away tears. 'I can't think about it too much. It's too much. I'm just carrying on like it didn't happen because I can't afford to do otherwise. I can't fall apart.'

'You shouldn't be here,' Jason said, wrapping his arms around himself. 'It's not safe.'

'Crows don't run,' Lydia said, looking him dead in the eye. 'And this is my home.'

Jason shook his head, his outline rippling. 'It's because of me, isn't it?'

Lydia forced a smile. 'Don't be daft.'

'You've come back for me.' Jason took a step toward Lydia and she felt the air cool around her.

'Well don't make a big deal out of it,' Lydia said. 'It's a good flat, too. Now, please can we get back to work. Distract me.'

Jason hesitated, and Lydia could see that he was torn between his desire to hug her or carry on arguing.

'Please,' she said. 'Help me to keep going.'

He nodded and picked up his laptop. 'You got the phone number?'

'Yep,' Lydia had written it into her little flip note-book and she opened the relevant page and read it out.

Jason's fingers flew over the keyboard. 'Numbers are linked to specific phones and every phone has a serial number. An ID. I reckon police can probably get phone records from relevant network. They'll be able to find out where it was bought, too. And when.'

'Any way to find out where it is now?'

'Not if it's switched off. If it's on, it pings the nearest mobile tower, gives a general location. The phone records will show which tower it was near when the text was sent. I think.' He carried on reading for a few seconds and then looked up. 'Unless they've left the GPS on, then we'd get a much more accurate location.'

'Don't think we'll get that lucky,' Lydia said.

'Yeah, if they know enough to use a burner...'

Jason was hunched over the computer, his body curved toward the screen. Lydia touched him lightly on the shoulder. 'How do you know so much about this already?'

He didn't look away and his fingers didn't slow. 'Google.'

LYDIA PUT on her jacket and hat and ventured out onto the roof terrace. It was a flat grey day with a bite to the air. A siren wailed somewhere in the distance and Lydia could feel dampness on her skin within seconds of being outside. She called Emma, trying not to think about how the records could still be found. No wonder Paul and Charlie were so hot on meeting in person.

'Sorry I haven't been in touch.' Lydia wondered how many times she had said that in the course of their friendship.

'What's wrong?'

'Nothing. I'm fine.'

Emma blew out a sigh. 'Don't phone me to lie at me.'

'I'm not-' Lydia began before stopping herself. 'Sorry. I'm sorry.' She felt tears in her eyes and told herself it was the cold air. 'Things are bad, here. Charlie has lost the plot.'

'What did he do?'

Lydia told Emma as briefly and unemotionally as

she could. 'I discovered I have a couple of aged relatives in jail. Or, I did. They were killed.'

'Oh God,' Emma said. 'That's awful. Are you coming home?'

When Emma said 'home' she meant the suburbs they had grown up in together. For a second Lydia felt its pull but then remembered that her childhood home now housed the shell of her father. And that her presence made his condition worse. She was a curse. 'I can't.'

'You need to get out of London, then. Put some distance between you and this mess. It doesn't sound safe.'

'I'm not running away,' Lydia said. 'I'm a Crow.'

'Come and stay with us, then.'

'Thank you, but no.' The idea of Charlie anywhere near Emma and her family made Lydia go cold all over.

'You're doing what you always do,' Emma was saying. 'Isolating yourself in the mistaken belief that it makes you stronger.'

'I don't think it makes me stronger,' Lydia replied. 'But I don't want anybody getting hurt on my account. I can't stand the thought that I will hurt people without even trying.'

'And there's the irony,' Emma said, her voice tight. 'The further you push us away the more hurt we get. Everybody loses.'

'You get to stay alive, though,' Lydia said.

Lydia made toasted cheese sandwiches, tidied her desk, and watched Jason work while trying to concentrate on a novel. She had checked the locks and stacked tins from the kitchen behind the front door, balancing a variety of utensils on top. It wouldn't stop Charlie from getting inside the flat, but it would make a hell of a noise. And inside her bedroom, she had dragged a chest of drawers in front of the door which led to the roof terrace. Her eyes kept straying to the hallway and the makeshift intruder-alert, a visual reminder that things were not okay. The words in the novel kept jumping around and her eyes felt gritty, so she went to bed, piling blankets on the bed and drinking a whisky nightcap to ward against the chill. The room was even colder when she woke up several hours later.

'I've made some progress.'

Lydia opened her eyes to find a ghost hovering next to the bed. 'Boundaries, Jason,' she said, rubbing her eyes and sitting up. He knocked over an empty whisky bottle from next to the bed as he came closer, and Lydia shifted so that he could sit down. 'What time is it?' She was rubbing sleep out of her eyes and trying to focus.

'Dunno. Early. It's not important.'

'Not to you,' Lydia said. 'You don't need to sleep.'

'You need to stop downing a bottle of whisky as a night cap.'

'It's been a stressful time,' Lydia said. 'Did you not even bring me a coffee?'

Jason put his laptop down between them. 'Will you listen?'

'Sorry,' Lydia knew that Jason wouldn't have woken her up without good reason. He looked tense and excited in the blue wash of the screen. 'I'm awake. I'm listening. Is it Malc's phone records?'

'No, nothing on those, yet. I went back to JRB.'

'Oh. That's good. Thank you.' Having an assistant that didn't need sleep was proving to be a real bonus.

'You know JRB is a shell company?'

'Yeah. I think so. I don't really understand how it all works.'

'Basically, it's registered as a business services company, but not in this country. The offices that you found are more like a PO Box, they evade all the UK listings and regulations by not being registered here. Anything that needs UK registration to operate, like trading, uses a subsidiary company which is owned by JRB.'

'Okay,' Lydia said, still not sure she fully understood. 'You said something about following the money?'

'I did,' Jason said. 'And I got a bit of help.'

'From SkullFace?'

'And others,' Jason nodded. 'There is a lot of money. It goes to offshore accounts for tax avoidance, as you would imagine. Everything is neatly squared away. But they weren't quite as slick when they first started.'

'When did they start?'

'A company called J.R.B. and Sons Ltd was registered with Companies House in 1887. Original registered address was a shop in Peckham and company director was a member of the Coster Guild.'

Lydia was awake, now. 'That sounds like Pearl business. They've always been more open to outside influences, though. Mixing up their Family. Dad used to say it was because they had always moved all over London as street traders, and dealt with people from around the world at the docks. Less parochial and closed than the Crows or Silvers or Foxes.'

'That sounds healthy,' Jason said. 'In-breeding is not a good look.'

'I agree,' Lydia said, 'but historically that hasn't been our official position...'

'And look where it's got you all.'

'I said I agree,' Lydia snapped, irritated. She was allowed to criticise her family, but nobody else could. That was the rule.

Jason moved the trackpad to wake up the laptop screen. He had a notes app open with a bullet-point list, which he read from. 'Founder and director is John Roland Bunyan, and it looks like the company passed from son to son for generations until it was wound up in 2001 which was when the new, off-shore company, JRB Inc, no full-stops, was formed.'

'Bunyan?' Lydia stared at Jason open-mouthed. 'And you're sure they're same company?'

'Not completely sure, I suppose.' Jason had a funny look on his face. 'Just internal memos confirming the fact. Accounting notes which reference trading done at J.R.B and Sons in the opening accounts of JRB Inc.'

'How on earth did you get those?'

'Any piece of information that is kept on a server is accessible if you know how to look for it.'

'Aren't things locked up?'

'Yeah, you have to know how to open certain digital doors.'

'And you know that stuff now?'

Jason grinned. 'It's amazing what you can learn when you don't need to sleep and you have no social life.'

'This is brilliant. Really well done.'

'It's helpful?' Jason said, looking hopeful.

'Definitely.' Lydia leaned close to read his list of notes, ignoring the chill of his skin. 'I take it, this information gathering wasn't strictly legal?'

'Not remotely,' Jason said cheerfully.

'We'll make a Crow of you, yet,' Lydia said, putting her head on his shoulder.

After a pause, in which Lydia felt the cold seep from Jason's shoulder into the bones of her cheek, Jason said. 'If JRB are linked to the Pearls, what does that mean?'

Lydia lifted her head to look at him. 'I think it means I need to pay another visit.'

'With a gift?' Jason's expression was terrified and Lydia felt like hell.

'If you can face it, yes.'

AFTER SPEAKING TO JASON, she burrowed back under the warm covers and dozed for a couple of hours. It was still early when she gave up on sleep. Light was coming through the thin curtain which covered the door to the roof terrace, cut off by the chest of drawers. She felt the sick fear in her stomach and wondered, for the millionth time, what Charlie was going to do. He had attacked her but she had won. He might decide she was more valuable than ever, a weapon to hone and control. Or he might have decided that she was a threat. Which would be very bad news. Lydia reached automatically for a fresh bottle of whisky, but realised as she began to twist the cap that she didn't actually want a drink. She got dressed and cleared the laundry off her floor, then moved into the bathroom, spraying cleaner around the sink and bath and scrubbing while she thought. There was so much going on, and she had to make a decision about what to deal with first. The Pearls were linked to JRB and JRB had been founded by someone with the Bunyan name. That couldn't be a coincidence. Lydia knew that she ought to focus on making nice with Charlie or on solving the murders of her Family members, but a fifteen-year-old girl was missing. As she used the shower attachment to hose down the bath, Lydia realised that it wasn't a difficult decision at all.

She found Jason in the kitchen. 'The Pearls might know something about Lucy Bunyan.'

'I don't want to do it,' Jason said immediately.

'I know, I'm sorry to ask. But she's only fifteen and the police haven't got anything.'

'You don't want me to do it, either. Hitch a ride, I mean.' Jason was making his fourth bowl of cereal. He had moved on from pouring cereal as a comfort activity, by and large, but things were clearly stressful enough to send him backward. 'You hated it.'

'I didn't hate it,' Lydia said, feeling the lie burn her tongue. 'Not all of it,' she amended. Mostly she had just been scared. Carrying the ghost inside was like swallowing death.

He folded the cardboard flaps of the cereal box back

down and put the box into the cabinet. 'You want milk on this one?'

Lydia didn't want any of the cereal, full stop, but she nodded. If Jason found making the breakfast of his childhood calming, she wasn't going to spoil his fun. After he had taken the seal from a new two-pint bottle and splashed milk onto the cornflakes, sprinkled sugar over the top and added a spoon, he wasn't vibrating anymore. He didn't take deep breaths, as he didn't need to breathe, but sometimes his shoulders raised and lowered, like he was emulating one, and Lydia knew he had come to a decision.

'I know it's important to get closer to the Pearls and if you think this is the best way, then I'll do it.'

Lydia started to say 'thank you', but Jason hadn't finished.

'You can't leave me there forever,' he said tightly.

'I wouldn't,' Lydia said, shocked. 'It will be ten minutes, maybe twenty.'

'Wait. What? I thought I was a gift,' Jason said. 'You usually give those. As in, for keeps.'

'Feathers, no,' Lydia couldn't believe how stupid she had been. She hadn't explained this right at all. 'I would never give you away. I couldn't, I don't own you in the first place. The gift is getting to meet you. That's the gift I'm bringing.'

Jason's face cleared instantly and he smiled with pure relief. 'That's fine, then. No problem. I mean,' he said. 'Some problem. I'm still scared and I won't like it, but that's okay.'

'You thought I was asking you to leave your home

and go and be the plaything or companion or whatever of some complete stranger for the rest of your... For eternity? And you were thinking about it?' Lydia was flabbergasted.

Jason gave a tiny shrug. 'You wouldn't ask unless it was really important.'

Lydia put her arms around Jason and hugged him tightly, ignoring the cold which flowed into her.

'Gerroff,' Jason said, after hugging her back for a moment. 'You need to eat your breakfast.' He looked at the line of cereal bowls. 'It's going to take a while.'

CHAPTER TWENTY-FIVE

Standing outside The Fork with a shimmering, fading, panicking Jason felt like deja vu. 'Quick,' Lydia said. 'Hop on.'

Having done it before, Lydia thought this time would be easier. She was wrong. It was just as unpleasant and alarming. The cold flowed through her body, highlighting every vein and capillary with traces of icy fire.

Lydia wasn't sure whether she would be able to drive while carrying a ghost, so she took a practice spin in the Audi. If she ordered an Uber, she would probably be safer during the journey, but might be left without a quick getaway at the other end. Time had behaved oddly on her last visit and Lydia wasn't confident that an Uber driver could be paid to wait for an undefined period. The journey to the north end of Hampstead Heath took forty long minutes. She could feel Jason's presence inside her mind, keeping politely and quietly to the edge, but undeniably there. And he was there in every movement, her body feeling both heavier than usual and also strangely untethered with a sense of fluttery panic. Every particle of her being wanted to push the interloper from the nest and fly high, high into the air. She controlled her instincts but it was exhausting and by the time they arrived at the gatehouse, Lydia felt as if she had run a marathon.

She wound down her window as the guard approached and arranged her face into what she hoped was a winning smile. 'I'm here to visit a friend.'

'No cars allowed through today, miss,' the guard hoisted his belt higher on his hips. He had a walkie talkie in a holster on the belt as well as a bulky flashlight and what could have been a multi-tool or an illegal taser, Lydia couldn't tell. 'Private event.'

'That seems extreme,' Lydia said.

The guard shrugged. 'Private road. Their rules.'

'I can walk along to see my friend, though?'

'Name?'

'Lucinda Pearl,' Lydia said, plucking the name from the air, and adding the address of the Pearl house. 'I'm Lydia Crow. I've got a gift.'

'Wait a moment, please'. The guard stepped away, reaching for the walkie talkie.

Lydia tried to look unconcerned as he carried out a conversation. She kept the engine of the car running, the stick in reverse and her foot poised over the accelerator. Just in case.

The guard was frowning when he walked back and Lydia almost slammed out of there, but it was regret. 'You'll have to leave your car here and walk, I'm afraid.'

Lydia forced a sigh.

The guard indicated a parking space marked out on the street. There was a sign which said 'No Parking – Drop Off Zone'. Lydia could feel the drag of carrying Jason as she exited the vehicle and made her way past the guard's cabin and on the pavement of the private road. Seen on foot, the houses were no less grand, but there was even less to see. High hedges and walls, gated driveways, and security cameras, the street was a testament to the privacy that wealth could afford.

As Lydia approached the Pearl residence, she saw a couple of kids standing outside the closed gates, looking pinched and pale in the cold. They were dressed in grubby, oddly-matched clothes, and had thin faces and sharp eyes, and looked more feral than residents of billionaires' row. Lydia gripped her coin for strength and straightened her spine. She had to hide any trace of tiredness and was glad she had thought to apply some red lipstick on the journey, rubbing a little into her cheeks to give the illusion of vitality. As she got closer, Lydia recognised the girl who had led the way last time, she was talking to her companion, a boy, in a low tone. The boy gave Lydia a blank look and then ran off in the opposite direction, his enormous hoodie flapping. 'I've got a gift for the king,' Lydia said.

The girl looked through her as if they had never met before. Lydia had hoped not to go through the whole production, again. She could feel Jason inside her body, the cold and brain fog and fear, and it wasn't improving her mood. 'I might have got you something, too,' she said.

'But only if you get me inside quick. It's cold out here and I'm a busy woman.'

The girl tilted her head, appraising Lydia with those unnaturally pale eyes. They were rimmed with red and Lydia felt a tug of concern and the urge to comfort the child, to hug her. A second later she recognised the impulse. Pearl magic.

'Is it sparkly?' The girl asked.

Lydia stared her down for a moment. Sympathy aside, you never showed your hand too early in a negotiation. She might not have been at Uncle Charlie's level, but she was a Crow through to her core.

After a few moments of staring right back – Lydia admired the girl's spirit – she turned and the gates opened. She walked up the driveway to the house and Lydia followed. She checked behind her, just once, and the gates were swinging smoothly shut.

Inside the house, Lydia recognised the giant tree growing through the centre of the entrance hall, but she could have sworn they were going a different route to the basement. Either the house was even bigger than Lydia had appreciated, or its interior had been changed since her last visit. Or it was all an illusion and they were in an entirely different construction. Anything seemed possible in that place. The air was thick with Pearl magic and Lydia could feel it reflecting and refracting off every shining surface. The walls of this stairwell were lined with black mirrors, pieces of shell, plates of metal. A hodgepodge collage of reflective surfaces which deceived the eye and clouded Lydia's senses until she felt like she was walking through treacle with every step.

At a wall that didn't look like it contained a door, the girl stopped and held out her hand. After thinking for a split second that the girl intended Lydia to hold it, she realised that the girl was demanding payment.

'It's through there?' Lydia indicated the wall. It was shining black ebony or painted wood, hard to tell in the dim light, and inlaid with thousands of tiny pieces of mother of pearl. It was as if the jewellery-box door she had gone through last time had morphed and grown, the pearl-encrusted-surface spreading through the house like a living thing.

The girl nodded.

'How do I open the door? There's no handle.'

The girl looked pointedly down at her outstretched hand, her lips compressed into a thin line so that they almost disappeared.

'Feathers,' Lydia said. 'You have trust issues, did you know that?' She reached into the inside pocket of her leather jacket and produced the heart-shaped locket she had bought in Ari's shop. It had an iridescent rainbow chain and a sparkly hologram picture on the front of the locket which changed from a cartoon kitten to a smiling rainbow when you tilted it. It was cheap, plasticky, kitsch and very, very glittery. Lydia had looked for something she and Emma would have gone nuts for aged eight and crossed her fingers that this girl wasn't so different.

The girl's eyes lit up and her hand darted out as if to grab the necklace. She stopped short, though, her fingers close to the jewellery without touching. Lydia pressed it into her hand. 'A gift from me to you, freely given.'

The girl put the necklace on immediately, tucking it safely inside her thin sweatshirt. 'This way,' she said, turning back to the black wall and putting both hands onto it, palms flat. She pushed and Lydia thought she heard a click. Or maybe she imagined it as a door appeared, swinging outward on well-oiled hinges. The girl caught the edge and opened it wide enough for them to pass through.

It might have been a different entrance, but the room Lydia arrived in was the same. This time, however, it was quiet. There was no music or dancing, just strobing lights reflected on the mirrored walls. And a crowd of good-looking people, wearing what Lydia assumed was high fashion as it was expensive-looking and a bit weird. A young woman to her left was wearing a white body con dress with a deep V-neck, exposing a bony sternum and shoulder pads which extended far past her own body, like fins. She hissed as Lydia walked past and it should have been comical, but it wasn't.

Walking through the crowd of almost-silent, eerily still bodies, was more menacing than Lydia would have imagined. She could feel Jason inside her, too, stirring uneasily through his own misgivings or because he was picking up on hers. She forced herself to breathe evenly and slipped a hand into her pocket to hold her coin. She could do this.

'Your Majesty,' Lydia said, bowing her head. She thought that she was prepared for the king's beauty this time, thought that she had remembered it from the last time and that it would make less of a toe-curling, mind-warping, sweat-inducing impact. That was not the case.

The androgynous figure lounging on the throne-like chair was, if anything, more beautiful and perfect than last time. More disturbing still, they were looking straight at Lydia this time, not merely giving her side-eye. The almond shaped eyes, edged in black with silver-painted lids and glowing skin and cheekbones; each feature was attractive and perfect. All together it was like looking at the sun.

'You again.' The king's voice was soft and mid-range. It was as gender-neutral as the rest of them. Not gender neutral, Lydia corrected herself. Gender-insignificant. Gender new. From where she was standing, gender perfect. Why be one or the other? Why not be this perfect blend of two, making so much more than the sum of two halves? Her mind was cloudy, she knew. Her hands were out of her pockets and her coin was nowhere. She could feel Jason, and thought that he might be trying to tell her something, to speak, but she couldn't hear his words. She just wanted to look upon the magnificence of the majesty.

Lydia.

Someone was saying her name. With a force of will, Lydia dragged her attention from the king's ethereal face. 'What?' She spoke out loud and the moment she did, the spell was broken. Her coin was in her hand, Jason was on board, she was standing in a night club in the middle of the day and the head of the Pearl Family was sitting six feet away, smiling at her like she was a performing monkey who was about to juggle.

'I have brought you a gift,' Lydia said. She flipped her coin over her knuckles, using it to keep her anchored in the moment. The Pearl magic had always pulled people in, made them want, made them need until they would be willing to part with any amount of cash in order to satiate that vast emptiness. This, however, was different. The rumours were true. Mr Smith hadn't been lying when he said the Pearls had evolved.

The king straightened a little, eyes lighting with interest. 'A gift from a Crow. What an unexpected pleasure.'

Ninety percent of Lydia wanted to throw herself down at the king's feet and beg to be permitted to stay within their perfect presence for all eternity, but the rest, helped by Jason, was keeping a watchful eye on the crowd, seeing who was circling behind her to block the exit. 'My gift is a show. A temporary performance, made all the more special by its fleeting nature.'

An incremental shift of a perfect eyebrow.

'If your friends are allowed to enjoy the gift, they need to be here,' Lydia indicated the space in front of her, 'in order to appreciate it.'

The king inclined their head and the crowd which had formed behind her, moved back to nearby, in front of Lydia. She took a step backward, toward the exit, trying to appear casual. 'Right, then.' She licked her lips and wished she had something to moisten her dry throat. 'I am pleased to introduce Jason Montefort. A man who died in 1985.'

There was a little ripple throughout the room, as people craned their necks and whispered to their neighbour.

'Okay,' she said quietly. 'You can come out, now.'

Feeling Jason leave her body wasn't quite as weird as feeling it enter, but it came close. She took several long slow breaths to get oxygen to her brain and make sure she didn't pass out or throw up. The latter would probably be tantamount to treason in the king's presence.

His form was thin and Lydia could see the king through his torso. She smiled at him reassuringly and took his hand. 'Ready?'

Jason nodded, his outline shimmering in the disco lights.

Lydia gripped her coin in her other hand and concentrated on focusing her energy. The training with Charlie had taught her that she wasn't a cup of magic that could quickly be drained, she was more like a dynamo, converting her human electrical energy into Crow force. She didn't know if it had an end or whether she could keep replenishing the fire, so to speak, forever. Charlie had said she could be limitless and maybe that was true. All she knew in this moment was that she could hear wings beating and feel wind on her face like she was flying, part of her was high above this building, in the clouds with the city spread out below. Once Jason was fully solid and stable, she pushed her energy out further, in a wave. She didn't know if this would work or for how long, but felt a core of confidence. It would work. She would push until it worked.

There was a gasp from the assembled crowd and, through her sweat-stinging eyes, Lydia saw Jason standing in front of the crowd. She could hear his voice and, from the reactions of the king and courtiers, they could, too.

'I'm honoured to meet you,' Jason was saying.

Very polite. Very proper. Good man. Lydia pushed a little harder, making sure that every person in the room could see and hear Jason. She could feel it like a net she had thrown out across the room, or a thin piece of fabric like a veil. She could see it loosely covering every person's head and draping down at the edges of the crowd.

The king clapped their hands, delighted. 'This is a very fine gift, very fine.' They beamed at Jason and then at Lydia and she felt, again, the Pearl-pull, the urge to throw herself at the king's feet and kiss their toes. Bleurgh.

'You may approach,' the king said.

Jason glanced at Lydia and she nodded encouragingly.

The crowd had got closer, people shifting forward, those at the back wanting to see better and their murmuring voices combined in a single, entranced song. Lydia was checking out the vast room, while simultaneously trying to pretend that she wasn't. There was a bar area along one wall with glittering glass bottles housed in a beautiful art nouveau cabinet and a row of stools in front of a polished slab of wood. The stools had carved wooden bases, shaped like twisted tree trunks and polished to a deep shine. Without the strobing lights, which had given the impression of a night club, Lydia could now see that the interior was far finer than your average dance pit. And it had to have cost a fortune.

The crowd were leaning in, their faces avid, and Lydia was checking that the veil she had cast was covering every member, when she spotted a figure who remained outside the circle. A female figure, young-looking and half-hidden in the shadows behind the king's fancy chair. Even in her mind, Lydia refused to say 'throne'. The figure wasn't looking at Jason, as he held out his hand for the king to shake, but was gazing instead at the king as if they were the most beautiful, mesmerising creature they had ever laid eyes upon. Even with her face made-up with rainbow glitter and wearing a prom dress, Lydia recognised the girl. Lucy Bunyan.

CHAPTER TWENTY-SIX

The king reached out and attempted to touch Jason's outstretched hand, but theirs passed through it. They laughed, thrilled. 'Very, very good. Thank you for visiting. I hope you will do so again.'

Lydia spoke before Jason could say something unwise like 'not on your life, mate'. 'We are very glad to have pleased,' she stopped short of saying 'your majesty' but dipped her head respectfully.

'And what is it you wish to request? Speak quickly, before I tire.' The king smirked as if aware they were speaking in a parody of royalty, but there was a haughtiness around the eyes which was entirely genuine.

Lydia swallowed. She couldn't ask the question she had planned upon. Not with the object of that enquiry currently making moon-eyes from the back of the room. She flipped to her other area of interest and hoped that the king would deem it sufficiently important not to guess that Lydia had actually come for another purpose. 'I would respectfully ask about the collective known as

JRB. I am an investigator, a business which is based on information, and that is an area where my knowledge falls away.'

The king regarded Lydia for a long moment. 'JRB is an incorporated company. It is registered with the proper authorities.'

Lydia's heart sank. She had started with the wrong question. And she needed more time. Extracting Lucy Bunyan was not going to be easy when she was so drastically outnumbered, but she was hoping to reassure the girl, at least. Lydia forced herself not to glance around.

'They are also a family, of sorts.'

Lydia looked up at the king, holding her breath, and momentarily distracted from Lucy.

'They keep us.'

Lydia waited, not wanting to interrupt. After the silence stretched on, though, she asked. 'Keep you?'

The king waved a hand. 'Pearls have always had a weakness for money and the pretty things it can buy. We would sew mother-of-pearl to our jackets to catch the light, pick a silver piece from a midden, fill our carts with polished tin and sell it for ten times its value.'

Lydia compressed her lips, stopping the urge to interrupt. She didn't want a history lesson or more stories but if it kept them talking, it bought her time.

The king smiled. 'You want the truth? The unvarnished reality, not this,' they waved a hand, indicating the large room, the beautiful people. 'The truth is this; JRB offered us a great deal of money and we took it. Now we are here. In this jewel box.'

'You're trapped?' The question was out before Lydia could stop it.

'I am a king,' they spoke in icy tones. 'And everybody is trapped in one way or another.'

Which wasn't a real answer. The king was looking increasingly impatient, however, and the crowd was shifting.

'Jason,' Lydia said, quietly. 'Come here. Walk backwards.'

Jason obeyed, backing away from the throne with small steps.

'We thank you for your time,' Lydia said. 'You have been most gracious and patient. I hope this can be the start of a friendship between our two Families.'

The king smiled with their mouth only. 'You wish an alliance? That will require a far larger gift. The coin you hold concealed in your hand, perhaps. Or this toy.'

For a second Lydia didn't realize the king meant Jason. 'I do not have the authority, sadly,' Lydia said. 'I will carry your message back to the head of the Crow Family.'

The king wagged a finger. 'You must not tell lies, Lydia Crow. I have a mind to teach you a lesson. I shall keep your gift, I think.'

With a speed and fluidity which surprised Lydia, the king was off their throne and in front of Jason, hands plunged into his chest.

He looked over his shoulder at Lydia, eyes wide and terrified.

'No!' Lydia said firmly. In her mind she added 'bad king' which was probably the product of fear, but it made her smile, which reminded her of an important fact. She wasn't powerless. She had always assumed that she was, had always felt like the spare part, the damp squib, the disappointment. But that wasn't true. It had never been true, she just hadn't known it.

She reached for Jason's hand and took it firmly in her own. It was solid and real under her touch and, as always, very cold. At the same time, she whipped away the veil she had cast over the crowd, removing their sight so that they could no longer see Jason. The king hissed displeasure, but she ignored them. She pulled Jason back and he stumbled against her. For a second he almost overbalanced her with his weight and in the next second he was insubstantial as a puff of air. Air she breathed in, gathering him inside for the trip home.

'That was very rude,' she said. 'You should not take things which do not belong to you.' Lydia let her gaze fall on Lucy Bunyan who was still gazing adoringly at the king with exactly zero comprehension on her face. 'There will be consequences.'

The king flicked a glance at Lucy before looking back at Lydia. 'You presume to threaten me, Crow?'

'I very much do,' Lydia said. 'And now I'm leaving.'

'Unlikely,' the king said, turning beautiful and terrible eyes upon her.

Lydia turned and realised that the crowd had encircled her. They no longer looked like a group of glamorous party-goers, their faces were twisted with anger and ugliness showed in every line. A split second more and Lydia realised something else. It wasn't just anger transforming their faces, it was age. Wrinkled skin sitting loosely over bone, milky-eyes, and gnarled fingers reaching. The king wasn't immune. They flickered between the perfection of youth and a well-preserved sixty-ish, black hair turning grey and then back again. A truth occurred to her. The Pearl court wasn't composed of newly evolved Pearls or the watered-down versions which she had encountered out and about in London, but of the old guard. The original, most powerful members of the Family. 'I see you,' Lydia said. 'And I am not afraid.'

The king laughed, but Lydia caught the flicker of uncertainty in their eyes.

'You will return what you have taken and I will forgive your transgressions. There is no need for the truce between our Families to be broken.' Lydia drew herself up to her full height. It wasn't very impressive, she would be the first to admit, and she could feel Jason's panic inside her mind, lapping at the edges and frilling her thoughts with sharp anxiety. The fear was good. When Charlie had attacked her, she had reacted instinctively, the terror of being choked had unleashed something wild and unknown. Now that she recognised the feeling, the shape of that something, she knew she could reach for it. Like the different powers she sensed in others, it had a signature. It was wings beating, it was the cushion of warm air lifting from below, it was sleek feathers shining in a noonday sun, and a sharp beak ripping into flesh. Not just one beak or two wings, though, hundreds. Thousands. A multitude of beating hearts. Lydia raised her arms, stretching them wide. She didn't stop looking at the king, keeping eye contact as she pushed the feeling out.

The crowd took a collective step back. Lydia could see the way out of the party basement. The door had a mirror attached and would have blended completely into the wall, becoming invisible, but Lydia had noted its position when she had come into the room and left it partially open. She backed toward it, keeping the Pearls in sight. They were frowning, uncertain as to why they hadn't rushed Lydia, as their king so clearly required.

Lydia didn't know how long this mass-whammy was going to work or how long it would hold if they all decided to push back. The basement club was covered in reflective surfaces and it made it seem as if the crowd were ten times larger than it really was. There were ten Pearls there, maybe fifteen, but their expressions were replicated and fractured in the multiple mirrors, polished wood, and mother-of-pearl inlay which formed the walls. With the lights, there were so many surfaces glinting and refracting light, so many areas shining, it was hard to keep your bearings, keep your thoughts on track.

Lydia.

That was Jason. Lydia tried to concentrate above the rhythmic beating of wings. The expressions in the crowd no longer looked angry, they looked excited.

Lydia realised that she had stopped moving toward the door. She didn't know when that had happened. She hadn't meant to, but she was rooted where she stood. She tried to move her feet, but they were planted. Was that the sound of wind in trees? How could she hear that?

The music was too loud. And they were in a basement. A fancy basement, sure, but a basement. There was no wind.

Lydia! Money!

Yes. Good point, Jason. Good man. Excellent assistant. Lydia reached into her pocket and found her coin. She held it between finger and thumb, arm stretched out in front of her body. All eyes in the room snapped to it. Lydia could see hunger. Faces that had seemed beautiful, now looked knotted and creased like old bark. For once, the assembled Pearls looked their age.

Lydia forced the power she had felt, those thousands of tiny pulsing hearts, those beating wings, and fractured the coin into hundreds of gold Crow coins. Then she flung the lot high into the air so that they clattered down on the Pearls. And then she turned and ran.

THERE WAS a roaring sound from behind, but Lydia ran up the stairs and into the grand entrance with the tree. Up here, Lydia could hear cracking and a low rumble, like something was moving deep under the ground. The floor began to shudder and the tree was shaking as if blown by an invisible gale. Lydia dived for the front door, yanking it open and throwing herself out, and running down the driveway to the closed wooden gates. She almost fell as the ground moved. Earthquake, Lydia thought, even as her mind told her that it was no such thing. Just ahead, a tree root broke through the stone chipping of the driveway and Lydia ran into air that was suddenly filled with earth and vegetation, and this time she did fall, catching herself on her hands and knees, the jolt of the impact traveling through her joints. Ignoring the pain, she forced herself back up and ran around the tree roots which were bursting through the ground, one four feet in the air and whipping around like the tentacle of a mythological sea monster.

The gates were closed but Lydia was pretty sure she would be able to climb over. There was a decorative lattice in the top half which ought to provide hand and footholds and, besides that, she had no choice. A moment later another tree root burst through the ground underneath one of the gateposts, spraying chippings and spitting earth, Lydia instinctively threw her arms in front of her face and felt sharp pains on the backs of her hands. The gate was splintered and sagging on one side and Lydia didn't break pace, pushing through the gap and stepping over the raw jagged edges of the broken wooden boards.

Lungs burning, skin stinging, and her breath coming in harsh rasps, Lydia forced herself to keep running as she emerged onto the street. She ran diagonally, putting as much distance between herself and the exploding grounds around the house as possible. Lydia felt as though she was still sprinting as she reached the end of the private road but, truthfully, she slowed by the time she made it to the gatehouse with its road barrier. She was dragging one foot in front of the other as every part of her screamed for rest, the weight and cold of Jason dragging her to the ground, but she ducked under the barrier and kept moving.

Lydia didn't want to be grateful to Uncle Charlie,

but right at the moment, she was extremely glad to see her new car, parked where she had left it. Once she was in the driving seat, all doors locked and shaking hands gripping the steering wheel, Lydia allowed herself a moment. Just a moment to take some deep, shuddering breaths.

The ground felt stable, now, which was a relief, but she could feel the ghost inside her and the strain of keeping him contained and stable. The beating of wings had receded and Lydia knew that whatever that power was it had turned down, like the volume on a television. She started the engine and kept her eyes on the rear-view mirror, ready to floor the accelerator if she saw even a single Pearl. She dialled Fleet and put the phone on speaker.

When Fleet answered she gave him the essential details. The address of the house he would find Lucy Bunyan. 'It's the Pearls,' she said. 'And they are pissed.'

'With you?'

Lydia could almost hear him resisting the urge to say something sarcastic. 'Yes. If you get here quick, you'll catch them on the hop. I doubt they'll expect me to call the police, they seem quite old fashioned.'

'Where are you now? Are you safe?'

'I'm at the bottom of their road in my car.'

'Well get moving. I'll call you when we have Lucy.'

'I want to help.' Even as she said the words, Lydia knew she didn't have a good follow up. She had barely got herself out of the house. 'They're strong.'

'An armed response is on its way,' Fleet said. 'Ten minutes.'

Lydia gripped the steering wheel. She should move. Get away. But what if the Pearls moved Lucy? If they were going to leave, she needed to see. Get a direction or a number plate. Something.

The minutes crawled past and Lydia's rear-view mirror remained devoid of action. She could feel the weight of Jason and wasn't sure how much longer she could hold onto him. Lydia didn't know what would happen if they separated in her car, but she knew one thing for certain; if the Pearls decided to come for her, she wouldn't be able to protect herself or Jason. She was exhausted.

At minute eleven, Lydia saw the first blue-and-yellow police cars. The guard didn't approach, just waved from his little cabin and raised the barrier. Three marked cars and two police vans headed up the private road and Lydia peeled away. She was still a little nervous of the police as an official entity and couldn't afford to get stuck giving a witness statement, not with a ghost onboard.

She drove carefully back to Camberwell, grateful that Jason was staying quiet, and, as soon as she had one foot through the door of The Fork, she pushed him out of her body. Lydia was glad that it was almost closing time and the place was deserted, but she honestly couldn't have waited for another second and would have ejected Jason even if the place had been packed in a midday rush.

'We made it,' Jason said, shimmering just in front of Lydia, his feet not bothering to connect with the floor. 'You look like crap.'

'I'm... Okay.' It was an effort to speak.

Angel pushed through the door from the kitchen, a mop bucket in hand, and stopped when she saw Lydia doubled over. 'You all right?'

'FINE.' Lydia managed. 'Stitch.'

'Well, that's running for you. Terrible idea.'

Lydia made her way upstairs. Jason had disappeared and she hoped it wouldn't be for long. She knew how much he hated blinking out of existence. She didn't need to worry as he was waiting for her in the office and his stoic silence in the car had given way to verbiage.

'I can't believe they... I don't think they were going to let us go. And how did the king do that? Put their hands in me. That was horrible, I felt them grabbing.' Jason shook his head. 'I never want that sensation again. Do you want some tea? I need to make tea.'

Lydia sucked in another breath. Every part of her body wanted to be asleep but she forced herself to breathe, to stay with the conversation. Another moment and she would go to bed. Or just pass out on the floor. That sounded nice.

Jason had been talking rapidly, expending nervous energy and Lydia understood the need. After he wound down, he took a step closer and asked: 'Did you really just give them your coin?'

Lydia straightened up. If Jason hadn't been a ghost she would have said he looked pale. Since he was, it felt like a redundant observation. He looked more dead than usual, though.

'No,' she produced her coin, after a moment of effort. Her finger tips burned as she held it, as if her coin was angry. 'I tricked them.'

Jason looked gratifyingly impressed and Lydia quickly pocketed the coin again. She sagged against her desk, exhaustion sweeping through her body.

'So, that was the Pearls.' Jason was trying for jokey, but his feet were still hovering an inch above the floor. 'Not sure I'm a fan.'

'I don't suppose we're on their Christmas list, either.'

'They all looked about a hundred and fifty years old. It was creepy.'

'That's how I spotted Lucy.'

Jason frowned. 'Lucy Bunyan was there?'

'You didn't see her? At the back? She was behind the king's ridiculous chair.'

'You're refusing to say 'throne' aren't you?'

'Damn straight,' Lydia forced a smile. 'Didn't you hear me call it in? That's why I was waiting for the police.'

Jason shook his head. 'Everything is dark after we got upstairs. We were running. I mean, you were running. And there was this noise like the earth was breaking apart and I just, sort of, blacked out.' He looked embarrassed. 'I'm a wuss.'

Lydia checked her phone. Fleet would call as soon as it was safe.

'So, the police arrived?' Jason was speaking hesitantly. 'They're going in, now, and they will rescue Lucy?'

'That's the idea.' Lydia wished she had been able to

grab Lucy herself, like an action hero from a film. If she was a big dude with a gun, she could have thrown Lucy Bunyan over one shoulder and muscled her way out. Of course, there had been the Pearl magic which would have rooted her in place, stopped her gun hand from moving, and then she and Jason would be deader than dead.

'What do we do?' Jason blinked at her, his feet still hovering above the floor and his edges shimmering in distress.

Lydia swallowed. 'We wait and we hope.'

CHAPTER TWENTY-SEVEN

I f Lydia had been smart she would have gone back to the Pearls and given them fair warning that Fleet and an armed response unit were going to burst through their front door and rescue Lucy Bunyan. She could have given them the chance to release Lucy, to maybe amend her memories and have her turn up somewhere neutral. In return for this favour, the king might have agreed an alliance between the Crows and the Pearls. It would have been, how would Charlie put it, 'a real world' solution. And one which would have elevated the Crows' power and position, secured their future.

Lydia wasn't clever. At least, not in the way Charlie wanted. She wasn't going to risk harm to Lucy Bunyan in order to curry favour with the Pearls. Not when a kidnapping charge was up for grabs. What if the king decided to dispose of the evidence by spiriting Lucy away or putting her six feet under? Charlie might believe that collateral damage was an acceptable cost of business, but Lydia did not.

Lydia paced the floor, gripping her phone in one hand and her coin the other. Like it was a charm that could ensure Lucy's safe return. What if the king had heard Lydia's threat and decided to do something violent, just to spite Lydia? To teach her a lesson. Lydia had fully convinced herself that she had signed the girl's death warrant when Fleet rang.

'We've got her,' he said. 'She's fine. Unharmed, thank God.'

Lydia crumpled to the floor, overwhelmed with relief.

'Nobody hurt our end, either.' Fleet sounded elated and Lydia knew that this moment was the culmination of many long days and sleepless nights for him. She knew how relieved he would be that Lucy was alive, because he was a good person, but also because the pressure from his boss would have been pushing down with unbearable weight. This was a result.

'Her dad's on his way to the hospital. She's being checked out, just a precaution. But she really does seem healthy. Bit confused, but physically well.'

'That's great,' Lydia said. She straightened up from her crouching position. 'Happy ending.'

'Thanks to you,' Fleet said.

There was a pause, and Lydia heard the background sounds quieten. He had moved away from whoever he was standing near. When he spoke again, his voice was quiet. 'You want me to keep your name out of this?'

'That would be best.' Lydia's mind was whirling, now. Had the Pearl King released Lucy Bunyan because of Lydia's visit? Had they been that impressed by Lydia's show of power?

'You won't want to give a statement.'

It wasn't a question and Lydia didn't answer.

'Will do,' Fleet said, raising his voice, his tone turning clipped and professional.

Lydia was about to end the call, but Fleet continued, his voice quiet. 'Bit odd, though. The place was just like you described, except there was nobody there. We bust through the door and searched the whole place. Found Lucy in an upstairs bedroom fast asleep and not another soul in the building.'

'Did you see the tree? In the hallway?'

'I saw a lot of rubble. Nice place, but looks like it's in the middle of a major refurb.'

Lydia swallowed. 'You went down to the basement?'

'I saw the swimming pool and the gym. And a bloody great hole in the wall. They must be planning an extension down there.'

'What about the party room? The private nightclub place?'

'Funny thing about that, Lyds,' Fleet said. 'There wasn't one.'

THE NEXT DAY, Lydia went downstairs to find some free breakfast. Angel came out from behind the counter, looking unusually anxious. 'Have you seen Charlie?'

'Not today,' Lydia replied. 'Why?'

'He's not answering his phone,' Angel said. She

pulled her dreads back into a ponytail as she spoke, wrapping an elastic tie to secure it.

'What do you need?'

'Nothing.' Angel's eyes slid left. 'Just wanted to ask him about opening hours.'

'Uh-huh. I thought he left operating matters to you.'

'He does, I just...'

'Angel,' Lydia said, tiredness eroding her patience. Her eyes ached. 'Just tell me.'

'I'm supposed to check in with him every day and he always answers.'

'You deliver him a report on me every day,' Lydia said, just for the sake of clarity and, if she was honest, to let Angel know that she was done pretending that everything was fine.

Angel's face went blank and Lydia produced her coin. 'It's unusual for him not to answer then?'

Angel nodded.

'But there's more to it. You're worried about Charlie because you've noticed he's become a bit erratic.' That was an understatement.

Angel looked like she didn't want to answer but she glanced at the coin held up between Lydia's thumb and forefinger and nodded again.

'What else?'

'Aiden was here,' Angel said, sounding aggrieved rather than worried. 'Said he had to pick something up for Charlie and then he took some of my good knives.'

Lydia's scalp tingled. 'What else?'

Angel really did not want to answer. Lydia felt her resistance and pushed it away like it weighted nothing at all. In a previous life, this would have pleased Lydia. It was evidence that she was stronger, her Crow abilities becoming more finely honed, but in this life it made her feel grubby.

'I heard him on the phone,' Angel said. 'As he was leaving. I think he was talking to Charlie and it didn't sound good.'

'Charlie's in trouble?'

Angel shook her head. 'Someone else is.'

'Connected with the Crow murders in Wandsworth?'

Angel winced. 'I reckon.'

'Hell Hawk,' Lydia swore under her breath. She still felt exhausted from her encounter with the Pearl King, but Charlie's behaviour was spiralling with no concern for her need for rest and recuperation.

'Where?'

'I don't know,' Angel said, her eyes sliding left.

'I won't ask again,' Lydia said, spinning her coin in the air and watching Angel's eyes widen in fear.

'He mentioned the arches.' Angel looked like she was trying not to cry and Lydia felt like hell.

'Close the cafe and go home,' Lydia said. 'Better yet, take a holiday out of London.'

'I can't-'

Lydia cut across her. 'Charlie is off the rails. We both know it. If you wait to see just how far off, it might be too late. I'll let you know when it's safe to come back.'

LYDIA LEFT Angel blinking and a little dazed and

headed to the railway arches on Camberwell Station Road. By some miracle, she squeezed the Audi into a space right outside the row of shuttered arches underneath the railway line. There was a lot of graffiti, mostly gang tags, and a few arches had brown metal shutters and rusted padlocks that looked as if they hadn't been touched in a decade or two. There was a place with fresh blue metal shutters and a poorly-painted sign advertising auto repairs and another one, further down the row, with a corrugated red garage door and no sign. Lydia walked back up the street, reaching out for 'Crow' with her senses. Every impression – the pavement under her feet, the pinkish sky as the sun set above the railway, the smell of cooking oil and diesel – were sharp and distinct. There it was. As she neared the blue auto shop again, the taste of feathers in the back of her throat. Crows.

The door had a brand new, high-end padlock, the kind that was a bastard to pick and not easy to saw through. It wasn't securing the door at the moment, though, which added to Lydia's assumption that whoever owned the unit was already inside. Lydia banged on the door with the side of her fist. It made a hollow booming sound. Nobody came to the door and she pressed her ear up against it, trying to listen. Nothing. She thumped again.

Lydia was just debating whether to try the handle, weighing up the advisability of surprising Charlie and whoever else was inside, against the possibility that she would be left standing on the frozen pavement indefinitely, when the door swung inward. Lydia had been expecting Charlie and it took her a moment to react properly to the sight of Aiden. He looked younger than when she had last seen him, and his skin was pale, his eyes wide and anxious.

'All right, Aiden?' Lydia said, keeping her voice light and friendly. The kid looked unwell, like he was going to throw up at any moment.

'You're not invited,' Aiden said. Then he looked over his shoulder.

Lydia took the opportunity to push past him. Immediately her nostrils were assaulted by the smell. Someone had recently voided their bowels. If Lydia had to bet, it was probably the man who was tied to a chair in the middle of the lock-up.

'What's all this?' Lydia spoke to the man in charge, her dear old Uncle Charlie who was crossing the cement floor to meet her. His bulk obliterated her view of the man in the chair and all she could see were his flat eyes.

'Head on home, Lyds,' Charlie said. 'This doesn't concern you.'

'I think it does,' Lydia said, squeezing her coin tightly in one hand, drawing strength and focus. 'Who's that?'

'Let's go outside a minute, yeah?'

Charlie hustled Lydia out of the room, half-closing the metal door behind him. 'It's necessary, Lyds. You know we're under attack.'

Lydia took a deep breath of fresh air and tried to order her thoughts. She kept flashing on the image of the man in the chair. His face was bruised and bloody, his nose clearly broken. More than the injuries, though, it was the expression in his eyes which stayed with Lydia.

The naked fear. 'Who is that?' Lydia indicated the lock-up.

'Big Neil,' Charlie said after a moment's hesitation. 'He's part of a crew I've had my eye on for a while and he just went to the top of my list.'

'He's Camberwell?'

'Peckham,' Charlie said.

'But the burner used to contact Malc was bought in Camden.'

Charlie shrugged. 'Originally, yeah, but it could have been sold on. How many phones were bought at the same time?'

'Ten,' Lydia said, conceding the point. 'And whoever bought it could have deliberately gone to a different area to do so.'

'Exactly,' Charlie formed a finger gun and pointed it at Lydia. 'Whereas my boy in there,' he jerked his head at the closed door. 'Is a little shit. Been mouthing off against us for months.'

'People talk,' Lydia said. 'It doesn't mean anything.'

'Doesn't mean nothing, either,' Charlie shot back. 'Everyone knows he's friendly with the Fox Family, too. Doesn't stack up well.'

Lydia felt a shiver of dread and the hairs on the back of her neck raised. 'What do you mean? Being friendly with the wrong person is a crime now?'

Charlie shrugged. 'Dangerous times. If you're friends with an enemy of the Crows, then you're an enemy of the Crows. You should think on that, Lyds, get your head straight.'

Lydia forced herself not to look away. It was an overt

threat and she wasn't going to bother trying to argue that Paul Fox wasn't an enemy of the Crow Family. That he had banished Tristan, his own father, for moving against them. Instead she asked: 'What are you doing to do?'

'Find out what he knows.'

Lydia glanced at the closed door, ice in her stomach. 'This isn't right. I will find out who ordered the killings, you don't need to do this.'

Charlie turned flat, dead eyes onto her. 'Don't tell me my business, Lyds.'

'I'm not,' Lydia said. 'I just want a bit of time. I can sort this. No blood spilled. If we retaliate like this,' she indicated the door. 'It will escalate. I'm right, aren't I?'

Charlie's shoulders lifted very slightly. 'Ever since you strolled back into Camberwell you've been telling me you don't want to be a part of Family business. Well, congratulations, you're out. Now off you fuck.'

BACK IN HER CAR, Lydia did the only thing she could think of and called Fleet. There was being a lone wolf and an independent woman and then there was good sense.

'I'm a bit tied up at the moment,' Fleet said. Lydia could hear voices in the background.

'The Bunyan case? How is Lucy doing?'

'Yeah,' Fleet's voice dipped and she heard a door close. When he spoke next, his voice was echoey like he had stepped into a stairwell. 'She's okay. Her dad has been praising us to the higher ups, so that's nice. They'll forget it by the next budget meeting, but still.'

'Things are a bit sticky here. I really need to find the person who sent the text into Wandsworth. I know it's not high up the list for the CPS and the case will probably get dropped, but I need-'

'You don't have to explain,' Fleet said. 'I get it.'

'Is there anything you can do?' Lydia was grateful that Fleet didn't ask her for details. She couldn't tell him that Charlie had a man tied to a chair in a lock-up. He was on her side, but he was still a copper.

'We didn't get anything else off the burner from Malc's cell. We've applied to get the records for the phone number which sent the text from the mobile provider, but it'll take a day or two.'

Lydia swore. Big Neil didn't have a day or two.

LYDIA PULLED on her jacket and wrapped a thick scarf around her neck. She was in the unusual position of actively wanting to speak to Mr Smith. She wished it was Thursday or that he had given her a burner, that would make things a little easier. Instead, she walked to Kennington Road. As always, she walked a slightly different route, doubling back on one of the side streets, and kept a sharp lookout for a tail, stopping once to window shop and once to pretend to tie her shoelace. Over the last few weeks she hadn't seen a single repeated figure, nothing to suggest surveillance was following her to her meetings with Mr Smith, but she wasn't about to get sloppy.

At the anonymous beige reception area, Lydia looked above the doors, in the corners of the room and the stairwell until she found the camera. It was small and higher-spec than you would expect in a council office building, but not hidden. Lydia stood in the middle of the reception area and waved. Then she pulled the piece of paper she had prepared before leaving the flat and held it up so that the words faced the camera and then sat on the bottom step to wait. She wondered whether there was another meeting going on in the flat upstairs with another source being hounded for information. More likely they used different flats for different operations. She wondered what was on her file and whether Mr Smith referred to her with a case code name, like the Met did for complicated operations.

Ten minutes later a telephone began ringing. Putting her ear to the door marked 'Kennington Council, Appointments Only' made the ringing louder. Lydia expected the door to be locked so was surprised when it opened easily. It was an office complete with box files, filing cabinets, standard furniture and a thirsty-looking spider plant. Lydia picked up the phone receiver. 'Hello?'

A woman's voice delivered four words and then there was a click.

'Vauxhall Bridge. Five minutes.'

Lydia was about halfway to the river, heading down Kennington Lane when a Mercedes saloon with tinted rear windows pulled up alongside. A large man in a suit was out of the car and taking Lydia by the elbow before she had time to react. 'This way, please, Ms Crow.' It wasn't a request.

Within seconds, Lydia was in the quiet, leather interior, the heavy thump of the door cutting off the sounds of the traffic. If Lydia had ever wondered what money could buy when it came to automobiles, now she had her answer.

'You wanted to see me?' Mr Smith was wearing a suit and he looked more intimidating than usual. Or perhaps that was the car and the staff sat up front.

'Is this bullet proof?' Lydia tapped the side window. 'And don't the tinted windows attract more attention than they deflect?'

'I assume it's important?'

Lydia was fiddling with the door, looking for the handle, and she didn't bother to reply. She wasn't frightened of Mr Smith, but she liked to know she could leave whenever she chose. 'Two Crows have been killed in Wandsworth nick.'

Mr Smith didn't reply.

'Police have got a burner phone used to order the hits, but it will take forty-eight hours to get the records from the mobile company.'

'You summoned me for another favour.' Mr Smith's tone was flat, his face unreadable.

'I'm not asking you for anything, just sharing information.'

'I see.'

'JRB. You know about them. More than you've told me. And I'm wondering if they might be stupid enough to kill a couple of Crows?'

Mr Smith tilted his head but didn't speak.

'They were founded by a Bunyan back in the nineteenth century, but that company was dissolved in 2001.

My understanding is that they had a special relationship with the Pearls. Something that has since gone a bit sour.'

'You've been busy,' Mr Smith said. 'And now you're wondering if JRB are in the market for some new friends?'

'It occurred to me that if they had fallen out of love with the Pearls, they might be keen to destabilise the truce. If the Families feel off-balance, they're more likely to partner with an outsider. At least, that's what JRB might think.'

'You think they're wrong?'

'I think they're underestimating the way the Families feel about blood. The Pearls have always been more open.'

Mr Smith nodded. 'Well done on finding Lucy Bunyan, by the way.'

'I had nothing to do with that,' Lydia said. 'It was DCI Fleet and his team.'

'Modesty is overrated.'

'Discretion is not,' Lydia countered. The Pearls hadn't vanished into thin air. There were thousands of Londoners with a little bit of Pearl in their blood and Lydia, like Charlie, had assumed that they represented what was left of the Family. They had been wrong. There was still a strong core to the Family. The powerful ancestors of the Pearl Family were, impossibly, still alive, and that alone had to take a lot of juice. They had to have moved somewhere and Lydia would find them. She didn't know if her aim was to make friends or burn their court to the ground, but she assumed she would figure it out along the way. In the meantime, Lydia had absolutely no compunction over using them as a bargaining chip with Mr Smith. 'Interesting thing about the Pearls, though. They are able to manipulate time. Or time behaves differently around them. Or something. I bet your boffins would be interested.'

'They would indeed,' Mr Smith said. 'I don't suppose you have an address for them?'

'As I'm sure you already know, they have cleared out.' Lydia tilted her head. 'Lucy Bunyan might be able to give some more information, though, once she's recovered.'

'She doesn't seem overly distressed,' Mr Smith said. 'Seems to think she was at a lovely party.'

'That's good, I guess. I might know someone who spent a little more time with them, though.'

Mr Smith went still. It was as much of a reaction as she ever got and Lydia mentally high-fived herself. 'It's another quid pro quo situation.'

'Of course it is.'

'I want you to find out who ordered the hits on Terrence and Richard Crow. And quickly.'

'And in return you will introduce me to your mysterious friend?'

'Well, there's a little more legwork on your part, but yes.'

'Deal,' Mr Smith's lips twitched in a smile. 'What have you got?'

'He went missing on New Year's Eve 1999.' Lydia took out her phone, navigated to the image she had taken in the Maudsley and passed it to Mr Smith. 'If you can find his identity, contact his family, and arrange some kind of financial recompense for twenty years lost time, he will tell you everything he remembers about his time with the Pearls.'

Mr Smith paused. 'How do you know he was with them? What proof do you have?'

'I can feel it,' Lydia said. She glanced at the figures in the front of the car and then raised her eyebrows at Mr Smith. He nodded. 'You know I can sense power in other people? Well I can tell which Family they belong to. With this guy, I know he isn't a Pearl, but their signature is all over him.'

He frowned. 'Like residue? Magic dust?'

'I guess,' Lydia said. 'And his entire body is covered in scars, just like the ones Joshua Williams will have when the cuts on his arms heal. Some of the partying evidently included writing on his body with a blade.'

'Interesting.' Mr Smith took out his own phone and took a picture of Lydia's screen. Then he reached forward and tapped the driver on the shoulder.

The car stopped and Lydia heard the mechanism unlock her door.

'You'll look into the hits? I'm on a tight schedule.'

'JRB,' Mr Smith said. 'I'd lay money.'

'Not the Silvers?'

Mr Smith pulled a face. 'They're not there, yet. And you're right. JRB are in the market for a new alliance. That means they want the four Families at each other's throats.'

'I'm going to need a name,' Lydia said. Charlie wouldn't just take her word and she couldn't even tell him about her connection to Mr Smith. She could imagine how well the news that she had been chatting to the secret service would go down.

'I'll see what I can do,' Mr Smith said. 'See you Thursday.'

LYDIA DIDN'T HAVE a name for Charlie, but she did have the strong suspicion that the hits taken out on Terrence and Richard would be the work of JRB, working to destabilise the Families. Or, also a possibility, the work of the Pearl King. In revenge for Lydia taking away their new toy.

Either way, it wasn't something she would expect Big Neil to have any knowledge of and that had to be enough to stop Charlie doing whatever he was doing. Lydia felt a lurch of nausea and she pushed away the thoughts and images her mind had readily supplied. Beating a man tied to a chair. Torture.

Swallowing hard, Lydia texted Charlie. 'On my way. Don't start until I get there.'

Lydia was driving to the lock-up when her phone buzzed with a return text. With a massive effort of will, she waited until she had parked on the street to check it.

Party over.

Well that wasn't good. Lydia's stomach was rolling as she made her way to the lock-up. She banged on the door but nobody answered. She swore at the metal door and the newly-installed lock and at her obstinate, terrifying uncle. It didn't help.

She texted Charlie back:

We need to talk. Where are you?

She waited for a reply and then, out of ideas, Lydia trailed back to The Fork. She parked as close as possible and, squared her shoulders, before heading inside. Maybe the text message didn't mean what she thought it meant. She had to keep an open mind, not jump to conclusions. And, most importantly, she had to keep her cards close to her chest. Whatever Charlie said, she would hide her feelings.

The cafe had the closed sign flipped when Lydia arrived and there was no sign of Angel. Lydia hoped she had taken her advice in full and was on her way out of town.

Lydia walked the empty cafe, checking the kitchen, the storage cupboard and the alley which ran behind the building. She had expected Charlie to be waiting for her, ready to issue some more orders or justify his actions. She had a cold feeling in her stomach that something was very, very wrong, but could not believe that he had meant she was cut out of family business altogether.

Her phone buzzed with an incoming text.

Home.

A ONE-WORD ANSWER. Well, that didn't bode well. Lydia locked the front door of the cafe and drove over to Charlie's house, trying to ignore her gut which was telling her not to visit Charlie on his home turf. Sitting outside the house, Lydia texted Fleet to let him know what she was doing. She finished with the words 'I will check in with you in one hour.' She didn't add 'if I don't, send help', didn't have to spell it out.

Despite Charlie's violence, the way he had spoken to her earlier, and the warning in her gut, Lydia still couldn't quite believe she was in real danger. It was Uncle Charlie. Her dad's brother. He was on edge, but Lydia couldn't help but feel that fences could be mended. There had to be a way to fix this. She knew he had crossed a line with Big Neil, but she still held out hope that he was redeemable. That it wasn't as bad as she imagined.

The path leading up to Charlie's front door was the first sign that things were not right. It was usually lined with corvids, but today it was deserted. The garden was silent, too, not even a breath of wind moving the shrubbery.

Charlie opened the door before she knocked. He must have been watching her approach from one of the front windows. 'Inside,' he said, and turned away.

Lydia followed Charlie into his living room. The fireplace still held the remains of the yule log and its ashes and the room didn't look like it had been cleaned properly since the party. There were piles of papers and books stacked on the sofa and chairs, mugs and glasses and dishes on the coffee table and sticky patches on the wooden floor where drinks had been spilled. It was cold and smelled of cigarette smoke and Crow.

Charlie leaned against the mantle and lit up, narrowing his eyes through the smoke.

Lydia couldn't remember seeing him smoke before and it didn't seem like a good sign. He was wearing a coat so she couldn't see his tattoos. She wondered whether they were moving or whether whatever she had done to him was permanent.

'It wasn't random,' Lydia said. 'But I don't think it's one of the Families. And I'm pretty certain it's nothing to do with Big Neil. When you said 'party over' what did you mean? What happened with Neil? Where is he?'

Charlie ignored her. 'I don't know why you're here, Lyds. I told you to keep out. You've wanted to be out of all this and now you are. Only thing I want from you is the keys to The Fork because you're pissing off back to Scotland.'

'There's a company, JRB. They're a client of the Silvers, but are effectively a shell company in the UK. Very dodgy. I've been investigating them for a while and it looks like they've been trying to make trouble between the Families. I think they want to destabilise the truce. Big Neil has nothing to do with them, no connection.' Lydia was going to tell Charlie more, but his face was weirdly blank and he looked as if he wasn't even listening.

'It doesn't matter.' Charlie dropped the butt onto the stone hearth and ground it out with his shoe. 'But, yeah, Big Neil is off the hook,' he said, finally.

'Good,' Lydia felt the knot in her stomach loosen. 'Do we need to smooth things over with Big Neil's crew?' Beating up Neil was bad, but it was salvageable. Lydia could walk things back. With the wider community and with Charlie.

Charlie shook his head. 'He's not going to run and tell tales.'

Lydia shivered as cold premonition rolled over her. She didn't want to say the words out loud, but she had to be sure. 'When you said the party was over... What did you mean?'

'Big Neil is no longer in attendance,' Charlie said. 'He's taken up permanent residence in a housing development in Brixton. Basement flat.'

It took Lydia a second to comprehend Charlie's words. Then she realised. Big Neil had been added to the concrete foundations of a new build, somewhere Charlie presumably had contacts.

'No windows,' Charlie was saying, 'but he's not in a position to argue.'

'I get it,' Lydia said. The nausea she had been feeling disappeared as she gripped her coin tightly in a closed fist. 'You murdered him.'

Charlie's face twisted into sudden anger. 'Don't you dare judge me. You've been in Camberwell for a year, I've been here my whole life. I've been keeping this family on top, keeping us safe, keeping us solvent. You have no idea what it takes.'

'I'm starting to,' Lydia countered. 'But I don't agree with your definition of essential action. You didn't have to end his life. He hadn't done anything to us.'

'You think he was nice guy, Lyds? Trust me, no one will be crying at his funeral.'

'That isn't the point,' Lydia spat. 'That doesn't justify-'

Charlie laughed. A short, humourless bark which would have made Lydia jump if she hadn't been gripping her coin in her palm so tightly it hurt. 'The ends always justify the means. Always. You think that's the hardest thing I've ever done? You think finishing that idiot ranks in my top five? It doesn't even register, Lyds. It's just business. I had to check out a lead because, in case you forgot, someone *murdered*,' he emphasised the word, throwing it back into Lydia's face like a weapon, 'two members of our family.'

'And if you'd knocked seven shades of hell out of the person responsible, I'd understand, but you knew Big Neil wasn't a big player, that he wouldn't have given the order even if he was linked in some way. What about a bit of restraint?'

Charlie went very still. 'A bit of restraint? You don't think I'm in control? I measure every single fucking action every single fucking time. It's not easy and you've got no idea what I deal with every day, Lyds. No clue.'

Lydia opened her mouth to argue, but Charlie was in full flow.

'When hard decisions have to be made, when certain things have to be done, I do them. That's what being a leader means. I learned that from my father and so did your dad, so don't think for a second that he's some sort of perfect angel. You do what you have to do. And I'm good at it. That's what makes me a leader, that's why I was trusted to take over when Henry retired early.'

'You were next in line,' Lydia said, fury overtaking her sense of self preservation. 'This Family is all about lineage, about blood. You were next in line and that's why. It wasn't some divine decree.'

'Like you would know anything about that time,' Charlie said. 'And I bet your dad hasn't filled you in, either. Not while he was busy protecting his precious baby girl, keeping her safe from us big bad Crows, all the nastiness he decided wasn't good enough for his princess.'

'Don't expect me to feel bad for you,' Lydia said. 'You love it. You were just telling me you're the natural leader of the Family. You can't have it both ways.'

Charlie's voice dropped low and it got dangerously calm. 'You need to watch your tone. What about a little bit of respect? I am the leader of this Family, something you seem to keep forgetting. Or is there more?'

'What do you mean?'

'You gunning for me, Lyds? Is that what this little performance is all about? You think you've got what it takes to lead the Family?' His eyes were flat and cold and Lydia wasn't sure she even recognised him anymore. 'You trying to take me down? Want to take your father's place?'

'That's not-'

'You've not got it. It's not just about Crow power, it's about balls.'

'Is that a fact?' Lydia could feel her anger returning, pushing the fear to the corners.

'Family wouldn't accept your authority. That is a fact. And neither would Alejandro.'

'What have the Silvers got to do with anything?'

'Allies are important.' Charlie seemed to catch himself. 'The right allies. Running around with your teenage dream crush doesn't count. Alejandro and I are bonded. You push me out, you'll have problems there, too.'

Lydia already had problems with the Silvers. And Maria had taken over as the head of the Silver Family, a fact that Charlie seemed to be ignoring.

'I don't think the Silvers are going to be our allies for much longer, anyway. Maria...'

Charlie waved a hand, dismissive. 'Alejandro is still in charge. Don't let that little PR stunt fool you. And he trusts me. He knows I will do whatever is necessary for the greater good. We go way back. You've got none of that. None of the history. He will never trust you the way he trusts me. We're bonded in a way you'll never match, because you won't make the hard decisions. I don't flinch and Alejandro knows that. When his father needed a problem sorting, he came to me. A Crow. And not your Grandpa, either, not Henry – me.'

'What problem?' Despite herself, Lydia was diverted. There was something tugging at the back of her mind.

'His own niece, Alejandro's little cousin, was stepping out with someone outside the Family. He left it run, hoping Amelia was just acting out, bit of young rebellion, but when they got engaged,' Charlie shrugged. 'He called me.'

Lydia felt as if a bucket of ice water had been thrown over her head. 'There was a Silver wedding at The Fork. Back in the eighties.'

'Amelia's wedding breakfast,' Charlie nodded, caught up in his own recollection. 'It had to be off Silver turf, make it easy for the cops to file it as natural causes. I had nothing against the guy, but I did the job. That's what I mean, Lyds. You have to be willing to do the unthinkable. The ends justify the means, even when the means are pretty bloody harsh.'

'You killed them? On their wedding day? The Silvers are that hung up on their bloodline that they ordered a hit?'

'Old Man Silver waited until they had actually got married, when it was definitely too late for Amelia to come to her senses and call it off. He gave the kid a chance.'

'How kind of him,' Lydia said, trying to keep a lid on her fury. She couldn't think about Jason, not now, it would make that rage boil over.

'But why kill Amelia, too? Please don't tell me it was some sort of honour killing.'

'No,' Charlie said, a flash of regret crossing his face for the first time. 'It was an accident. That was a shame. When her new husband had his heart attack, Amelia went mental. She went for her father in front of every-one. It wasn't discreet. Alejandro pulled her off him and into the kitchen, away from the crowd, to calm her down. I tried, too, but she wasn't having it. She went for me, then, and I pushed her back. Bit too hard, as it happens,' his face clouded. 'That was an accident. I do feel bad about that one. She went back, slipped on the floor and cracked her head going down.'

'How did you do it? Kill...' she almost said, 'Jason' but caught herself, and finished with 'him?'. She felt physically sick.

Charlie rolled his shoulders, like she was asking him out of admiration. 'Now that was a neat bit of work. I stopped his heart.'

'Just like that?'

Charlie tilted his head. 'I have my moments.'

Lydia was trying very hard not to picture Jason and Amy on their wedding day. Jason young and vital and alive on what should have been one of the happiest of his life. The start of his marriage to his beloved. All of that happiness, all of that potential, snuffed out in an instant because Charlie wanted to make powerful friends. Charlie had made a calculation and carried out a professional hit on an innocent man. He had murdered Jason in cold blood. Lydia had been trying to convince herself that Charlie was under stress and acting poorly because of the hits in Wandsworth, but this changed everything. Charlie had been dangerous for a very long time. At once, Lydia's nausea had disappeared. It was replaced with a cold, clear mind and one thought. Charlie had to be stopped.

CHAPTER TWENTY-EIGHT

It was one thing to realise that your uncle was a murderer and that he had to be stopped and quite another to take action. He was Family. More than that, he was 'family' with a small 'f'. He had swung her up high in his arms when she was five, taught her card games at seven, and slipped her £20 notes when her parents weren't looking when she was a teen. Lydia had been brought up away from the Crow Family and their business, but Uncle Charlie had visited his big brother every couple of months and those visits had always been memorable.

Back at the flat, Lydia brought Jason up to speed on what had happened with Big Neil. She didn't know how to tell him about Amelia. Amy. How did you tell a person that a member of your own family had murdered them and then accidentally killed your new wife? There wasn't a handbook for that conversation.

Jason was remarkably calm about the news that Charlie had tortured and killed Neil, though.

'You don't seem surprised,' Lydia said. 'Why aren't you more shocked?'

Jason shrugged. 'Sorry. It kind of fits with my idea of Crows.' Seeing Lydia's face, he apologised again. 'Just the rumours I heard. The stories. I thought they were just stories, but then I met your uncle and they didn't seem so far-fetched.'

'Hell Hawk,' Lydia sank on to the sofa and put her hands over her face. She wanted to block out the truth. She couldn't continue as a member of the Crow Family with Charlie in place. Which left her with two options. Leaving or taking over. She was tingling with nervous energy and could feel her Crow power, too, beating wings and the taste of feathers. She pulled her shoulder blades back. Could she forge a real alliance with the Fox Family? Or perhaps they could go quiet? If Charlie agreed to retire to the countryside, somewhere far from London, maybe she could wind down his businesses and just run Crow Investigations, quiet and legit. No big centre of power, nothing to threaten anybody else.

Even as her mind ran down these possibilities, she knew it was futile. Nobody would believe that the Crows were stepping away. They would be seen as weak and somebody, a Family or JRB or an unknown threat, would attack. People believed in Crow power and that meant that people feared it. Fear made people strike out, to seek to destroy.

She removed her hands and found Jason hovering uncertainly in front of her. 'I was just trying to come up with an exit strategy.' She couldn't even bring herself to tell Jason the thoughts of a moment ago. Maria Silver wanted Lydia dead and buried. Putting Paul Fox to one side, the rest of the Fox Family weren't her biggest fans, and she had just pissed off the Pearls by taking away their latest toy.

Her head was spinning and she had several calls from Fleet on her mobile. She texted to tell him that she was fine. 'I'm going to sort this,' she told Jason, hoping that sounding confident out loud would magically translate into certainty within.

'I know,' Jason said. 'But if you can't, I'll run with you.'

Lydia paused. The Fork was Jason's home. More than that, it was the place he was tied because it was where he died. She felt tears pricking her eyes and she hugged Jason in a quick, chilly embrace.

Lydia placed her phone in the middle of her desk and looked at it for a long moment. There was a full bottle of whisky on her bookshelves and she looked at that for a moment, too. A calmness filled her centre and, instead of pouring a drink, she walked out onto the roof terrace and lifted her face to the sky. The city lights and a full moon meant that the winter sky was navy blue, not black, and the clouds silvery grey where they met the lunar glow. Lydia reached inside and felt the edges of her power. She produced her coin and made it spin out beyond the railing, holding it suspended high above the street below. Then she made more and more coins appear, dotting them around the terrace, above the street, and up, up into the air until they were sprinkled up as high as she could see, catching the light and shining like stars.

. . .

Lydia went downstairs and headed out the back exit and along the alley which ran behind the building, joining the main street away from The Fork. She called Paul's burner.

'I haven't got anything,' he said. 'Nobody is talking about Malcolm Ferris or the move against the Crows. I'm sorry, Little Bird.'

'Not on the phone,' she said. 'I'm heading in your direction.'

'Potters Fields?'

Being back in the park and spotting Paul waiting for her at the entrance, brought home to Lydia how much her loyalties had shifted. She was done with following her Family blindly, just because they shared her blood. And she was done being pulled along in their wake.

'What's happened?'

Lydia checked that nobody was within earshot and filled him in. The loose plan she had been formulating coalesced as she spoke. She wasn't going to run, which meant Charlie was going to have to take a holiday.

'He's not going to go lightly,' Paul said. 'You might have to consider a permanent solution.'

This was not news to Lydia, who had barely been able to think about anything else since the death of Big Neil. She felt her stomach turn over again. 'I can't hurt him.' She had been going to say 'I can't kill him' but she couldn't even form the words. She couldn't murder anybody. She wasn't a killer. 'And we don't have banishment in our Family.'

'Don't you?' Paul said.

'What do you mean?'

'There is a place which has always contained Crows. Not many of you, admittedly, but it's not unheard of.'

The penny dropped. 'I can't have him locked up.' She heard the slam of the door in the police cell, the wave of sheer panic which had rolled over her. Crows didn't belong in cages.

Paul shrugged. 'He's been running an OCG his whole life. Gotta have considered it an occupational hazard. And it's not like he would be powerless inside. No one would touch Charlie Crow.' Paul's eyes widened as he appeared to remember recent events. 'Sorry. That was stupid. I just mean-'

'I know,' Lydia said. 'And you're not wrong.' Especially if she sorted out whoever had attacked Terrance and Richard. And there might be an alternative to a place like Wandsworth. Somewhere more secure from ordered hits. 'I just need to know that the head of the Fox Family would formally recognise Lydia Crow as the head of the Crow Family.'

Paul's lips twitched into a smile. 'The kids are taking over,' he said. 'I approve.'

BACK AT THE FLAT, Lydia knew she couldn't put it off any longer. No matter what else was going on, she owed it to Jason to be honest with him. Lydia found Jason in his bedroom, typing on his laptop. He was absorbed, content. Should she break that peace? Barge into his world with information that would bring pain? Worse still, pain without the hope of resolution.

'Do you believe in what I do?' Lydia sat on the bed cross-legged.

Jason looked up. He must have seen something in her expression as he shut the lid of the laptop and pushed it to one side. 'Investigating?'

'Yeah, my business. Do you think it's a good thing?'

'Where is this coming from?'

'Spending all this time with Charlie,' Lydia said. 'I don't like a lot of what he does, what the Crow Family business looks like, and it's made me wonder about my own business. Am I any better? I cause people pain all the time.'

Jason shook his head. 'You don't cause the pain. You give information. You solve things. You give closure to people or details about their relationships which help them to make decisions about their lives.'

Lydia twisted her fingers together. 'You make it sound like a public service. I snoop for money.'

He smiled. 'Yeah, but you've got a free-loading housemate who gets through a lot of cereal, you've got to make bank.'

'Make bank?' Lydia raised an eyebrow. 'You're really picking up the lingo. Is that your online friends?'

'Don't do air quotes,' Jason said. 'They are my friends.'

'I'm teasing,' Lydia said. 'I'm happy for you.'

There was a short pause, while Lydia wrestled with her conscience. Then she said, 'do you think the truth is always better than not knowing? For our clients, I mean.'

'Yes.' Jason spoke without hesitation.

'I've got something to ask you, but it's about your life. You've seemed much happier and I don't want to rake up things up if it's going to upset you.'

Jason went very still. Usually, when he was upset he vibrated slightly and, if he got very emotional, he became less and less 'alive-looking' and more and more 'definitely ghost'. Right now, however, he was sitting very still and looking very solid and holding her gaze. 'I am much happier but I still want answers. Even if they aren't very nice.'

'Right-'

'I mean,' he smiled suddenly. 'I'm dead. My wife is dead. I already know it wasn't a happy ending.'

Lydia reached out and took his cold hand. 'You told me before that you didn't know Amy's parents very well. That you hadn't spent much time together.'

He nodded. 'They were always nice to me, though.'

'Were they?'

'I told you before, they seemed fine. Amy said they left her alone, had done ever since she was a teenager and they realised that if they tried to control her it would just make her more rebellious.'

'Smart move,' Lydia said.

'Exactly. And they were. Really smart. Really clever, I mean. So was Amy. She was incredible, could have done anything she wanted.'

'They were at your wedding?'

He frowned. 'Of course.'

'And at the party, here?'

'What are you getting at?'

'You still don't remember anything about that day?'

'No,' Jason was vibrating, now, and Lydia squeezed his hand tighter, hoping to anchor him. If he got very upset, he might just disappear. It had barely happened over the past few weeks, since discovering programming and hacking and an online social life, but it had used to happen with alarming regularity. He would disappear and when he returned, hours later, he had no memory of where he had been. It was something out of his control and Lydia knew it frightened him.

'I think Amy's parents made a deal with Charlie.'

'What sort of deal?'

'Alejandro is like Tristan Fox in one regard, he doesn't believe in diluting the Family's bloodline. And his father was just the same.' Lydia took a deep breath. 'Amy was Alejandro's cousin. Her uncle was the head of the Silver Family.'

'No, they were fine with us,' Jason said. 'I told you.'

'I know,' Lydia said. 'I'm sorry. This is hard to hear, but I don't think they were as accepting as they pretended.'

Jason held up his hand. 'You've found something out?'

'Yes,' Lydia said. She was about to say 'from Charlie'.

'Don't tell me.'

'Are you sure?'

'What if it gives me closure or something and I disappear? I'm happy. I have a life.' He tried a smile which didn't quite work. 'I mean, I have a kind of life. I don't want to lose it.'

'Okay,' Lydia said. 'Let me know if you change your mind.'

'Have you worked out what you're going to do about Charlie?'

For a split second Lydia thought she might have accidentally told Jason about his murder, anyway, but then she realised that Jason was just trying to change the subject from his untimely death. 'I think so. It involves asking for a favour, though.'

'Well that should go well,' Jason said, deadpan. 'You're really good at asking for help.'

'Hilarious,' Lydia said, pushing him lightly on the shoulder.

LYDIA IGNORED a call from Charlie as she walked over to Miles Bunyan's house. The pressing issue of her homicidal uncle aside, she knew she had to speak to Miles. Besides, it was a bright, crisp day and she wanted to enjoy London in the winter sunshine. Walking usually helped to calm her mind, but today her thoughts kept going churning, searching endlessly for a new way out of the problem. She couldn't work with Charlie and she couldn't let him carry on as the head of her Family, not after the things he had done, but she didn't know if she was willing to step up and take his place. Charlie was wrong about a lot of things, but he was right there.

The Bunyans' Victorian terrace looked the same as on Lydia's previous visit, but the atmosphere inside was entirely different. It was light and happy and Lydia wondered if that was something anybody would be able to sense, or whether it was her Crow power. Since the confrontation with the Pearl King, Lydia had been wondering just how different her abilities made her, and how far they might go. It was a novelty after years of ignoring, denying or being embarrassed by them.

She followed Miles down the hallway and into the kitchen, as he explained that Lucy was napping but that she was welcome to stop for tea. 'If she wakes up, you can see her, but I'd rather not disturb her.'

'That's fine,' Lydia said. 'It was you I wanted to speak to, really.'

'Is that so?' Miles was bustling around the kitchen, getting mugs and opening a packet of biscuits. He shot her an astute look. 'No Charlie today?'

'No Charlie,' Lydia said. 'I'm following up on something.'

'I thought he would be here, wanting to collect his dues.'

Lydia frowned. 'You were paying him to investigate?'

'No, no. Nothing like that.' Miles shook his head. 'He likes to receive thanks in person, that's all. Not that I'm not grateful,' he added hurriedly. 'Tell him I'm very grateful. Eternally grateful. I assume he pulled some strings with the police...'

Lydia forced a smile. 'I'm really not here on Charlie's behalf. There's something I wanted to ask you.'

'Sugar? Milk?'

'Just milk,' Lydia said. 'It's about a company called JRB.'

Miles had been taking a teabag out of a mug and his hand jerked, splashing tea across the counter.

'You've heard of them?'

Miles looked at her, then. 'Is this about Lucy?'

'Why would JRB have anything to do with your daughter?'

'No.' Miles shook his head. 'This is ridiculous. It's just a story.'

'What is just a story?'

Miles turned back to the tea. He put his hand on the milk carton but didn't lift it to pour. He was thinking and his jaw was tight. Lydia guessed that he was about to ask her to leave. She spoke quickly. 'I just want to make sure that you and Lucy stay safe. I know who took her and I think I know why they gave her back, but I want to be sure it doesn't happen again. The house where she was found, the people there have a link to JRB, a company that used to bear your family name. This is just between us. It's not for the police or the press, it won't go any further than this room.'

'Nobody would believe you, anyway,' Miles said. 'It's completely mad.'

'J.R.B and Sons was started by John Bunyan. Relative of yours?'

'It's nothing to do with me,' Miles said. 'I was never on the board. My father was a director, but the company was dissolved twenty years ago. It doesn't exist.'

'What happened?'

'My father passed away ten years ago. He would be

the one to ask. I don't know anything about it.' Miles was getting increasingly agitated.

'What was 'mad'?'

'Sorry?'

'About the company.'

'There was a disagreement, I think,' Miles said. 'With their business partners. Or fellow directors, I'm not sure which. A big blow up, though. The company had always been very successful and I know that it would have been better for dad to stay and for it to keep going, so it must have been over something pretty serious. He came out with money, of course, but he always said it was a shame it had ended. He had wanted me to join at one time, but I had other ambitions and, well, you don't always want to just follow in your parents' footsteps, do you?'

Lydia kept quiet.

'So they wound it up and that was that.' Miles dropped the teaspoon into the sink.

'What aren't you telling me?'

'I told you, it's nonsense. Dad got quite confused at the end. He didn't know what he was saying.'

Lydia crossed her arms and leaned against the counter, indicating that she was willing to wait.

'He said there were some weird terms. Some of the people involved had taken the split very personally, very badly. Dad said they made a joke document but it wasn't very funny. It was full of these pretend terms which were supposed to apply as a result of dissolving the company.'

'Can I see it?'

Miles frowned. 'No. I've got absolutely no idea where it is. Probably lost. Or it might be in the attic. Or it might have been shredded when we cleared dad's house.'

'You read it, though?'

Miles shook his head. 'Dad said it was a spoof. Made out to look like a legal document but full of daft fairy tale things.'

'Such as?'

'Oh, I don't know, I can't remember.'

'Try,' Lydia said, squeezing her coin in her palm.

Miles closed his eyes. 'Floral bounty. Freedom below. Your first-born girl.' His eyes flew open. 'My father didn't have a girl.'

'No, but you did,' Lydia said. 'If I were you, I would find that document and burn it.'

CHAPTER TWENTY-NINE

The next day was Thursday and Lydia made her way to her meeting with Mr Smith. She stopped on the way and bought takeaway coffees and two large slices of chocolate fudge cake. She didn't bother to arrive early to sweep the flat for bugs, having accepted that it was futile. Mr Smith belonged to a world with far greater resources and tech than she did.

He was already in the kitchen, the bakery box of Pasteis de Nata on the table.

Lydia put down her cardboard tray. 'I brought a farewell gift. Cake.'

'But we're just getting started,' Mr Smith said. 'This will cheer you up. I found your friend's family and the reunion went very well. I filmed it on my phone, if you want your heart-warmed.'

'He's leaving the hospital?'

Mr Smith nodded. 'Discharged and on his way to his parents' home. I can give you the address. FYI, his name isn't Ash. It's Simon.'

Lydia lifted the lid on her coffee and blew on the liquid inside. 'I'll take his details. And I'll follow up to make sure he stays safe and well.'

'I don't know what you're implying,' Mr Smith said. 'But he has volunteered to speak to us about his experiences. And he will be well compensated for his time.'

Lydia used the shark smile she had been practising. 'You're giving me your word?'

A small crease appeared between his eyebrows. 'Has something happened? You seem a little...'

Lydia took a sip of her coffee and pushed the tray toward Mr Smith. 'Have some cake. It's not poisoned.'

'You said 'farewell gift'. You know that's not how this works, right?'

LYDIA PUT HER COFFEE DOWN. 'What would you say if I said I could deliver my uncle into police hands with enough evidence to put him away?'

'I would be surprised,' Mr Smith said. 'Can you?'

'There's a bigger problem. Two Crows were killed in Wandsworth. I don't think prison is safe.'

'Agreed. Your uncle must have many enemies.'

'Your department,' Lydia said. 'Do you detain people?'

'Sometimes,' Mr Smith said. 'Are you suggesting that my department would handle the incarceration of Charlie Crow. Keep him safe while he's locked up?'

'I don't know,' Lydia said. 'Is there a deal to be made? One which protects Charlie and gives him more freedom than prison, but still...'

'Removes his civil liberties?'

'That's not exactly what I... Something like that.'

'No halfway house on that, I'm afraid,' Mr Smith said. 'We could give him comfortable accommodation, treat him with dignity and respect, only include experiments with his full consent, allow him visitation rights and communication tools, but a locked door is a locked door.'

Lydia closed her eyes. The mutilated body of Big Neil filled her mind, snapping into horrific focus. 'If I delivered Charlie to you, would you heal my father?'

Mr Smith inclined his head. 'I assume he wouldn't be coming willingly? He may not cooperate with our research?'

'Not willingly or knowingly. He won't walk into prison quietly. As for research, I don't know. He's curious about the Crow powers, too, so he might cooperate if you offer to share results. I honestly don't know.' She clasped her hands together. 'You would do things without his consent, wouldn't you?'

'Absolutely not,' Mr Smith said. 'We have a code of conduct, same as any branch of the civil service.'

'But we're talking dark ops and without seeing a copy of that code, that doesn't mean very much.'

Mr Smith nodded. 'True.' He didn't elaborate.

Lydia had turned over this in her mind ever since it had occurred to her, sometime after she had finished throwing up. Big Neil had not been a good person, but he hadn't deserved to die in fear and pain. And Lydia could not belong to a Family which acted in that way. She had to do something. She had to change the rules and that was never going to happen with Charlie in charge. Even if she took over from him, he would continue to pull the strings, to order people around. He had been doing it for longer. He knew how the game was played and Lydia barely knew what the game was. 'I'll bring you the evidence you need. You'll have to act fast, though. He can't see you coming. And in return, you will heal my father. If you can't do that, the deal is off.'

'I can do it,' Mr Smith said.

'You said before that you would only be able to try, that you couldn't guarantee it would work. What's changed?'

'You have sufficiently motivated me. Good job.'

'How do I know I can trust you? If you lied about that...'

'I didn't lie. When I heal somebody, it takes something from me. It's not something I do lightly. I said I would try, but I was keeping the proviso that it might not work or work completely so that I could stop the process if I felt it was taking too much from me.'

Lydia nodded. That actually made sense and Lydia found that she believed him. It was possible that Mr Smith's powers or the prize he offered was interfering with her judgement, but Lydia didn't think she had a choice. She had to believe him. Believing him meant that she might be able to save Henry Crow. 'We have a deal, then.'

'Are you really going to do this? Swap your uncle's freedom for your father's life?'

Lydia swallowed. 'I think so.'

'Better get more sure than that,' Mr Smith said, his voice gentle.

SAYING the word and meaning it were two different things. Standing outside in the cold air, tasting car exhaust, Lydia knew that she had to be absolutely certain. There would be no going back from an action of this magnitude against Charlie Crow. And she had to make sure everything was tied up before she pulled the trigger. There was a chance things would go poorly, even allowing for the mighty power of the secret service. She used the contact details from Mr Smith and called Simon's home phone number. A woman answered and Lydia asked for Simon.

'Are you a journalist?'

'No, a friend.' Lydia felt a stab of guilt. She had no right to that label. 'Lydia Crow.'

'Simon? There's someone on the...' The woman's voice became muffled as she put a hand over the receiver. A moment later, Simon's voice said 'hello'.

'I just wanted to check in on you. See how you're doing.'

'I'm okay,' he said. There was a pause as if he was waiting for something and Lydia could imagine his anxious mother retreating to another room, Simon watching her go. 'I mean, it's weird,' he said, finally. 'They're old. I still feel, I dunno, pretty much the same. I don't know why I expected everything to be the same. It's not like I hadn't seen my own face in the mirror. I knew time had passed, but I still... It's stupid.'

'I'm sorry,' Lydia said, feeling helpless.

'Don't be. I'm glad you called, I wanted to say thank you.'

Lydia physically flinched. 'Don't-'

'That guy, the one who found my parents. He's giving me money and he said that you...'

'It's nothing. Don't thank me.' Lydia took a deep breath and crossed her free arm around her middle, hugging herself. 'I'm sorry. I should have helped you sooner. I was caught up in my own stuff and I thought you were...' She broke off before she could say 'delusional'.

'I saw something on the news,' Simon said. 'A girl went missing in Highgate but she's been found.'

'Yeah,' Lydia said. 'That's right.'

'I was in Highgate.'

'What?'

'I'm remembering a little more. Just pieces. But it was Highgate Woods we went to on New Year's Eve. I drank a lot of Mad Dog and some vodka, I was pretty out of it, but I remembered something else.'

'What?'

'There was this little kid. A girl. She was holding my hand, I think. I got lost from my mates and it was really cold and I was drunk, but like, not so drunk that I didn't know I was seriously freezing and that I might end up with hypothermia or something. And then there was this little kid and she said she knew a really good party. It was weird, because she wasn't old enough to be out at that time. Or partying.'

Lydia thought of the Pearl girl outside the house.

'She said something really old fashioned about me going of my own free will. And I think we went underground.'

'Underground? Where was that?'

'The woods. I don't remember going anywhere else. Everything after was underground. Different rooms, different places, but no windows.'

'Do you remember any of the people at the party? Anything else about what happened?'

'I'm not allowed,' Simon said, his voice cracking a little. 'I mustn't. I know that. But I was thinking about that girl. Not the little girl, the one in the news. If she went missing same place as me, maybe the same people took her. And that means maybe they've done it before or will do it again.'

'Maybe,' Lydia said, squeezing her coin in her palm. 'I wouldn't think about it. Just concentrate on getting better. I mean, you've got your life back.'

'What's left of it,' Simon sounded angry, now, and Lydia couldn't blame him. 'I've lost twenty years.'

'It's not fair,' Lydia said. 'I'm sorry.'

'It's not your fault. It's them. The people who kept me. They can bend time or wipe memories, because I can't remember much, but I know I feel like I was only with them for, like, months. A year tops. They can't get away with it. They've stolen years of my life.'

'You can't look for them. Best thing you can do is to forget about it.' Lydia felt the uselessness of that statement and wasn't surprised when Simon laughed.

'I'm going to find out who they are and stop them from ever doing this again.'

'That's a very bad idea.' Lydia pushed a little bit of Crow whammy into her words. The poor guy had been manipulated enough by magic, but this was definitely for his own good. The Pearl King and their court were extremely dangerous and, thanks to Lydia, extremely pissed off. Simon needed to stay well away. To her surprise, her power seemed to bounce right off him.

'I'm serious,' Simon was saying. 'I need something to live for and getting back at the bastards who stole my life is as good as anything. Do you know I can't sleep? And I can't get used to my name. I mean, I kind of remember that I was called Simon, but it doesn't feel right.' He lowered his voice. 'Every time they use it, mum and dad, it makes me flinch. I miss the name 'Ash'. That's insane, right? I hate the people who gave me the name and I miss it at the same time. If I don't do something I'm going to lose my mind.'

'Let me help you,' Lydia said. 'Let me look into things.'

A pause. 'You'd do that?'

'I told you, I should have helped you before. This is my atonement.'

'I can pay.'

'No pay,' Lydia said. 'Just promise me you'll sit tight until I can do some digging.'

There was a short pause and then Simon agreed. 'How long will it take?'

'I've got an urgent matter to attend to today, but I'll get started as soon as possible. And I'll keep in touch. Don't do anything until you've spoken to me first.' Lydia stared across the street for a moment after hanging up, not really seeing anything. She had let Simon down and had to make it right but, more than that, the man had a point. How many others had the Pearls abducted over the years? How many little playthings had the king taken? And had Simon just been unlucky, a case of wrong place at the wrong time, or had he been chosen?

LYDIA KNEW that she was teetering on the edge of a cliff, and before she jumped off, there was one final thing she had to do. She rang the buzzer on Fleet's building and waited for the door to unlock. When Fleet opened the door to his flat, he was in shirt sleeves, his tie loose. 'You can use your key,' he said.

'I didn't want to presume,' Lydia said. 'We're still...' She had been going to say 'broken up' but the words got stuck.

Fleet nodded and turned away. 'Can I get you something to drink?'

'I'm fine, thanks.'

He turned back. 'Is everything all right? Did something happen with Charlie?'

Lydia didn't know how to explain and she felt her eyes aching with unshed tears. She shook her head. 'He's not going to be in charge anymore.'

'You quit?' Fleet said, one eyebrow raised. 'How did that go down?'

'That's not really...' Lydia stepped into Fleet, trusting that he would hold her, and let her head rest on his chest for a few precious seconds. She had been so angry and hurt, had felt that Fleet had let her down. He had chosen his job, his position as a copper over Lydia and, when she as in custody in Camberwell nick, she felt he had sided with his profession. Deserted her in her hour of need. Now, she had seen the true meaning of betrayal. Betrayal not just of Lydia, but of everything she had thought a person was capable of. It really put things into perspective.

'What's happened?' Fleet was rubbing small circles on Lydia's lower back. 'What's wrong?'

She looked into Fleet's steady brown eyes and read the love and concern which lived inside. 'I'm going to take over as the new head of the Crow Family.'

His frown deepened. 'What does Charlie think about that? Is he going to go after you?'

'He won't be in the picture,' Lydia said. 'I'm calling in a favour from MI5. Turns out,' she smiled a little, 'the official channels have their uses.'

Fleet was searching her face, his frown still very much in evidence. 'There will be repercussions. Charlie isn't going to take this quietly.'

Lydia shook her head lightly. 'You're not listening. I'll be the head of the Crow Family. I'll be the new Charlie. Nobody is going to move against me.'

Fleet opened his mouth to argue but Lydia ploughed on. 'That's not why I'm here, though. I'm not asking your advice or your permission. This is my work, my Family, and I don't think I've got a choice.'

'Okay, but-'

'I wanted to ask you something. It's the final thing I need to work out before I go ahead.'

'What's that?'

Lydia took a deep breath. 'Would a London copper consider a steady romantic relationship with the head of the infamous Crow Family?'

Fleet's frown smoothed away and a smile like sunshine appeared. 'This one would.'

Lydia sat at her favourite table in The Fork. It was one at the back, giving her a good view of the whole cafe, and the wall behind meant that nobody could approach without her knowing about it.

She hadn't turned on the overheads, so the room was lit with the glow of the streetlights and the headlights of passing cars. Lydia flipped her coin over the back of her knuckles and waited. The cafe had been called The Fork after a fork in the road. A place where two diverging paths met. Charlie had given so many people stark choices in this room, often two terrible options. He wouldn't have hesitated. And, if Lydia knew her uncle, he wouldn't have lost sleep about them afterward. She wasn't her uncle, but she was a Crow. And Crows don't flinch.

Lydia felt the brush of a wing on the back of her hand just before a noise from the kitchen alerted her that she was no longer alone. The door behind the counter opened slowly and there was a pause before Charlie walked in. Lydia imagined he had been peering out through the gap, assessing the situation, probably wondering if she was stupid enough to meet him alone.

'It's just us,' Lydia said. 'For now.'

Charlie moved through the dark cafe like a shark

cutting through water. Everything about him that Lydia had once found terrifying - his certainty, obvious power and those dead eyes – were still very much in evidence. Lydia felt the urge to run away or to bend to his will, and shoved it down.

Charlie sat opposite her and leaned back in his chair, assessing. 'Not very bright, Lyds. You can't summon me.'

'Clearly, I can,' Lydia said.

Charlie's expression didn't betray anything but Lydia felt the tension in the air increase. 'This isn't a pissing competition,' she said. 'I'm not trying to score points or disrespect you. I'm just telling you that you need to step down from your position and head out of town. I don't care where you go as long as it's far away from London and you keep very, very quiet.'

Charlie smiled then. He gave a little head shake, like she was a pet that had learned an amusing trick. 'You're giving me an ultimatum? This is...' He waved a hand while pretending to think. 'What? A threat?'

'Not a threat,' Lydia said. 'A chance. I wasn't going to give you one. You've crossed too many lines and I'm having you removed. I made a deal with the secret service. Agents are at your house right now. If you hadn't come to this meeting, you would already be in their custody. They've got a room in a secure facility with your name on the door.'

'What are you talking about?' Charlie was going for bluster, but there was something moving behind his eyes. Something which suggested that the penny had dropped.

'That was the plan, honestly. I've given them the

lock up and Neil's whereabouts and they exhumed his corpse a couple of hours ago, gathered the DNA evidence required from your torture party. Not that the secret service need much in the way of evidence.'

Charlie was on his feet, looking around as if he expected soldiers to rappel down from the ceiling.

'But I decided to give you one final chance. Turns out I'm not as cold as you. It's not as easy as I thought it would be to sell out a family member, even when they're a killer. So you've got a tiny window of time. Get out now, go far away. It's your only chance.'

Charlie narrowed his eyes. 'You're lying.'

'Look at me,' Lydia said.

Charlie's eyes bored into hers. After a moment he swore.

Lydia glanced at her phone, which was face up on the table. 'You don't have long to decide. When they don't find you at your place, this is the next place they'll look.'

Charlie lunged for her without warning. His hands thudded down onto her shoulders, his thumbs digging into her windpipe, squeezing. Lydia jerked back instinctively, smacking the back of her head against the wall. She tried to stand up, but Charlie was pressing down with his whole weight and Lydia knew that she would never win in a strength contest.

'I don't know what you're playing at, Lyds, but it's not clever to threaten me.' Charlie's voice was completely calm. 'I'm not going anywhere.'

Little bursts of light were appearing across Lydia's darkening vision. The instinctive panic, pain and lack of oxygen, working together terrifyingly fast to cloud Lydia's thoughts. Luckily, she didn't have to think about producing her coin. It was just there. A comforting shape in the palm of her hand, anchoring her to consciousness. Her head pulsed with pain, in time with her hammering heart, but she ignored that and reached out instead to feel for the nearest Crow heart that didn't belong to her. It was thudding pretty fast, too. Adrenaline. Excitement. Exertion. Whatever the cause, it made it even easier to find in the dark than Lydia expected. She reached out and held it. The edges of her coin dug into the flesh of her palm as she closed her power around Charlie's heart and squeezed.

The pressure on her neck released instantly as Charlie clutched his chest. He crumpled to the floor, his face drained of colour and lips rapidly turning blue. Lydia let go of his heart, feeling it fluttering back to life as she tipped her head back and dragged ragged breaths through her bruised airway.

Her head cleared as the oxygen flooded back, and the pain of her throat began to make itself known. She touched the back of her head gingerly and found a lump. She should probably get checked out in hospital, but Lydia felt a fistful of painkillers and a lie down in a dark room would do the trick. Charlie was unconscious on the floor. Lydia eased herself into a crouching position until she could press her fingers to his neck and feel for pulse. The movement made her head swim and her headache intensify. After checking that he was breathing, she pulled Charlie over into the recovery position.

The stairs to the flat felt like a mountain, and Lydia

had almost made it to the top when she heard a thump from the floor below. It was a quiet thump. Discreet. But was followed by the sound of a door crashing open, thudding feet, and shouted orders. She had left the front door unlocked, deliberately, and hoped Smith's retrieval team would collect Charlie without smashing the cafe up too much. Considering she had knocked him out cold, she had provided them with the easiest possible job. The least they could do would be not to make a mess.

Lydia made it inside her flat and she locked the door. Halfway along the hall, her limbs were barely moving, but she forced herself onward. Just a few more steps. The pounding in her head had amplified to a continuous all-encompassing globe of pain. She hoped it was a mild concussion and not a sign that she had pushed her power too far too quickly.

In her bedroom, Jason's form appeared in her narrowing vision. His icy touch was like a balm and she felt him support her weight, helping her to the bed. Her phone buzzed as she lowered herself to the pillow, its cool softness almost making her weep. She held the phone in front of her face and forced her eyes open just enough to see the text message. Unknown number, of course. 'It's done.' And then she let go of the phone, closed her eyes and let the waters of sleep close over her aching head.

WHEN LYDIA WOKE up the next day, she felt remarkably well. Her throat and head both still hurt, but they were perfectly manageable and some more painkillers and a pint of water helped. After showering and getting dressed, Lydia accepted a mug of tea from Jason. As she sipped it and contemplated breakfast, she realised what had changed. She was free. Not of dealing with her family, of course, but of dealing with Charlie. She probably ought to feel more conflicted about his fate with Mr Smith, but it was difficult. Charlie had made the choice and there was no doubt in Lydia's mind that he had intended to kill her last night. That really helped with the guilt.

Her phone rang with her parents' number and she snatched it up.

'Lydia?' There's a man here. He says you sent him.'

'What's he look like?'

'Young, very short hair,' her mother said. Then she lowered her voice. 'Handsome.'

'Mr Smith?'

'Yes! You know him? I assumed it was a made-up name. It sounds like a joke.'

Lydia decided not to explain. 'No, he's fine. He's visiting dad.'

'That's what he said. I told him I would check.'

'You did the right thing. Sorry. I didn't know he would be with you so quickly. I would have warned you. I'm on my way.'

'You don't have to if you're busy...'

'I'll be as fast as I can.'

LYDIA PULLED up outside her childhood home just in time to see the front door opening and Mr Smith leaving.

She got out of the car and met him as he approached his own car. The Mercedes with the tinted windows. Lydia waved at the suited man in the driving seat who ignored her.

'Did you do it?'

'And good morning to you, too, Lydia Crow.' Mr Smith's skin was ashy and he had dark circles under his eyes. He looked at least ten years older.

'My dad?' Lydia hated the raw hope in her voice.

'I did my best,' he said. 'You're hurt.' He was looking at her neck.

Lydia stepped back. 'I'm fine.' The last thing she wanted was another favour from Smith. 'So, you and I are done.'

Mr Smith nodded. He was clearly exhausted, swaying slightly on his feet. 'Until next time.'

'There won't be a next time,' Lydia said. 'It's over.'

'As you wish.'

She expected a little more resistance, but perhaps her spook was as knackered as he seemed. Lydia watched as Mr Smith got into the car and it peeled away.

She took two steps toward the house and then doubled back to her own car, rummaging on the back seat for a scarf. Once she had arranged the material around her neck, hiding the bruises, she went inside.

The front door hadn't been closed properly and Lydia walked into the empty hall.

Her mother appeared at the top of the stairs. 'Come on up, he's asleep.'

Lydia couldn't remember the last time she had been inside her parents' bedroom. It looked and smelled the same. Floral curtains, dark furniture, the mix of her mum's perfume and her dad's aftershave. In the double bed, lying perfectly still, was Henry Crow. He had a bit of grey stubble which was rough on Lydia's lips as she kissed his cheek.

'Who was that man?' Her mum was whispering and her eyes were bright with unshed tears. 'He just sat here. On the bed. And held your dad's hand. Was it something religious?'

Lydia shook her head. 'Nothing like that. Just someone I thought might be able to help. Did dad wake up at all?'

'No. He's been sleeping a lot recently.' She tried a wan smile. 'I think it means he's more relaxed, more comfortable.'

Lydia noticed the things in the room which were different. The line of medication on her mum's dressing table. A plastic cup of thick pink liquid with a straw. Something that looked suspiciously like a commode in one corner. It was the bedroom of a very ill person.

'I'm sorry I haven't been helping,' Lydia said.

Her mum sat next to her on the bed and put an arm around her. 'It's all right, love. We've been fine.'

Lydia rested her head on her mum's shoulder for a moment and blinked to make sure she didn't start crying. That wasn't going to help. She felt the disappointment settle in her stomach like a dead weight. Mr Smith hadn't promised he would be able to cure her father, but Lydia had still hoped.

Her mum stood up. 'Tea?'

'Thanks,' Lydia turned back to her dad. His

breathing was so shallow she could barely see his chest move. 'I'll sit here a while longer, if that's okay.'

Henry's hands were outside of the covers, lying neatly on top of the duvet. Lydia adjusted her position so that she was a little more comfortable and then picked up his nearest hand and held it. Maybe there would be an improvement. Mr Smith had looked like hell, so perhaps he had managed some kind of cure. Lydia felt the hope and the fear and the urge to cry got stronger. Give me a sign, Dad, she said silently. Please wake up.

Henry Crow opened his eyes. He blinked and then turned his head on the pillow until he was looking at Lydia. She formed a smile, squeezing his hand at the same time. She would not hope. She would not cry.

Henry Crow frowned a little as if surprised to see her and then he said: 'Hello, Lydia, love. It's been a while.'

THE END

THANK YOU FOR READING!

I hope you enjoyed reading about Lydia Crow and her family as much as I enjoyed writing about them!

I am busy working on the fifth book in the Crow Investigations series. If you would like to be notified when it's published (as well as take part in giveaways and receive exclusive free content), you can sign up for my FREE readers' club:

geni.us/ReaderClub

If you could spare the time, I would really appreciate a review on the retailer of your choice.

Reviews make a huge difference to the visibility of the book, which make it more likely that I will reach more readers and be able to keep on writing. Thank you!

ACKNOWLEDGMENTS

Some books are trickier than others and this one put up a bit of a fight. My eternal gratitude to Dave, Holly and James for putting up with me while I wrestled it into submission.

I love writing books (even the tricksy ones!), and I am deeply grateful to my lovely readers for enabling me to do my dream job.

As ever, thank you to my brilliant author pals; Clodagh Murphy, Hannah Ellis, Keris Stainton, Nadine Kirtzinger, and Sally Calder. Thank you for the support, camaraderie and understanding.

This book was largely written during the Covid-19 pandemic and ensuing lockdown. Like everyone, I've been anxious and discombobulated for much of the time and, more than ever, I want to thank my friends and family for their love and support.

On that note, special thanks must go to the internet. Thank you for the video chats, streaming content, and the ability to carry on working.

Thank you to my editor, cover designer, early readers, and wonderful ARC team. You are all wonderful.

In particular, thanks to Beth Farrar, Karen Heenan, Melanie Leavey, Jenni Gudgeon, Geraldyne Greenwood, Ann Martin, Caroline Nicklin, Judy Grivas, Paula Searle, Deborah Forrester, and David Wood.

And, as always, love and thanks to my Dave.

ABOUT THE AUTHOR

Before writing books, Sarah Painter worked as a free-lance magazine journalist, blogger and editor, combining this 'career' with amateur child-wrangling (AKA motherhood).

Sarah lives in rural Scotland with her children and husband. She drinks too much tea, loves the work of Joss Whedon, and is the proud owner of a writing shed.

Click below to sign-up to the Sarah Painter readers' club. It's absolutely free and you'll get book release news, giveaways and exclusive FREE stuff!

geni.us/ReaderClub

Printed in Great Britain
by Amazon

82701504R00205